ZELINA
THE FIRST GLYPH

ZELINA
THE FIRST GLYPH

STEPHANIE FAYE

MAIN PUBLISHING

For information contact:
author@authorstephaniefaye.com
authorStephanieFaye.com

Published by:
Main Publishing

Cover Design: Biserka Designs

Interior Design: Francine Platt • www.edengraphics.net

Interior Illustrations: Samantha Sheafer

ISBN   13: 978-1-7340543-0-9

This book is a work of fiction. Names, characters, places, and incidents either
are products of the author's imagination or are used fictitiously. Any resemblance
to actual events or locales or persons, living or dead, is entirely coincidental.

This book is dedicated to my family; my wonderful and patient husband who pushed me to keep writing, and helped keep me focused, my two younger kids who were excited to read the finished story, and my oldest who sat through me bouncing ideas off of her, and playing "catch the owl" when I had writer's block. To my mom who has always believed in me and supported my writing even as a child with my silly, nonsensical stories.

Lastly, my beautiful grandmother—I miss her so much. She is such an inspiration to me. I love you Beebs!

From Rune's notebook, page 1

Chapter One

ONFUSION. Zelina rubbed her eyes and opened them slowly, looking around. Where was she? Above her the sky was cloudy and gray, the sun fighting to shine through. She sat up slowly from the wet grass, wiping the mist from her face. Glancing around, Zelina found herself surrounded by stones in the middle of a green field. The stones reminded of her something, a distant memory she could not quite place. A flash behind her eyes; a bright circle with intricate design, set in stone and made of fire. She rubbed her eyes. As quickly as the image appeared it was gone. *What was that?* She wondered. She stood slowly, her legs shaking and heart pounding. The massive stones all around her were so old; some stood while others had fallen, probably ages ago. What was it about them that made her feel trapped? Zelina's head began to pound behind her eyes and she closed them tight, once again, to shut out the image of the stones. Maybe it was all a nightmare, and if she squeezed her eyes tight enough, she would wake up and everything would be all right once again. She tried desperately to make sense of where she was; tried to recall her last memory. What was the last thing she was doing before she woke up in this strange place? Nothing. All Zelina saw was blackness, and other than her name, she had no memory. She opened her eyes in alarm.

"Hey, young lady! You aren't supposed to be over there!" A coarse voice yelled from behind her.

Zelina turned to see an elderly couple walking, arm in arm, around the outside of the stones. "You need to come out of there before you get into trouble."

Zelina looked around and saw several other people walking around the stones, taking pictures. She did not want to get into any trouble, so she slowly walked toward the old man. "Sorry, I'm not sure how I wound up in there."

"Are you alright, dearie? You look a bit shaken." The older woman looked up at Zelina and held on to the old man's arm a bit tighter.

"Yes, I'm all right. Thank you." Zelina smiled at them and turned to face the stones, hoping for some answers.

"All right, well, the weather is just going to get worse, so you better be heading home." The old man squeezed his wife's hand, and they walked off, leaving Zelina to the mist and the unnerving stones. She closed her eyes once more, willing a memory to come forward. Through the fog of her mind she was running from something—she didn't know what—tears running down her face, then nothing.

The wind began picking up. The gray sky above began churning and Zelina felt a chill run up her spine, not from the weather, but from her blank mind; from being in a place she knew nothing of. She had no idea where to go, or what to do. Zelina brought the hood of her sweater up, trying to cover her face as she stared at the stones.

A voice as loud as thunder came out of nowhere, making Zelina jump. "Young lady, we've been searching everywhere for you! This is the farthest you have gone! What have we told you about taking off like that?!"

Spinning around, Zelina saw a stern-looking woman with salt-and-pepper hair pulled in a tight bun at the back of her head, approaching her. Her dull, gray clothes made her look ashen. She was rather tall and terribly thin; sickly looking. Her cheeks were sunken in, and she had dark circles under her eyes.

Zelina's first thought was that the woman was yelling at someone else, because Zelina had no idea who she was. She stared at the woman as she approached, thinking she would pass by to yell at another young lady.

"Young lady! I am talking to you! What have you been told? You will be taken to another home, one not as nice as ours, if this continues! Now, you don't want that do you?" The woman took Zelina's hand and started walking her away from the stones.

Zelina pulled her hand away. "I'm sorry. You must have me confused with someone else. I have no idea who you are." The lady grabbed her wrist and squeezed it tightly so Zelina could not pull away again. The woman looked frail; however, the look in her eyes said otherwise.

"Darling, your name is Zelina and you reside in a home I take care of. You've taken off, as you've done many times in the past. Now, if you will please come along, the weather is turning rather nasty, and I'd like to be back home before the storm rolls in."

The lady began pulling Zelina once more, and Zelina felt she had to go along. She did not know the woman, that much was true, but there was something inside her telling her to go, that it would be all right.

They walked a short distance to a car where an enormous man, dressed all in white, waited. As they approached, the big man began walking toward them, pulling his hands from his pockets. Zelina stopped walking; the big man standing next to the car made her stomach sink. The woman looked at the big man, shaking her head and raising one hand to have him stay back. "Zelina, dear, listen to me. It's happened again." She looked at Zelina, shaking her head. "This is normal for you; this why you have been sent to us. You have blackouts from time to time. You lose certain parts of the day, having no memory how you got places, or even, at times, who you are. Come on, dear, the rain is starting to come down, and we need to get you home where we can help you. Please, don't make this more difficult than it needs to be. I promise you; we are here to help."

With that, she waved to the big man to come forward and help get them to the car. The woman may have been speaking sweet words, but they were bitter to Zelina's ears. This lady was in no way sweet, and somehow Zelina knew it, yet she knew she had to go with her.

"I'm honestly sorry. I have no idea who you are. You say this has happened before?" Zelina's head was pounding hard now; it hurt so badly she felt she might cry. She did not want to go with them, not really, but felt she had no choice. There was something deep inside her that felt pulled to go with the pair; she thought maybe it was a deep memory, like that of the stones and the circle of fire.

The lady huffed. "I'm Ms. Nyx. I run the home you have been living in for the past few years." She sat beside Zelina while the big man got in the car and started driving. "This is Damon. He helps when things don't go as planned." She smiled creepily at Damon in the mirror. "It will all come back to you soon enough, dear. For now, just relax; we'll be home soon.

"As I said, this is the farthest you have ever travelled. It took us two days to find you. How ever did you get this far?"

"Ms. Nyx, I have no idea where I am. What is this place?" Zelina asked, pointing back to the strange stones in the empty field.

Ms. Nyx rolled her eyes, letting out a loud huff and pulling Zelina's hood off before stating, "That is Stonehenge. It's just been around, well, forever it seems. Really, Zelina, this is the worst I think I've seen you. You have no memory of how you got there? Child, you could have been seriously injured."

Zelina shrugged her shoulders; she could not remember traveling to Stonehenge. She found it strange that she remembered her name but had no memory of anything else. Nothing. No, she did remember something. She remembered her age; she was sixteen. However, she did not know when her birthday was, or who her mother was or —.

"Don't try to think too much, dear. It always hurts your head and delays the memories from returning. Just relax. We will get you some food and be home in a couple of hours. Once we get home, things will be better." Ms. Nyx smiled, but that smile was not warm or caring. It gave Zelina a chill up her spine, just as when she was standing in front of the stones.

Zelina tried to relax a bit and looked out the window, hoping a memory would come to her as they travelled. Maybe she would remember how she got there, where she had taken off from, and where she was trying to go. Stonehenge was a strange place to run to. There were no shelters or towns nearby; there was no place she could hide. Zelina hoped Ms. Nyx was right and that when they got back to the house, she would get better and remember. It alarmed Zelina to not be able to remember anything. Her last memory was running. Running from what? Was she running from Ms. Nyx and the house?

They pulled up to a quiet little place and grabbed some food to eat while they drove home. Ms. Nyx said she didn't want to stay away too long, as they had already been gone longer than expected. "Many things to be taken care of. I must get back to Ankerstone. You will eat in the car; just don't make a mess." She stared down at her cell phone, texting frantically.

"Ankerstone?" Zelina asked as they drove off into the oncoming storm.

"Yes, Zelina, Ankerstone, it's where we live. Now no more questions, eat."

The food wasn't too terribly bad. It was some kind of minced meat with spices, wrapped in baked bread. Zelina didn't really want to eat it as she wasn't very hungry; however, she also didn't want to make Ms. Nyx or Damon angry. He was just as intimidating as Ms. Nyx. His one arm was the size of Zelina's head. His blond hair was cut way too short; Zelina could see his pink scalp. Damon was as wide as he was tall; however, his size was not the scariest thing about him. The most frightening part was his eyes. They were small, beady eyes that seemed to have no pupil, just pure blackness. When he smiled, she half expected to see fangs instead of teeth.

Zelina never wanted to see him angry.

The rest of the ride was silent. They passed through a lot of countryside before hitting a bigger town. There was much more traffic and Damon honked the horn at several cars moving too slowly for his liking. They hit the country roads again, where all she saw was green grass, no people or cars. Zelina ate slowly, and when she was done, she went back to staring out the window. Watching the towns fly by, Zelina wondered how she had travelled so far from home. *So many pastures leading to big cities, so many places to hide and never be found. Why Stonehenge?* she thought.

What felt like an eternity, was actually only three hours. They pulled up to a long, winding dirt road, at which time Ms. Nyx hummed and poked Zelina's arm. "We are home, dear. Damon will be taking you to your room, where you are to wait until the director comes to get you."

Zelina nodded, not saying a word nor taking her eyes from Ms. Nyx. They pulled up to a massive, rusted ornate iron gate. The gate looked as if it had stood there for a century or two. It was quite beautiful, even covered in rust. Damon grunted as he rolled down his window and punched in some numbers on a keypad; the gate crept open. They slowly moved forward, coming around a curve in the dirt driveway. Zelina stared out her window, taking it all in, and did not hear Ms. Nyx talking to her.

"Child! Did you hear me?" Ms. Nyx poked Zelina in the arm again, bringing Zelina out of her stupor.

"Sorry, I was just looking at this place. It's massive."

"Well, you will get to see it all soon enough. For now, you need to listen to me. Damon, please pull to the side; we will take her in that way. Now, Zelina dear, as I said, Damon will take you to your room. You will not leave the room; you will not talk with anyone until the director comes to get you. Do you understand?"

"Yes, Ms. Nyx."

The home was an enormous structure. Zelina did not have much of a chance to see the front, other than some pillars and an immense green garden. To her right was the entrance to the side of the house. Just seeing one side of the place gave her chills. There was no color; similar to Ms. Nyx's clothes, it was all gray. Some stones were covered in green moss, which was the only splash of color to the building. The side door, looking as if it were made of stone as well, stood open and inside people were working in the kitchen. *Perhaps they're making dinner*, Zelina thought. Off to Zelina's left was a four-car garage with three cars sitting in stalls. It was a newer building, made of brick, and its architecture did not match the main structure at all. There were no houses or buildings around them. The house was quite secluded.

Damon pulled Zelina out of the car; interestingly, his grip was not as strong as Ms. Nyx's. Zelina looked down at his hand and up at his face. Forcing a smile, she willingly walked with him into the kitchen.

The kitchen was a cook's dream come true: everything in it looked brand new. Three ovens and a long serving counter were along one wall, and across from them were two cook tops at the end of an island. Two stainless steel refrigerators were to Zelina's right and two sinks sat beside them. A girl stood cutting vegetables at the island, which ran almost the full length of the kitchen. Hanging from the ceiling were two pot racks. There were two other girls in the kitchen cooking. All the girls stopped what they were doing and looked up at Zelina, wide-eyed. Ms. Nyx walked in, at which time their heads all went down and they resumed their work.

"Please, girls, continue working," Ms. Nyx told them as she waved Zelina and Damon out of the kitchen.

They walked quickly out and into the dining hall where Zelina saw eight long tables with benches. Two massive chandeliers hung from the ceiling, but most of the light came from an entire wall of windows at the back of the dining hall. Damon yanked her into the entryway, and up the stairs. Zelina could hear people talking and laughing but saw no one. As she looked back, she saw Ms. Nyx go straight ahead to a door, knock, and then walk in.

Zelina and Damon trudged up the stairs. "Just in case you don't remember, right is for the boys and left is for the girls. No girls allowed over there and no boys allowed over here," Damon stated emphatically.

At the top landing, the hall split. A long hallway went left, while to her right, Zelina could see several boys' rooms, as all the doors were open. There was a dim wall sconce at the very top of the landing; it looked as old as the house itself. "Also, there is no leaving your room after ten p.m. on the weekdays, eleven p.m. on the weekends. Understand?"

Zelina nodded. Damon simply grunted and led her to the left, down the long skinny hallway, and then went right down another long hallway. Zelina tried to look in the open doors, but Damon was making her walk much too fast to be able to see anything. They stopped at the end of the hall. "This is your room," Damon said, opening the door to the last room on the right and pulling her in. "Do not leave. I'm tired of chasing you." He slammed the door. Zelina stood there listening to his footsteps fade away before she dared to move.

Just like the rest of the place, her room was lacking color. *What do they have against color?* she smirked. It was a good-sized room and one she did not share, as there was only one bed. On her bed was a blanket the color of the dark sky. She ran her fingers over the blanket, it was velvety and felt warm. A small lamp was on and sat atop a dark wooden nightstand next to her bed. On the other nightstand was an opened book and a clock. She noticed there were no pictures anywhere. She did not remember seeing pictures in the few rooms she walked through downstairs, nor in the rooms she passed so quickly. She thought it strange. Her room had no decorations of any sort, no drawings or even mementos. If she had run away, wouldn't her room still have her belongings in it? Yet, the room seemed as if it had not been used in years. Directly across from her bed was her closet. She opened it and saw a few pieces of clothing inside. She had two pairs of jeans, three blouses, and one light blue dress. Next to the closet was her dresser, with a hairbrush and some hair accessories on top; a plain mirror hung just above the dresser. She opened the dresser drawers, looking in each one, finding a few pieces of clothing there as well. There was one window with white curtains pulled back; she glanced out and saw the massive backyard. The grass outside was the only vibrant color in the entire place; there were no flowers anywhere she could see. The green grass in the back made her want to run through it barefoot. It looked soft and lush; she thought she could lie on the grass for hours watching the clouds go by. Zelina turned from her window, looking around her room. Next to the window was an old green chair with a tan blanket thrown over the back. The chair seemed almost as old as the wall sconce in the hall. It looked as if it once had a floral pattern, but now it could barely be seen. She felt cold and empty, just like her room.

What is this place? Where exactly am I? she wondered as she walked to her bed. She was sitting with her back to her door, trying to remember something, anything, when there was a knock. "Yes?" Zelina murmured, looking over her shoulder. The door slowly opened and in slid a boy. Zelina jumped from her bed, "No boys are allowed in here."

"Calm yourself." He shut the door quietly. "I'm not here to cause problems. Just let me look at your eyes."

"What? No! Damon is already mad at having to chase after me again. I don't want to get into more trouble. I was told—"

The boy approached Zelina quickly. "I will leave as soon as I see your eyes. Stop being scared! They can't do anything to you."

Zelina backed up to the wall. Having nowhere else to go, she just glared at him. "I will scream if you come any closer. I'm not kidding."

He either did not believe her or did not care as he walked right up to her, inches from her face. He took her face in his hands and looked down into her eyes. He was just slightly taller and had short, black curly hair and bright blue eyes with a hint of yellow close to the pupil. His full lips spread into a smile and she noticed an indent on his chin. He had a square jaw line and was broad-shouldered. There was something about him that made her feel safe; she wasn't sure why. Was he a friend she could not fully remember? She had to know him; she could feel it.

He took a step back, looked at her and said, "Did that hurt? No. Thank you." With that, he turned from her and walked to the door. "I'm Rune, by the way. See you at dinner."

He shut the door gently behind him and Zelina stood against the wall, staring at the closed door, listening for his footsteps to fade away, but she did not hear anything. She had no idea what that was all about, but she had to see why this guy was so interested in her eyes. She ran over to her dresser and leaned as close to the mirror as possible to examine her eyes. She had a hard time pulling her attention from her curly, unruly red hair. It was a mess. "Now, why didn't anyone tell me how crazy my hair was?" she said as she tried to push the out-of-control curls closer to her head. Giving up, she grabbed a hair tie to pull the mess back and give her a better view of her eyes. She stood on her tiptoes, elbows resting on the top of the dresser and leaned into the mirror to see what the big deal was. To her, there was nothing remarkable or interesting about her eyes. They were a light color, nearly yellow, with specks of dark brown. She shifted her gaze down to her lips; there were dry and thinner than Rune's. She had a few freckles across her nose and under her eyes. Looking down at her hands, she saw dirt under her nails; her fingers appeared short and stubby. "You need to get some color; you are scary white," Zelina said quietly to herself as she backed away from the mirror, trying to keep a few stray hairs from her eyes. Before she could sit down on the bed, her door opened and an older man walked in, leaving the door open behind him. She wondered if he had seen Rune leave her room. Would she be in trouble now?

"Hello, Zelina. I'm Mr. Jared; I'm here to help you remember, as I always do." He sat on her bed, patting an empty spot beside him for her to sit. "Now, tell me the last thing you remember."

Zelina sat in silence for a moment, as she studied Mr. Jared. He was a smidge taller than Zelina and was slender, with only a slight belly.

She shrugged her shoulders and said, "Nothing. I can't remember anything. I was at Stonehenge; Ms. Nyx had to tell me what it was called. I have no idea how I got there—I don't remember this place, or even you. I'm sorry." Zelina hung her head, staring at the floor.

"You have no reason to be sorry. This is why you are here, my dear. We are helping you so that you can go out and live a normal life one day." He patted her leg softly. "I want to help you remember everything." His light brown eyes twinkled; his smile was a true smile. Unlike Ms. Nyx's, his was almost comforting, and there was a genuine sweetness there.

"Well, where are my parents?" She looked at him, hoping for answers.

Mr. Jared got up from the bed, scratching his salt-and-pepper hair. The sides were cut short while the top was curly. He pursed his extremely thin lips together as he walked to the window and breathed in deeply before answering. "Zelina, you are an orphan, as is everyone here. You were sent here because we deal exclusively with children such as yourself." He turned from the window to look at Zelina. "People with memory loss and no family to help them." He scratched his well-trimmed moustache and walked back around the bed to stand in front of her. "We help you to remember and to learn how to deal with the blackouts, such as those you are suffering from. We have a very high success rate here, I might add." He smiled at her, took her hands and pulled her to a standing position. "I will help you with this. I will make sure by the time you are eighteen and leave here, you'll be ready and perfectly able to live a normal life. You just have to trust me. Okay?"

"Yes, sir."

Mr. Jared walked Zelina to her open door, her hands still in his.

"You can head down to dinner. I want to see you first thing tomorrow morning. I would prefer you not speak to anyone; I need to be able to work with your mind empty, as it is now." He smiled at her, letting go of her hands. "I don't want people filling your mind with nonsense or make-believe. Okay? Can you do that for me?"

"Yes, I think so," Zelina replied. Mr. Jared motioned for her to head downstairs. He stood there, just outside her room, as she walked down the hall.

The dining hall was noisy, but surprisingly there were only about a dozen kids, varying in age, sitting at different tables. Zelina had no idea what the rules were or even how she was to go about getting her food, although she was not hungry. As she walked past the full tables to find the food, people stopped talking to stare at her. She tried to keep her gaze straight ahead and not look at anyone.

"The food line is to the left; grab a tray over there." Rune was standing behind her. She did as he told her, getting some food and heading to a semi-empty table. "What's your name?" he asked as he sat down across from her.

"I'm not supposed to talk with anyone." She put her head down, picking at her food.

"You can't even tell me your name?" Rune smiled at her, and it made her smile.

"I'm Zelina," she said, looking around to make sure no one was watching them. "Really, though, I can't talk to anyone right now."

"That's fine; I'll do all the talking then. What do you remember?" Rune had his mouth full of bread and it grossed Zelina out to see him talking with little pieces of bread flying free. She wrinkled her nose at him and said nothing, turning her gaze back to her food.

"Okay, well then tell me what you think of this grand place," he said as he took another bite of his food. It seemed to Zelina that Rune did not chew his food; instead, he just kept shoveling it in his mouth, and she continued to snarl at him. She had a hard time answering his simple question.

"I don't know. It's huge and cold, not very homey. Hey, how did you get past Mr. Jared earlier?" Zelina asked, putting her fork down and pushing her tray of food away.

"I don't know what you are talking about. I've been down here all day." He winked at her and then motioned with his eyes to the people at the other end of the table. She turned to look at them and found they were listening to their conversation. Zelina smiled and pulled her food back toward her, forcing a bite into her mouth, but it did not taste very good. The fish cakes were cold, as were the potatoes and carrots.

Rune did not ask any more questions and Zelina only ate the carrots while watching other kids return their dishes and trays to a certain area and then head out of the dining hall. She was not sure where she should go or what she should do once she finished eating. She only knew that Mr. Jared did not want her talking to anyone the rest of the evening.

"Food was delicious, as always," Rune said as he patted his stomach and let out a small belch. He got up from the table to put his tray away. He looked back over his shoulder, watching Zelina. She was uncertain of what to do, stay there and finish her food or follow Rune. "Come on, put your stuff over there and come with me," Rune said as he headed out of the dining hall, past Zelina. She did just that: she put her tray away and hastened out of the hall to catch up with Rune.

He was heading out the front door when she caught up with him. "I'm not really supposed to be talking to anyone, though. Mr. Jared said   "

"And how was your little chat with the great Mr. Jared?" Rune interrupted. Out the front door was a massive porch that stopped to the left, where Zelina was brought in. It wrapped around the right side of the house. Zelina could hear voices coming from that side, although she and Rune were completely alone out front. Four pillars ran along the front; there were two swings, at least a dozen chairs, and several small tables sitting on the porch. Rune sat in a chair to the left, almost where the porch ended, and Zelina followed, sitting in a chair next to him. For a few moments Rune stared out at the lawn while Zelina stared at him, unsure of what to say.

"You don't like Mr. Jared?" Zelina had to break the silence; it was killing her.

"What?" Rune never took his eyes off whatever it was he was looking at in the distance.

"It's how you spoke of Mr. Jared. It seems to me that you don't like him much. Why?"

Finally, Rune turned and looked her in the eyes; she felt herself blush. "The great Mr. Jared. Yes, he's helped many kids here with their memory problems and helped them to become stable, responsible members of this society."

She could hear the sarcasm in Rune's voice and was unsure why he felt this way. He leaned closer to her. "Whatever he tells you, don't believe it. I'm serious." He took a deep breath and returned to looking out at the front lawn before continuing. "Whatever is told to you here is a lie. Except, of course, what I'm telling you. I'd like to talk to you more, but people are coming, and they can't hear what I have to say. I'll come by your room tomorrow when you're done meeting with Mr. Jared." With that, Rune got up from his seat and headed to the other end of the porch, turning the corner and leaving Zelina to herself. She watched him go and was slightly annoyed that she never got to find out why he was so against Mr. Jared, who seemed so genuine.

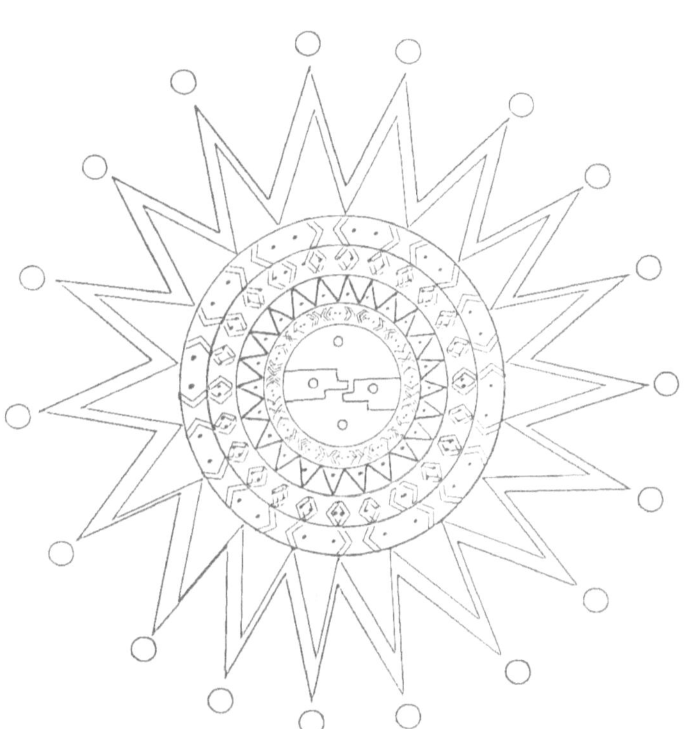

From Rune's notebook, page 67

Chapter Two

NOT EVEN A MINUTE later, Ms. Nyx and Damon walked out the front door. "Ah, good, dear, you're alone. How was your dinner?"

Ms. Nyx sat by Zelina while Damon stood behind her. Without giving her a chance to answer, Ms. Nyx simply started talking once again. "That's good, dear. I have your appointment with Mr. Jared tomorrow morning at nine a.m. You need to be up by seven, head down to breakfast and be showered by eight-thirty. Damon will take you to Mr. Jared's office at eight-forty-five. Mr. Jared has many appointments tomorrow and wishes to see you first thing. You mustn't be late. Do you understand?" She did not wait for a reply; instead, she simply patted Zelina's leg as she got up from her chair. "Good, dear. I'm glad we understand each other. Now, I think you should head to your room and relax the rest of the night."

Ms. Nyx and Damon walked down the porch, in the same direction as Rune, and turned the corner. Zelina sat outside a bit longer, watching the rain fall and thinking. It had been such a long day: Stonehenge, this house, Rune, Mr. Jared, Ms. Nyx, Damon and the horrible food—it was so much to take in. She could not keep her thoughts on track; they were all over the place. What had Rune been talking about, anyway, when he said not to believe anything Mr. Jared told her? And earlier that evening, in her room, Rune told her they could not do anything to her—what did that mean? Three people that day asked her about the last thing she remembered, one being Rune. Now, why would *he* ask that question? How had she made it as far as Stonehenge? Where was she going? Why did she leave here in the first place and where exactly was she? Why did she not remember anything, other than her name and age? If she had been living here for years and took off for two days, wouldn't she have had friends here to greet her when she returned? Instead, it seemed no one knew her.

Well, maybe Mr. Jared can answer those questions tomorrow, she thought to herself as she got up and headed inside. Her head was beginning to pound; she could feel it behind her eyes and thought maybe Ms. Nyx was right, she should head to her room for the night.

As Zelina walked through the entryway, she heard voices coming from down the hall and decided to explore that end of the house before turning in for the night. Straight ahead of her were the stairs leading up. She walked past the stairs; Mr. Jared's office was the first door on the right. Past the office were two other doors: a girls' restroom and a boys' restroom. Straight ahead, at the end of the hall, was the door leading to the back; she could see out the window that there was a porch there as well. Just beyond the two restrooms and to the right was a big archway that opened to a vast open room. As Zelina walked in she was greeted by a warm fire burning in an enormous stone fireplace at the far end of the room. Two girls sat on one of two tan sofas facing the fireplace, talking and laughing. They seemed oblivious to Zelina's presence. She walked quietly around the room, behind the girls. Along one wall were six wooden desks with flat screen computers; between each desk was a tall bookshelf filled with books. On the other side of the room were some electronic games she did not know the names of, a Ping-Pong table, and a foosball table. In the center of the room were two empty white tables, big enough to seat ten people at each of them. Along the other wall were three small shelves that held board games like checkers and chess. It was strange to Zelina that she remembered those games yet struggled to remember her home and her friends. As she looked around the room, she realized there were no pictures hung on the walls and the room also lacked color.

Beside the fireplace in the corner of the room were two over-sized brown chairs and two more bookshelves. Zelina thought about curling up in a chair and reading for the rest of the evening.

"What do you want?" a blonde girl barked.

Zelina looked down at her and thought she was rather pretty, with big blue eyes and full pink lips. Her hair was short, not quite to her shoulders, and fell flat against her head.

"Nothing. I was just looking around. I didn't mean to—"

"Whatever. Just move on."

The other girl waved at Zelina to leave the room. Her blonde hair was pulled up into a loose bun and her green eyes glared at Zelina as she pursed her very thin lips, she seemed highly annoyed. They both stared at Zelina, waiting for her to leave.

Once Zelina turned and walked away they went back to talking once more. Instead of continuing to look around, she decided to head to her room; she was too exhausted to run into anybody else that snippy.

Up in her room, Zelina sat on her bed. She desperately wanted to remember everyone and everything again. She wanted this day to be over and to wake up tomorrow knowing everything she should know. She pulled off her shoes, lay back in bed and stared at the ceiling, willing herself to remember something, anything. Her head began pounding worse, and her eyes started watering. She promised herself that when her memory came back, she would not take off again. She would do whatever it took to not have the blackouts ever again and to do her best with what Mr. Jared told her to do. She did *not* want to go through this ever again. Her thoughts raced as she drifted off to sleep.

Her sleep was restless. She woke in a sweat, gripping her blanket with both hands, her heart racing. What had she been dreaming? Zelina took a few deep breaths, then lay back on her pillow. Using her blanket, she wiped the sweat from her forehead and tried to relax. "Relax Zelina, it was just a dream," she whispered to herself. She closed her eyes, willing herself to calm down and sleep. She was so exhausted; she wanted to get some rest. She closed her eyes, concentrated on her breathing and began to relax once more.

She must have fallen back to sleep because the next thing she knew, the alarm was going off. Rolling over, drained, she sat up slapping the nightstand, trying to figure out how to shut off the awful noise.

"The big button on the top will shut it off. Good grief, girl." Rune was sitting in the chair next to the window.

Zelina hit the button, shutting off the alarm. She was shocked that Rune was in her room yet again. "What are you doing in here?! How did you—How long have you been here?!" she asked in a hushed tone, getting up from her bed, moving to the door.

"You're way too uptight. Calm down. We only have a few minutes. One question: what did you dream last night?" His eyes lit up and a goofy grin spread across his face.

"You need to leave. I have to meet with Mr. Jared, and I'm not starting my day off by getting into trouble." Zelina's hand was on the doorknob, except she did not turn it, nor did she truly want to. There was something about Rune that made her feel calm. He felt like, for lack of a better word, home. She had to have known him—that must have been it. Her memory was returning; she was remembering who Rune was and a small smile played across her lips.

"Please, Zelina, just sit down for a minute and tell me about your dreams last night. I promise I'll leave right after." Rune did not move; he sat in the chair staring at Zelina, waiting.

Huffing and rolling her eyes, Zelina walked over to the bed, sat down, and stared at her feet. "I honestly don't remember my dreams last night. What I do know is that I woke up scared, sweating and out of breath. It was like I was running from something, but I'm not sure what." She continued starting at her feet, wanting

Rune to leave, yet at the same time wanting him to stay.

Rune made no movement and she could feel his eyes on her, which made her a bit uncomfortable. She could hear him breathing. *What is he thinking?* she wondered.

"You remember nothing else? No colors, noises, or shapes?" He got up from the chair, crossed his arms over his chest, and walked slowly to the door.

Zelina raised her head to watch him go. "I'm sorry, Rune, I really don't—Wait. I remember hearing some chanting...odd, almost soothing chanting. Not from one person but multiple people; there were several voices. Does that mean anything to you? Is that what you were looking for?" Zelina was up from her bed without even realizing it and standing right in front of Rune. Home—yes, was it, he felt familiar to her, as if she had known him her entire life.

He smiled at her; he had a dimple on his right cheek, something Zelina had not noticed before. "It's a start, a good start. Whatever you do, don't tell Mr. Jared about that. Promise me." He took his hand from the doorknob and put it on Zelina's shoulder.

"Why? Tell me why I can't tell Mr. Jared about this. Tell me why I can't trust him or anyone else here, for that matter. Aren't they trying to help me, help us all?" Zelina shrugged off Rune's hand and backed up several steps.

"Zelina, I don't have time to explain it all today, but I will, I promise. You have to trust me. Please, just promise me you won't talk about the dream to anyone else, please."

Rune looked genuinely worried, his brow furrowed, and his lips thinned.

"Fine, I won't tell him today. Eventually, I might have to though. I want to remember, Rune, and if it will help then I have to tell him."

"Okay, just don't tell him today. I better get out of here. You know where the showers are?" His hand was back on the doorknob, ready to leave her room.

"Yeah, I found them yesterday. Downstairs, third door on the right." She smiled at Rune. He kept his eyes on her until he turned to leave.

She was a bit shaken by the whole confrontation, but she had a schedule to keep, and she did not want to be in trouble.

Zelina rummaged through her dresser, finding a pink tank top and a pink and purple-striped T-shirt to wear over it. She then found some ripped jeans in her closet and ran downstairs for a quick shower before heading to breakfast. Breakfast, which consisted of some eggs, baked beans, toast, and sausage, was better than dinner the night before. Zelina actually ate some and was not entirely disgusted. She did not see Rune in the dining hall, so she sat by herself at the back of the room, closest to the big window. The dining hall was pretty empty; only two other girls were eating. Zelina enjoyed the silence, as it let her relax a bit before her meeting with Mr. Jared.

Damon knocked twice at Zelina's door precisely at eight-forty-five, just as she was putting on her shoes. "It's time to go," he grunted as he opened the door.

Zelina looked up from her shoes, smiled and stood from her bed. It seemed that her clothes were a bit too big. She wanted to ask Mr. Jared about that, among other things.

"Good morning, Damon," Zelina said with a forced smile as she walked out her door and headed down the stairs.

Damon grunted and walked slowly behind her. When they got to Mr. Jared's office, Zelina raised her hand to knock on the door. Damon slapped her hand down, hard.

"Ouch! That really hurt," she said, rubbing her hand and biting back the tears.

"I'll knock on the door. You have a seat over there," Damon said, pointing across the hall by the front door. There was a rather uncomfortable-looking plastic chair sitting up against the wall. "Mr. Jared will come and get you when he is ready; otherwise you sit there and stay quiet." Damon did not move until Zelina was seated in the chair.

Damon knocked and Mr. Jared poked his head out and said something to Damon, who immediately went back up the stairs, stomping the entire way. He reminded Zelina of a small child throwing a tantrum after his parents told him to clean his room. Mr. Jared shut the door without even glancing Zelina's way. As she sat, her mind raced. She wondered where the other kids were; it was so quiet. She wondered what this meeting was going to be about, what they would talk about and what she would learn. She also thought about Rune and what he told her about not believing anything Mr. Jared said, and she was still unsure what he meant by, "They can't hurt you." She stared at the faded gray walls, not realizing that Mr. Jared was standing in the door of his office, watching her.

"Lost in thought, are we?" Mr. Jared smiled. It was a rather unpleasant smile; he seemed more annoyed to see her than he had been the previous night. It reminded her a bit of Ms. Nyx's smile, unsettling. "Well, come on and let's get you started."

Zelina shuffled into his office. The evening before she had imagined Mr. Jared's office as dark and dank, with steel chairs that made her legs fall asleep. However, when she walked into his office, she found it quite the opposite; the only color in the entire place seemed to be concentrated in that room. The office was bigger than it looked from the outside. There were four massive cherry wood bookshelves reaching almost to the ceiling, two on each side of the room and two more behind his desk. They had incredible, ornate designs at the top and the bottom. Mr. Jared sat behind the biggest desk Zelina had ever seen. It, too, was a cherry color, with a darker red chair that looked to be the most comfortable chair. She wanted to curl up in it with a warm blanket and a good book.

"Zelina, please sit there," Mr. Jared requested, gesturing to one of the two light tan, oversized chairs that sat in front of his desk. On the backs of the chairs were blankets with swirls of dark red and different shades of blue. The blankets looked warm and inviting.

Sitting down, Zelina could see several picture frames on his desk;

however, she could not see who or what was in them. The frames were all different colors. She was tempted to turn them around; she wanted to see someone's face in a picture, something personal. This place seemed so odd to her, nothing personal from anybody.

Zelina sat with her hands in her lap, playing with her fingers, unsure of what was expected of her. Mr. Jared was looking at papers on his desk, every once in while looking up at her and then writing on a paper next to him. Finally, when he spoke, it actually made Zelina jump. "Well, how did you sleep last night?" There was no expression on his face. No smile, no frown, just a straight question.

"I slept fine." Zelina lied.

As he wrote, she looked around the room. Close to the door, on the right, was a white sofa with one blue pillow and one red pillow. Behind the sofa was a large window with tan-colored curtains that were pulled back, letting in the sun. In front of the sofa was a cherry wood glass-top coffee table with magazines and a notepad sitting on top of it. Two white Victorian-style chairs sat in front of the coffee table; a cherry wood end table sat between them and a floor lamp behind it. On the walls hung stunning paintings: one was of a nearly collapsed wooden house with snow covering the crumbling roof. In front of the home was an old, hourse-drawn carriage, waiting for its passengers. It looked so peaceful. Next to it was a painting twice the size; it had odd shapes and colors that didn't make much sense, but Zelina liked the varying colors. There was also a still life, which was so lifelike that Zelina could almost feel the fuzz of the peach skin and taste the juice from the orange. It made her mouth water a little. Another was of a landscape in the fall. The office was very different from the rest of the house. She felt she could sit in there for hours, never getting bored. A smile spread across her face.

"So, no dreams or nightmares?" Zelina shook her head. "Any waking in the middle of the night, for any reason?" Again, Zelina shook her head. Putting down his pen, folding his fingers together and putting them under his chin he studied Zelina, smiled a bit and asked again, "What is the last thing you remember before Ms. Nyx found you?" He sat back in his chair, seeming to relax, and waited for her answer.

"I told you and Ms. Nyx that I have no memory of anything before yesterday afternoon. Honestly. I don't remember this place or anyone here. The only things I seem to remember are my name and age. Which, Mr. Jared," Zelina sat forward a bit, straightened her back and looked him in the eyes, "I can only remember my first name, not my middle nor my last. Can you help me with that?" She felt a surge of confidence, not knowing where it came from or why it hit her at that moment. "I do find it odd, very odd, that I have supposedly been here for—what? Years? And yet no one greeted me when I arrived. I have no friends?" She sat back in her chair, the same as Mr. Jared, like she could sit there all day.

"Zelina, where is all this coming from? You have a bit of an attitude, huh? I will not have that here. Do you understand?" Mr. Jared sat back up, fire in his eyes, and rested his elbows on his desk. He stared at her for a moment. Zelina nodded her agreement and he wrote something on the paper next to him. Sitting back once again, he said, "Now, I don't know about your friendships here; however, I do know that when we have a runaway, such as yourself, the others here get tired of it. Possibly at one point you had friends, and now maybe they're tired of your drama, always running away, always causing problems. I can't say for sure, my dear."

A fake smile played on Mr. Jared's lips. Zelina really wanted to slap him, hard. She clasped her hands together and put them between her knees. He seemed so genuine when she first met him, with real smiles and sincere concern for her. At the present moment, she wanted to knock the fake smile right off his face. She had no idea where that feeling came from either, but it made her smirk for a moment.

"As for your other names, yes, I know them," Mr. Jared stated. He flipped through the papers on his desk, searching for something, possibly her name. After a moment, he let out a quiet huff and then made a clicking sound with his tongue. Zelina was unsure what that meant. "Smith. Your last name is Smith. I am sorry; I don't see a middle name here. So possibly your parents did not give you one or it was lost with your papers when you transferred here."

"Transferred? What does that mean?" Zelina sat back up, arms on the chair's armrests, hands in fists. "So, I lived somewhere else before coming here?"

"Yes, Zelina, that's precisely what that means. However, we're not here to discuss your parents, their deaths or the orphanages you lived in before you came to us. We're here to discuss what happened last week; what happened that sent you running out of here and sent us on a frantic search for you for two days."

Zelina began chewing on her bottom lip, something was not right. Maybe what Rune said was true—no one here could be trusted. Her name did not feel right, either. Smith did not fit. Deciding she would play the game, she forced herself to relax a bit. "Smith. Sounds right. Do I have any siblings?"

"Not that I've seen in your papers. Now, let's get back to Friday morning, shall we?" Mr. Jared grabbed the paper he had been writing on, put it directly in front of him, took his pen and began writing. "Please, Zelina, tell me about Friday morning."

Friday morning? Had she not already said a million times that she had no memory before Stonehenge? Okay, that was a lie; she remembered the ladies chanting and the smell of fire. That was new to her; it just came to her as she sat there, the smell of fire. She needed to make sure she told Rune about that when she saw him again. "Mr. Jared, I'm being honest here. I have no memory of anything. I'm sorry. I'm really trying to remember what made me run off." She started to whine a bit, slouching her shoulders, hoping that Mr. Jared would believe her.

"Well, let's see what we have on file for you." He picked up the stack of papers again. "Yes. Damon and Ms. Nyx, as well as Lexy, gave written reports as to what transpired Friday morning. Would you like to hear what they have to say?"

She wanted to say, "Not really. Move on." Instead, she bit her tongue, smiled and said, "I guess so. I will do whatever needs to be done to help with the memory loss and blackouts."

"Good to hear, Zelina. Why don't you lie down on the sofa and we can talk about what happened, not only this time but other times as well? We can also discuss how you can prevent this from happening again."

Mr. Jared stood from his desk, grabbing his pen and the stack of papers. He nodded to Zelina, who rose from her chair and walked back to the sofa, where she sat straight up, hands in her lap. Mr. Jared sat in one of the white Victorian chairs, putting his papers on the end table next to him except for one. "Go on, lie down, get comfortable and let's chat a bit."

Zelina was reluctant to lie back, but Mr. Jared stared at her, waiting patiently. Finally, she succumbed and stretched out. Clearing his throat, he began, "Now according to Ms. Nyx, you awoke early Friday morning, around five." Mr. Jared peered over the top of the paper, looking at Zelina. "That's quite early around here."

Zelina stared at the ceiling; she understood that was early. Mr. Jared stared at her for a few moments, then continued when Zelina did not say a word. She was not going to participate in the conversation. "It states here, 'Zelina began throwing her belongings around her room, breaking a mirror, which brought me running up the stairs and into her room. When I entered the room, she was standing by her open window, breathing heavily. Zelina spun around, glaring at me screaming that it was time for her to leave. This place was not helping her and she felt like a prisoner with all the rules. I walked cautiously to her, both hands out in front of me, promising if she calmed down, we could talk her through this. The closer I got to Zelina, the more agitated she became so I stopped by her bed. She screamed as she threw a book at me, I ducked out of the way so I would not get hit. It was then that she ran by me, pushing me completely over and onto the floor. I heard her running down the stairs and out the front door. I yelled for Damon's help. As I got up from the floor I saw Lexy, staring wide-eyed, outside Zelina's door. She asked if she could help in any way and that is when I told her to inform Mr. Jared as to what had transpired. Once Mr. Jared was told, that is when our search for Zelina began. I don't know what set Zelina off this time.' Zelina, does any of this sound familiar?" Mr. Jared put the paper back on the table, sitting forward, elbows on his knees, staring at Zelina.

Zelina heard Mr. Jared speaking to her but it seemed he was speaking from a tunnel. She could hear everything he read from Ms. Nyx's report, but it seemed the more he read, the farther he got from her and the less she could actually understand. She kept her gaze on the ceiling, not sure what fascinated her about it, but she could not tear her gaze away. She knew she needed to show some response, so she shrugged her shoulders and grunted.

"Shall I continue with Damon's explanation of the events?" Zelina shrugged once again, continuing to stare at the ceiling as Mr. Jared took another paper from the pile next to him. "Damon states that he heard Ms. Nyx yell…" His voice droned on until Zelina could not make out a word he was saying; she could only hear a faint voice. She felt as if she was floating, free and almost giddy. It felt like only a few brief seconds before Mr. Jared's voice was, once again, coming in loud and clear. It must have been longer, though, since he was finished reading Damon's and Lexy's accounts of what took place the previous Friday morning.

"Does any of this help you with what made you leave Friday morning? Does it help you remember what upset you?" Mr. Jared asked.

"It doesn't sound familiar. No, I'm sorry, but it doesn't help, Mr. Jared." Zelina kept her eyes on the ceiling, hoping that she would float away again. "I wish I could remember what got me so upset that I felt I had to run. I'm sorry." She finally turned her head to look at Mr. Jared, who was writing something. She huffed, turning her eyes back to the ceiling. "What else can we do?"

"Well, I think at this point we need to talk about your blackouts, how you can tell when they are coming on, and what you can do to stop them. Why don't you sit up now, and let's go over a few things?"

The meeting lasted another two hours. The entire time Zelina's eyes would wander to the ceiling. All she could think about while Mr. Jared was talking was what happened. How did it happen, and why? She did not hear a word he said the rest of their meeting; she had no idea what he was talking about, so she simply nodded her head every now and then so he would think she was listening.

Mr. Jared cleared his throat, causing Zelina to jump slightly, bringing her out of the reverie. "You've done very well, Zelina. This is the best I've seen you behave after one of these episodes, so I've decided you can go back to school tomorrow. How does that sound?"

"Really? School? Yeah, that sounds good." Her eyes lit up and she smiled from ear to ear. She started to get up from the sofa when Mr. Jared shook his head and put one hand up to stop her.

"Now wait a second, I do need to explain a few things to you. Have a seat once more, please." He sifted through the pile of papers that sat on the table. Finally pulling one out, he looked it over and looked back at Zelina. "We have switched schools for you. I'm sorry to have to do that; we felt it was best with this whole situation, a chance to start anew."

She was not sure what she felt at that moment; she knew she needed to act excited so she could get out of there. She smiled, agreed with Mr. Jared, and asked, "What time do I need to be ready?"

"School begins at eight-thirty. You will need to leave here about seven-thirty and walk to the nearest bus stop which will take you to school. I do believe that nearest stop is only about a five-minute walk from here. We are trusting you with this, Zelina, so don't let us down. If you run away again, we'll have to school you here on the grounds. Is this understood?"

Zelina nodded her head.

"One last thing: as a reminder, eventually you will be required to get a job. Ms. Nyx will help you with that when the time comes. We require all the children here, sixteen and over, to get a job so that they'll be able to live on their own at the age of eighteen. It shows us they are ready to be contributing citizens in the community." He smiled slightly. Zelina shivered faintly and nodded again. "Until you're ready for a job outside the house, you will be required to help around here. Ms. Nyx will assign chores for you to do." He put the paper back down on the stack and cleared his throat. "You may go. Lunch will be simple today and you may eat in the dining hall in an hour. As for now, you may relax and enjoy the quiet. Trust me, it all ends by four o'clock when most of the children return for the day."

Zelina stood from the sofa at the same time Mr. Jared stood from his chair. He reached out his hand to shake hers; she followed suit and shook his hand. "Thank you, Mr. Jared, for helping me through this. I will do my very best to not let you down again." She smiled as sweetly as she could, then turned and headed for the door, where she stopped, and turned back. "Mr. Jared?"

Mr. Jared stopped in front of his desk, set down his papers and turned to Zelina. "Yes, Zelina?" he answered with a huff.

"May I use the computers anytime I wish?"

"They are to be used for school purposes only. If there is research you need to do, you'll need to get permission from Ms. Nyx or myself. Someone must be present when a child is using a computer. We do not play on them."

"Yes, sir. What about cell phones?"

"You may purchase a cell phone when you are eighteen and leave here. We don't like the electronic distractions; we've noticed they hinder progress."

"Thank you." She left, closing the door behind her, and decided to explore the house. She honestly had no idea how to use a computer; she knew what it was but was clueless how to operate one.

Zelina walked all around the house, looking at the books in

the common room, even reading a little bit before heading outside. The grass was still wet from the night before; birds were singing in the trees, and leaves were beginning to change colors and fall as the cooler air began to move in. There was something so peaceful here, yet something so wrong. The outside felt right, normal and peaceful. She felt she could breathe when she was outside. It was more the inside of the house that felt out of place. No, not the house itself, but some of the people there did not seem quite right. Zelina felt like she was being lied to, but she could not figure out why. She made her way to the side door that led to the kitchen and made some lunch (leftovers from dinner the night before); she was the only one in the dining hall, which she enjoyed. After lunch she sat outside on the front porch, thinking back to her meeting with Mr. Jared, deep in thought about how she seemed to float away, not hearing much of what was being said and she wished it would happen again. The idea of that brought a smile to her face.

The rest of the afternoon was quiet. She never saw Ms. Nyx or Damon. The door to Mr. Jared's office remained closed. She did not see Mr. Jared leave or anyone go in. She spent most of the day outside, where she felt at peace.

From Rune's notebook, page 10

Chapter Three

AROUND FOUR O'CLOCK, a few kids started showing up. Some went to the kitchen while others went to the common room. Zelina sat on the porch steps, enjoying the sunshine and watching the leaves drift down.

"Well, if it isn't Little Miss Freaky," said the snippy blonde girl from the night before. "Did you enjoy your day off?" She and the other blonde with green eyes ambled over to Zelina, both smirking as they approached.

"Yes, I did actually. It *was* peaceful." Zelina's eyes never left the tree in front of her; she was watching the top of it sway in the breeze. "Did you enjoy your day? Um…I'm sorry, I don't know your name."

"My name is Lexy. Oh my gosh, you have totally lost your mind." She looked to her friend, who was picking at a string on her shirt, not making eye contact. "Let's get out of here before she ruins our brains, too."

As the pair began to walk up the stairs, Zelina stood, hands on her hips. "Oh, you don't have to worry about that. I can't ruin what you don't have." Zelina pushed between the girls and headed down the steps to the yard. She heard one of them huff, but she did not turn to see who it was.

"That was decent." Rune was walking up the path; she had not seen him approach. Lexy and her friend stomped up the steps and went inside without another word. "That's Lexy and her follower, Sloane, and they are the worst here. Lexy is Ms. Nyx's pet, so you need to be careful with that one." He smiled and sat down on the top step, patting the empty space next to him without looking at Zelina.

Zelina stood for a moment, a few steps from where Rune sat, debating whether or not to sit with him or walk around to blow off steam. She decided that maybe Rune could calm her just as easily, so she turned around and sat next to him, hands between her knees, and asked, "What did I do to invoke her wrath?"

"Lexy?" he asked gesturing his thumb to the door. "You don't have to do anything to make her pick on you. She's like that to everyone. She's mean and doesn't need a reason. Maybe she was born a mean girl. Don't waste your time or energy on her, she's not worth it."

"So, did you go to school today?'

Rune looked over at her and smiled broadly, the biggest smile she had seen on his face. "Um…Sure, yeah, I did. It was thrilling. I wanted to talk with you about—"

At that moment front screen door slammed opened and Ms. Nyx stormed out. "Zelina, get inside; you need to start helping around here. I thought Mr. Jared talked to you about that today. Get in here." She stood in the doorway wit her arms crossed over her chest and tapped her foot.

Zelina rolled her eyes. "We'll finish our conversation later, I suppose. Have fun." With that, Zelina stood and followed Ms. Nyx inside.

Zelina was led to the kitchen. "You'll help prepare dinner for everyone tonight," said Ms. Nyx. "I trust you remember how to cook?" She had an evil smirk on her face as she turned and walked away. There were two other girls in the kitchen. One was much younger than Zelina, about twelve years old, and the other was about the same age as Zelina. They had their aprons on and were cutting some vegetables on the counter. The two girls did not even look at Zelina.

"Where do I begin?" Zelina asked with a smile. Both girls kept their heads down and continued chopping the vegetables as if they did not see or hear her. "Okay then, what are we making tonight?" she asked as she looked around for an apron.

"Stew," the youngest one answered without looking up. "Grab the big pot up the there." She pointed with her knife to a huge pot sitting on top of a hanging rack above them. After several failed attempts to start a conversation with the girls, Zelina decided she was done trying and just did as she was told by the older girl, which came in short huffs, especially when Zelina did something wrong.

Ms. Nyx showed up as they were finishing the dinner. "Smells wonderful, girls. I hope you taught Zelina a thing or two about how to work in the kitchen and how to work with others." Ms. Nyx glared at Zelina. "It's almost time to begin serving, so get ready for everyone to start lining up. Stand there and be ready to serve them one scoop each and a piece of bread. They will get their own drinks and extras down there." Ms. Nyx smiled at the other girls and left the kitchen.

Several moments later, the kids arrived and grabbed their trays, Zelina started filling their dishes with the stew. She looked up and saw Lexy with her faithful sidekick, Sloane.

"Oh look, Sloane, they found the perfect job for Little Miss Sass: a lunch lady." They giggled and moved on. Zelina rolled her eyes and kept her remarks to herself; she did not want to get in trouble again. *The girls were ridiculous and not worth her time,* she told herself.

Zelina and the other two cooks got their food last, after hanging up their aprons and putting the leftover food away. Zelina sat at an empty table; she could not find Rune and realized she had not seen him in the food line either. She wondered where he was.

The stew was much better than the last meal she ate. She ate it slowly, watching everyone leave the dining hall until she was the last one there. She sat for a while, staring into her empty bowl.

"Anything interesting in there?"

Zelina looked up and saw that Rune was sitting across from her.

"Hey, where were you? You didn't eat." She pushed the bowl away, crossing her arms over her chest.

"Sorry mum, I was busy. I'm here now, although not hungry for this. What was this, anyway?"

"Stew. I helped make it. It wasn't half bad, really."

"Yeah, glad I skipped it, especially with you in the kitchen." He pushed the bowl back in front of Zelina and wrinkled his nose in disgust.

Zelina stuck out her tongue and laughed. "So, where were you?"

"Like I said, I was busy. I can't hang around here all day. So, tell me about your day, here in this glorious place, by yourself."

"What is there to share? I had my meeting with Mr. Jared and then read a little bit. Mostly I sat outside. It was so nice out there."

Looking over his left shoulder, Rune leaned closer to Zelina. When Zelina did not lean in, Rune stared at her. "What, Rune? What's with the secrecy?" With a huff, Zelina finally leaned closer, resting her elbows on the table and her chin in her hands. "What?" she whispered softly.

As Zelina was beginning to tell Rune about the whole floating thing, she remembered the smell of fire from her dream. "Wait. I want to tell you I remembered something—or really, I had a dream, but I only remember part of it. I told you about the chanting ladies, right?" Rune nodded his head, his eyes fixated on her. "Well, I remember the smell of fire. There was fire burning and not a little fire but more like I was surrounded by it. What do you make of that?" She smiled proudly.

"That's great, Zelina. It'll come back; fast it seems. Now on to the meeting."

Zelina was a bit annoyed. She thought Rune would be more excited, more interested in her memory of the fire, but he brushed it off for the meeting with Mr. Jared. "What will come back fast? Come on, Rune! You have to tell me what's going on! Since the moment I met you it's been all mystery and everyone wants to know what I remember and if I'm having dreams. I think it's all strange, very peculiar. If you are truly my friend, then help me."

"Who said I was your friend?" Rune's face showed no emotion, she was unable tell if he was serious or not.

Zelina was unsure what to say to that. She was assuming they were friends before she ran away and he was trying to help her get her memory back, but he never actually said they were friends.

"I'm just kidding. Relax," he said. He looked around the dining hall once more and leaned forward again. "This really isn't the time or place to talk about any of that. We only have a few more minutes. Now please tell me all you can—the important stuff, that is—about your meeting with Mr. Jared."

Zelina took a deep breath, trying to remember only the important parts of the meeting. "Let's see." She started chewing on her top lip. "I can head back to school tomorrow, although it's a new one. I found out my last name is Smith, which doesn't feel right to me. He said I take off all the time. He had me lay on the sofa while he read reports from Ms. Nyx, Damon, and Lexy." Zelina wrinkled her nose in disgust as she mentioned Lexy's name. "She really doesn't like me, does she?"

"We're not discussing Lexy, stay on track here. The meeting with Mr. Jared. Continue, please."

"Sorry. Okay, well I heard him read the report from Ms. Nyx, but none of it seems real, like it was made up. After that, I don't remember a whole lot. I mean, I remember Mr. Jared continued to talk to me, reading the other two reports, but I zoned out; I didn't hear anything he said."

"Zoned out? You just tuned him out, started thinking about other things?"

"No." She thought for a moment, trying to figure out the best way to describe what had happened to her. "More like I wasn't really in the room. Like, what is that called? An out-of-body experience type of thing. I could still hear him talking, but more in the distance. He sounded like he was on the other side of a tunnel. I didn't see my body or anything; I felt like I was floating away."

Rune sat back, placing his hands on the table and looked up at the ceiling. "Yes! This is great. I will meet with you tomorrow morning, I promise. I have to go now, though." He jumped up out of his seat and hurriedly left through the kitchen, out the side door.

Zelina sat a moment longer, wondering what was so great about feeling like she was floating. She giggled a little, thinking maybe Rune was the crazy one and not her.

"Zelina, they need to finish cleaning up in here, so you need to finish up."

She was so lost in her thoughts that she never heard Ms. Nyx enter the room. "Don't I need to help them clean up?"

"No, you've done enough for tonight. You may go." Ms. Nyx looked down on Zelina, raised her eyebrows, and gave a dismissive wave of her hand

Zelina got up slowly. Ms. Nyx never took her eyes off her as she placed her empty dish in the correct bin and headed upstairs. Had Ms. Nyx seen her with Rune? And if so, what was she thinking? Zelina hoped that she would see Rune in her room, as he seemed to show up there. She wanted to talk with him some more and find out more about what she experienced. She also wanted to find out about the smell of fire and what it all meant. However, she did not see him for the rest of the evening. She kept to herself; she had taken a book from the common room earlier in the day and read until she fell asleep.

Her dream was the same as the night before, and just like the night before, she woke up breathless and in a sweat, gripping her blankets. She sat up, and slowing her breathing, wiped the sweat from her forehead with her blanket and turned on the light on her nightstand. She swung her feet over the bed and sat staring out her window. She wondered what the dreams meant, if anything. She wondered if it was normal for her to wake with these nightmares. Dreams did not wake a person like this; these had to be nightmares. As she sat there, concentrating on her breathing and slowing her heart rate, an image flashed in her mind so suddenly that it scared her. She jumped from her bed, turning around to face the door, half expecting to see someone there. There was no one. She backed slowly to the chair, sat down and pulled her legs up to her chest, hugging her knees, shaking.

The image was vivid: the three women chanting softly, as she saw before, only this time Zelina was seeing it more clearly, with more detail. She closed her eyes, rested her forehead on her knees and tried to relax. As she did, the image came back slowly, zooming out as if she was floating. Below her was a circular room and she could see herself standing in the middle. In the center of the room, where Zelina stood, was a circular decoration made of stone inlaid in the floor; it was nearly surrounded by water. There were three other circular pieces of different-colored stone. Those pieces seemed to come from different doorways; Zelina could not see where the doors led. On those stones stood three women dressed in all white, arms out to their sides, one palm facing up while the other faced down. Between the three women, and running the entire length of the room, were long metal troughs of fire. She could feel the heat from the fire on her face. As the women chanted, the water began rising. Small waves moved out toward them, barely hitting their feet, and splashed up, while the flames grew higher. The more the ladies in white chanted, the higher the waves went. Eventually, the fire and water met midair. It amazed Zelina to watch since the water did not extinguish the fire; instead, they seemed to fuel each other. The water got deeper and the fire grew. As this happened, Zelina could see a white, foamy substance floating in the air just below the chanting women's palms. The white substance looked sticky and thick. As the substance grew, the three women lifted their heads. Although Zelina could not see their faces through the thick white veils over their heads, she could feel them looking at her. The three women then brought their hands in front of them, the white substance following them. Their hands were barely in front of their chests. They pushed their hands forward, all at the same time; the white substance flew and hit the platform, knocking Zelina off her feet and bringing her out of her trancelike state. She was sweating again, heart racing, hands shaking. Was this a memory? Surely it was not real, it had to be a nightmare.

Zelina sat curled up in the chair until the sun shone through her window. She never fell back asleep; she sat in the chair, trying to remember every detail of what she saw. The dream continually replaying in her mind and she kept trying to figure out what it meant.

She had an immense headache as she headed downstairs to shower for her first day at her new school. She was not excited about the new school and she wondered if her friends at her old school would be worried about her. The warm shower felt good on her back and neck, which were stiff from sitting in the old chair for so long. She ate dry toast and drank some water for breakfast before heading out to the bus stop. Ms. Nyx gave her the name of her new school and directions as she headed out the door, in case she had forgotten how to get around town. Zelina made it to the bus stop with some time to spare and sat next to an elderly woman while she waited.

"Off to school, dear?" the old woman asked, smiling at her. The elderly woman was hunched over and wore big white sunglasses and a sunhat. It was hard to see the woman's face. Zelina noticed her finely manicured nails, a bright red that matched her long red dress and the red and white scarf she had wrapped around her shoulders.

"Yes, ma'am. First day at a new school, so I'm quite nervous." Zelina was wringing her fingers; it struck her how nervous she was.

"Don't be nervous, dear. You have a very nice face; beautiful eyes as well." The woman patted her leg. "Bus is here."

They climbed onto the bus and sat next to each other without speaking another word. Zelina looked over the directions Ms. Nyx had given her for several minutes, memorizing them, and then stared out the window. She knew she had to have seen all this before. The cars zooming past, people walking, all the buildings, but still it seemed so new to her. She was in awe of everything going on around her.

She was on the bus for about fifteen minutes when it came time for her to exit, the elderly lady still sitting beside her. "Excuse me, ma'am, I have to get off here."

Zelina smiled, stood from her seat, and squeezed past the lady, who suddenly grabbed her wrist, looked her in the eyes and said, "Be a good girl today. Enjoy your time while you can." She dropped her hand back to her lap and smiled up at Zelina as if she had no idea what just happened. "What, dear? Did you forget something?"

"No, ma'am. Thank you." Zelina stepped off the bus, shaken. She did not know what the lady meant by, "Enjoy your time while you can." It was all so strange. She remembered, at that moment, that Rune had said he would meet her that morning. Maybe he would shed some light on what was happening to her. She was beginning to feel a bit insane. She had expected him to show up in her room before she left that morning. He was not at breakfast either, although she had to leave earlier than anyone since she did not know her way around, so maybe that was why. Her head was starting to pound again; she did not want her first day of school to be like this. She took a couple of deep breaths, rubbing the back of her neck, and watched the bus drive away. She looked at the directions once again and began walking toward the school.

The school was a massive stone and brick edifice. It looked as if it had been there for hundreds of years; it was three stories tall with arched, stained glass windows. Directly out front were two sets of stone steps, one leading from the right and one from the left, curving around to meet at the front door. The building reminded Zelina of a castle from many centuries ago. A bit of moss grew on the side, the grass was still a beautiful lush green, and a few students stood in the shade of some trees to the right.

So many kids were standing out front, talking to each other, listening to music and clowning around, that no one noticed her.

She climbed the stairs, keeping her head down; she did not see Rune sitting on the middle step. He grabbed the leg of her jeans as she stepped past him, making her trip slightly and scaring her. "You really need to watch where you're going." He smiled up at her.

"It's not funny. I could've fallen on my face. What are you doing here? How did you get here?" She stared down at him, her brow furrowed, slightly annoyed.

"Now, now, little one." He stood, still smiling, and put his arm through hers. "Let's get some tea and have a nice chat, shall we?" He started to walk off. Zelina stood where she was, making him stumble back. "Come on. We can't talk here," he said.

"I have school and I will not get in trouble again. So, we can talk after." She turned to walk up the stairs, following most of the other students.

"You have got to trust me. They won't even know you weren't here; I've taken care of everything. Just trust me." He pulled her arm slightly as he walked away.

Zelina watched all the other kids go in the front door; she and Rune were the only two left outside. She slumped her shoulders, feeling defeated, and let out a loud huff. "Fine, Rune. If I get in trouble, I'll make your life truly miserable." Rune's whole face lit up, which infuriated her. "I mean it. I can do it," she warned.

They walked down the stone steps together and across the street to a charming little café at the corner of the two roads, called The Enchanting Cafea, where their specialty was their many teas. Zelina found the name of the café cute, mixing café with the fact that they serve so many different kinds of teas; it put a smile on her face. She loved that the outside looked rustic with peeling paint and the old stone showing through. The two round tables out front were already taken by people reading newspapers. The entire front of the shop had big windows that she glanced in; there was only one door to the place and on it was the name of the shop, written in beautiful antique writing. Rune held the door open for her and as she stepped in, she was greeted with a soothing mix of different scents.

Her favorite was cinnamon. The inside was decorated the same as the outside, with the chipped paint and the old stone showing. She liked the small vintage countertop and the food in a refrigerated case looked delicious. The tea shop only had one other patron inside. Most people were either on their way to work or at school.

Zelina sat at a table by the window, facing the school. She was a bit nervous that Ms. Nyx would find out she ditched school, but she desperately needed to talk with Rune about her dream and the old lady on the bus. He knew more than he was letting on and she had to know what was happening to her. She sat down while Rune got them some tea; she stared out the window thinking about her dream, trying to keep all the details fresh in her mind. The sky was turning dark as gloomy clouds rolled in. The wind picked up slightly and she watched a few leaves twirl and fall to the ground.

"Looks like it might storm again." Rune set a steeping cup of tea in front of Zelina as he sat down. "I didn't get you anything to eat. I figured you ate already."

"Yeah, I had some breakfast, thank you though." She was unsure of how to begin telling Rune about the dream. Should she blurt it out? How does one ease in to sharing such things? She did not want him to think she was losing her mind; right now, Rune was her only friend. She took a sip of the tea and it seemed to calm her nerves some. "Rune, I need to tell you about a dream I had last night, although it doesn't seem like much of a dream, it's so unbelievable." She looked down at her tea; she could not look him in the eye as she began.

"Well, go ahead. We honestly don't have all day, you know." He smiled; he seemed to know she was having a hard time talking. He never took his eyes off of her. "Just take your time. I promise I won't think you're a freak. I already know you are one." His smile grew as he punched her lightly on the shoulder. "Relax and tell me about what happened."

Taking another sip of her tea, she tentatively began to recount the images she had seen in her dream the night before. As she described the events to Rune, she began to talk faster and her heart began racing. She realized, though, it was not out of fear of the events; instead, it was out of fear of what Rune would say to her or think of her. She was afraid to look at Rune, afraid to see disgust in his eyes, so she kept her eyes on the trees across the street while she described the dream.

As she sat in her room during the previous night, she wondered if she would remember all of it: the sights, the smells, everything. She contemplated writing it down and letting Rune read it. She realized that was no good; if anyone found it, especially Ms. Nyx, she could be in severe trouble, so she decided to keep replaying the images in her mind for this very moment, to share with Rune. She had to stop several times to catch her breath. She wanted to make sure she did not leave anything out; he had to know every detail.

Finally, taking a deep breath, she turned away from the window to look at Rune. "Well, what do you think? Should I tell Mr. Jared? I mean, it did really scare me—it still scares me. What if this starts—"

"No. You cannot tell anyone at the house about this. Change that—you should tell no one about it." Rune was shaking his head, bringing his face closer to hers. "You're going to have to trust me. Do *not* tell anyone about that dream. I can see that it's left you shaken, so let's change the subject to something better, shall we? Let's talk about—"

Zelina put her hand up in front of Rune's face to quiet him. "Yes, let's talk about how you get around the house without getting caught. Let's talk about how you skip school and how I won't be getting into trouble once I return to the house. How no one even knows I didn't attend school. It's time for you to share with me." She slapped her hand on the table, causing Rune to jump. She sat back, crossing her arms over her chest, her brows drew together.

Rune laughed. "Well that, my dear, is a long story and definitely one that should not be told here. I can tell you that I'm smart and quick. Finish your tea and we'll go for a walk." He turned to the window and started drinking his tea. Zelina sat, arms crossed, glaring at Rune. He obviously was not going to talk, so Zelina, continuing to stare at him, drank her tea.

"So, can you at least answer me this? Was it a dream or a memory? Real or not?"

"It's a memory; however, I can't explain any of that here. Finish your tea and let's get moving."

Once they were both done, they headed out of the tea shop, up the street and around a corner. The clouds were moving in faster, and the wind picked up so much that it was blowing Zelina's hair into her face and mouth. "Rune, where are we going?" she questioned, holding her hair back.

"You'll see. It's close." He had his arm looped through hers again and was practically dragging her down the street. They walked down some cobblestone streets, down two alleys, and past a very posh neighborhood before finally reaching their destination. "Here we are," he said with a smile, letting go of her and sweeping his arms in front of him like this was his masterpiece.

"Are you kidding me? You dragged me out of a cozy tea shop for miles in this insane wind for this?! What is this place?" Standing in front of her was an old, crumbling, two-story brick building. It looked as if it had been a factory of some sort many, many years ago. The windows were either busted out completely or boarded over. The ground was a mud pit from the last rainstorm and nothing seemed to grow there; everything around it was dead. "We aren't really going in there, are we?" Zelina enquired.

The "front door" was actually a huge board hanging from a few screws. Rune started walking toward the building, leaving Zelina behind.

Rune never said a word; he did not even turn around to see if Zelina was following him. He pushed the board to the side and slipped in. Zelina stood outside, chewing her bottom lip and looking at the place, afraid it would collapse any second. She wondered why the town had not torn the eyesore down. A very upscale neighborhood was only a few blocks away; surely they did not like having that monstrosity so close.

Rune poked his head out of an empty window. "It's going to rain. You better get in here or you'll get drenched." Then he disappeared behind the door.

Throwing her hands in the air and realizing she had nowhere else to go, Zelina headed into the dilapidated building. She pushed the board aside and peered in.

"Rune?" She did not see or hear him. "Rune, where are you?" She walked in, just far enough to let the board slide shut. There was barely enough light in the entry for her to see her surroundings. In front of her was a reception area. She stood still, taking in her surroundings, trying to locate Rune. To her right were swinging doors and to her left was a long hallway. There was trash and leaves on the floor; a few pieces of paper lay undisturbed on a table by the reception area. She could hear the wind kicking up outside and hoped it would blow over before they had to head back. She decided to head down the long hallway. She hoped this was not a joke and that Rune would not jump out at her. As she walked down the hall, she saw old offices with papers on the floor, and one room had blankets thrown on an old couch. "Someone sleeps here," she said in a whisper. "Rune, you better answer me. This isn't funny," she said as she turned away from the office. Frustration rose in her and her stomach knotted. "Rune, I'm leaving. I'll figure out how to get back home without you. This really isn't funny!" she yelled. As she turned to leave, she heard Rune call her name from the opposite end, closer to the swinging doors. She ran down the hall and through the swinging doors, slamming into Rune, knocking them both to the floor.

"What is wrong with you, Zelina?" Rune asked, sitting up and running his fingers through his hair. "Something chasing you?" His eyes got wide and he put his hand to his mouth, mocking her.

"No. You left me out there. I didn't know where you were and you didn't answer me. It wasn't funny." She was livid and his making fun of her was not helping. She stood up and dusted herself off, preparing to leave him in the dingy building. She had had enough.

"I didn't hear you calling me. I'm sorry. I didn't do it on purpose. Come on over here; I want to show you something." Rune took her by the hand and led her deeper into the building. They passed an old locker room and went through the main floor of the factory. "I'm not sure what they used to make here. It's interesting, don't you think?" You could see where the machines once sat; small machine parts were scattered on the floor. Other than that, the place was entirely empty.

"Not really. This place is creepy and should be torn down." Zelina gripped his hand, afraid of somehow getting separated from him. "Why are we here, Rune?"

"Look at this place." He stood in front of a set of stairs, beaming. He swept his free arm out in front of him. He was honestly proud of the place. "There is so much history here, a history we don't even know." Zelina was not amused by him. "All right, come on. Up this way."

Rune led her up a flight of stairs, then turned left before he stopped and turned to look at her. "Back over there is another part of the factory. That's where the roof is caved in so I don't go that way." He grinned, like a little boy telling his mother how good he has been. "We're almost there. It's just right across this walkway."

Ahead of them was a narrow hall that led to a covered second-floor walkway. The glass was broken out of most of the windows there too, with only a few shards remaining. Zelina stopped for just a moment to look out one of the busted windows. She could not fathom why Rune would be taking her here or why she even trusted this boy. She rubbed her palms together. She had no memory of him before a few days ago—how did she know he was not some crazy person? "Come on. You said you didn't like it here, so why are you stopping?" Rune was standing beside her, poking her upper arm, eyebrows raised and eyes wide. "Let's go, let's go, let's go."

"I just wanted to…I don't know. Let's go, lead the way." Zelina put her arm in his, walking beside him. "Rune, you've got to tell me what's going on. I know you know more than you're letting on."

Zelina looked up at Rune's face; he was looking straight ahead and seemed to be ignoring her. He turned right at the end of the covered walkway. "Everything will make sense soon enough. You just have to trust me," he stated in a melodious way and it made Zelina grin.

"How long have we known each other? How is it you remember so much?"

Rune continued to lead her around, weaving in and out of hallways until they stopped in front of a set of double doors that looked fairly new compared to the rest of the building. They seemed odd and out of place.

"We actually barely know each other now. I can tell you this: we lived near each other when we were younger, and we really didn't get along very well, we picked on each other a lot."

Zelina did not have time to contemplate what Rune told her; he closed his eyes and whispered, almost inaudibly, a word that Zelina never heard before: "*Demitto.*"

The doors creaked loudly as they opened inward. The room beyond the doors looked like any other room in the building, old and run-down with trash scattered on the floor. It appeared as though someone lived in the room. There was a mattress with a couple of blankets against the farthest wall, near a busted-out window, and food wrappers were strewn across the floor, some old, some new. Zelina also noticed there was no building debris and hardly any dust on the floor.

"Rune, I don't think we should be in here."

Zelina began to turn to leave when Rune grabbed her arm and winked at her.

"You? This is your mess?" she asked incredulously. "Why would you be staying in here?"

They entered the room, which was quite big—about the size

of the two offices downstairs—and warm, considering the busted window and the storm brewing outside.

Rune turned toward the doors once again and murmured something; the doors shut on their own. "This is my sanctuary. Nice, isn't it?"

Zelina was unsure whether he was being serious or joking with her, so she gave a half smile and shrugged.

"I know it's no palace, but it's away from the house and the prying eyes of Ms. Nyx." He sat on his blankets, leaning back against the wall.

"Well, you could at least pick up the trash," Zelina said as she bent down to pick up a food wrapper and throw it in a nearby bin. "Slob." She walked a few steps over to an old brown dusty chair and sat on the very edge; she had so many questions she wanted to ask him.

"Before you start asking questions, let me get a few things out of the way. I can't tell you everything. As much as I want to, I just can't. Most of it has to come to you naturally. It'll help if you don't fight it, as you didn't fight the memory from last night. Ask away. I'll answer what I can."

"Okay. How do we know each other? You said out there that we lived near each other when we were younger. I don't remember you or where we lived, so how do you remember?"

"Good questions. Not ones that I can answer right now. Another?"

Zelina shook her head and looked up at the ceiling, remembered the meeting with Mr. Jared, and smiled. "Yesterday, when I had my meeting with Mr. Jared, as I lay on the sofa and he was telling me about running away, I felt as if I was floating. What do you know about that?" Zelina crossed her arms and waited; she knew he was holding back.

Rune sat up, puffed out his chest and beamed; he was loving this. "Well, that was me."

Zelina, eyebrows raised, looked at him. "You? How…?"

Rune stood from his bed, put his hand up to stop her from talking and winked at her. "It was actually very simple. Even the slowest of us can do something like that." He walked closer to the doors again and turned around to face her. "I knew what Mr. Jared was going to do—he was planting ideas or memories in your head. I couldn't let that happen. If he had gotten in your head, then there would be no coming back; I would've lost you for good. So, I left for school, as I normally do." Rune took a deep breath.

"You mean you didn't go to school?" Zelina interrupted him, getting up from the chair and sitting on the bed, which was quite comfortable—more comfortable than it looked.

"Yes. Well, I have to make it look as if I am attending school. Now, no more interrupting." Rune began pacing the room. "I doubled back to the house, hid out front, and waited. Mr. Jared always, *always* opens the window by the sofa. It's his job to install these memories in each new person."

Zelina raised her eyebrows, about to ask him what he meant when he shook his head. "Yes, Zelina, you are new here. You have not been here for years; you have not run away before. That's all I can say about that, so please don't ask. Now, back to your meeting. Once I saw you enter the office, I sat behind the shrubs in front of the open window. I could hear everything he told you. Some of it made me laugh; I had a hard time keeping quiet." He stopped in front of the door and turned to Zelina, who was watching him, her brow furrowed and chewing on her nails. "You okay? You seem a bit tense."

Zelina dropped her hands to the bed and relaxed her shoulders. "You told me not to interrupt you, so you shouldn't be allowed to stop. Now continue! Tell me how I was floating! Explain! Explain!" She waved at him to continue, put a pillow behind her back and crossed her arms over her chest.

"Okay. Sorry." He began pacing again as he continued, "When he brought you over to the sofa and started reading you Ms. Nyx's statement, I started helping you. I have certain, for lack of a better word, abilities. I knew what Mr. Jared was about to do and I couldn't let it happen. I put something around your mind, like a shield. I didn't know you would feel like you were floating—never heard of that happening. I need to look into that; it could mean something…"

"Stay focused here. Rune, you are saying you have powers? Really? Do I look stupid to you?" Zelina shot up from the bed and stood, glaring at Rune.

Snapping out of his thoughts, Rune jumped slightly. "Well, that outfit isn't the best." He smiled at her, trying to lighten the mood. Zelina stood with her arms crossed over her chest, eyes boring into him. Rune walked to her. "Zelina, I really did that. I put a protection spell around you so Mr. Jared couldn't plant ideas or fake memories in your mind. The floating, I'm not sure what that means, but I do know it worked. You don't remember anything he told you, right?"

Zelina nodded her head, agreeing with Rune.

"So that's all that matters. It worked. It kept your mind clear so your memory can fully come back now. See?" His eyes were full of concern and he bit his lower lip.

Zelina huffed, lowering her arms and looking out the window. She relaxed a bit. "I don't understand any of what you just told me. None of it. So, what are you?" Zelina turned from the window, walked to Rune and stared into his eyes. "An alien or something?" She laughed and strode to the door. She tried to open it, but it was locked. "Rune, unlock this door. This is ridiculous." The tension slowly rising back in her shoulders.

"I'm not an alien and neither are you. Sadly, there are things I can't tell you. You have to find out for yourself. If I were to tell you everything, it could prevent your memory from fully returning or it could turn your brain to mush, and we can't have that happen, any worse than it already has." He gave a half grin; she kept her back to him. "Oh, stop being so stubborn. Just sit down, really think about things." Zelina glanced over her shoulder, he gestured to the chair and nodded his head. "Please."

She whirled around. "Just unlock the door, Rune. I thought you were going to tell me the truth about everything. I thought you were my friend." She turned back to the door and banged on it several times. "Unlock this door, Rune, before I scream." Her hands were now in fists and she could feel the anger rising in her.

Rune put his hands up in front of him. "If you would think about your dream, try to remember anything before seeing Ms. Nyx! Think about all you've been told since you showed up, how you've been living here for years, yet no one knows you or talks to you. Please give me a few more minutes." Rune approached her gingerly. "Zelina, I am your friend and I'm telling you the truth." When Zelina did not look at him, he relented, muttered something and Zelina heard the doors unlock. "There you go. I unlocked the doors for you. You're free to go and discover the truth on your own. I'll be here if you need me."

Zelina did not move as she was unsure of what to do. A part of her desperately wanted to leave, but another part of her wanted to stay, wanted to believe everything Rune was saying was true. He was right; nothing since she first saw Ms. Nyx made sense to her, not since she awoke to find herself at Stonehenge. She opened the door slowly and looked over her shoulder at Rune. "I'm sorry, Rune; this is all a bit mad. I need time to process things." She smiled weakly and walked out.

As she headed down the hall, Zelina heard the door shut and lock. She sighed and felt utterly alone. She hated that feeling, but she felt she made the right decision, until she realized she had no idea how to get back to the house or the school. Rune walked her there; she had no idea where they were. She needed to go back and ask Rune to take her home, but she did not want to see him, so she decided to wait for him to leave; then she would simply follow him.

She found her way back to the front door and sat on a chair in the reception area. She did not know how long Rune would sit up there and the place was rather creepy. She sat back in the chair, trying to relax. As she waited, she started thinking about everything that Rune told her upstairs, about him having special abilities, and how he had protected her mind. That brought a slight smile to her face; his story was too fantastical to be real. She then turned her thoughts to the moment when she had first seen Ms. Nyx. Ms. Nyx knew exactly who she was, as did Damon; however, no one else seemed to know. She thought back to when she first entered the house and how the other kids there did not seem to recognize her. She mentioned that to Mr. Jared in their meeting and he told her it was because she had caused so much trouble, which was quite plausible. Maybe she had no friends there because of the trouble she caused; maybe their stares were not from her being new but from them being annoyed with her attitude. She put her head down on the desk in front of her. Her head was beginning to pound; none of it made sense. How could she not even have one friend, besides Rune? She thought about that too. When he came into her room, he wanted to see her eyes. He didn't ask if she was okay, how much trouble she was in, or even how far she got. No, he wanted to see her eyes. As a friend, would he really care about the color of her eyes above everything else? Surely not.

"You have a memory block on you. Basically, they erased all your memories; however, with some people it doesn't take completely."

Zelina looked up to see Rune standing in the doorway of the reception area. He had a look of concern on his face. "Come on. I'll take you home."

Zelina remained seated. "A block? How—? Why did I get my memory erased?"

Rune looked around the room. "Let's head upstairs where it's safer to talk."

"No, I want to talk here. Please, Rune, help me to understand." She put her head back down on the desk; she wanted to cry.

"Is your head hurting?" He walked over and knelt beside her.

"Yes. The more I try to put the pieces together, the more it hurts. I want to understand. I need to understand this, but it hurts."

"Hold on. Give me a few minutes." With that he walked out of the room. Zelina could hear him walking back and forth just in front of her. She lifted her head long enough to see him walking from the board that was the door to the reception area; she could see his mouth moving and hear his voice, but she did not understand what he was saying. He walked back into the room. "Okay. We have a few minutes, then we have to go. I'll make this as quick as possible." He knelt beside her again. "Zelina, everything they've told you is a lie—everything. I promise that all I'm telling you is the truth. I have no reason to lie to you. I need your help as much as you need mine."

Zelina raised her head to look at him, tears in her eyes. "What do you mean?"

He took a deep breath in. "You can help me get back home. I know you can, and I can help you as your memory starts coming back. We need to work together."

She wiped her eyes and said weakly, "Rune, I don't get any of this. My head really hurts. Maybe we should go back now." She started to get up, but Rune put his hand on her shoulder, keeping her in the chair.

"I know you don't understand it yet, but you will, and when you do, you will need my help. That's what I'm here for. I promise I will help you as I was once helped." Rune put his finger to his lips to quiet her as she was about to ask a question. He spoke softly. "Just lay your head down and listen, no interruptions." Rune got up and started pacing. "I remember waking up at Stonehenge when I was about eleven years old. Ms. Nyx and Damon showed up, shouting at me about running away and causing all kinds of problems. The only real problem was that I still had a bit of memory left. I remembered the three ladies chanting; I remembered the water and the fire and being transported here. I remembered my family, somewhat, and the street I once lived on. Some of my memories were fuzzy or gone altogether. I was taken into Mr. Jared's office, just as you were, and was told my last name was Johnson, which I knew was a lie. Right there, at that moment, I knew those people were not who they said they were. I knew who they were working for and what their job was. I told them I remembered nothing, just as you did, and just like you, they told me how this happened all the time to me and how I had to learn to control it. I didn't know I had a special ability at that time, but did know not to listen to anything Mr. Jared was telling me so I let my mind wander and thought of my dreams or of my real home. Well, as time went on, I began to have more dreams, and more memories would return. On my way to school, sometime in the winter, it had to have been at least six months since I had first arrived, I met an old lady at a tea shop. Yes, even then I skipped school. She bought me tea and talked with me for hours. As we were leaving, she whispered to me to meet her again the next day; she wanted to show me something. Now, normally I wouldn't have shown up to meet a total stranger so she could take me somewhere—I knew not to do such things— but there was something in her eyes that I trusted, that felt like home. There was something there that I recognized."

Zelina's head snapped up and she turned to look at Rune. That is exactly how she felt about him. She never told him that, either, so how could he know?

He winked at her and continued. "We are running out of time; I'd better hurry. I did meet with her and she brought me here to this factory, to that room up there, and told me the same thing I told you. She told me about the house and what they do there, how they plant memories in kids who are sent here, and how they help them become accustomed to living here and being part of this society. The only difference between you and me is that I came here with more memories than you. I'm telling you exactly what I was told. It'll come back to you, and when it does, I'll be here to help." Rune knelt beside her, looking Zelina in the eyes. "I promise it'll all make sense. You need to trust me and know that I'm telling you the truth." He stood up, offered Zelina his hand, and together they walked out of the building.

They meandered as the sky churned above them. The sun was completely gone. Dark clouds rolled overhead and thunder crashed, scaring Zelina several times. They walked in silence most of the way, both lost in thought. Zelina's headache eased and she finally broke the silence. "Rune, what happened to your friend, the old lady?"

"She was killed. Long story—I'll have to share that with you another time."

"I'm sorry." She bit her lower lip and looked down at her feet. "Okay. Easier question, I think: How can you, or we, skip school every day and not get caught?" She glanced up at him.

Rune stopped and gave her a mischievous grin. "Now that one is fun. It's a spell I use; it makes people see what I want them to see. Also, I hack into the school's main computer and change my grades and attendance. I'll do the same for you. You don't need to attend school here; you have a school back home, and I'll teach you all you need to know. You can call me Professor Rune." He started walking off with a slight strut. "Yes. 'Professor', I like that. This is my new name."

Zelina watched Rune walk away and she laughed; he had a way of taking the stress out of any situation. She caught up with him. "I'll never call you professor, just so we're clear on that. So, what do we do now?"

They approached the bus stop that would take them home, and both sat down on the empty bench. "I'd like to meet here daily, go over to the factory and discuss dreams or memories that come back to you."

"What if nothing comes back to me?"

"Well, then we'll just hang out. Eventually, memories will come back and we can begin working. When we are at the house, we really shouldn't talk about this stuff; it's not safe."

School let out and groups of kids waited at the bus stop. None of them seemed to notice Rune and Zelina sitting there, they were all looking down at their phones.

Rune and Zelina did not say another word until they reached their stop. As they wandered up the road toward the house, Rune slowed even more. "You should go in ahead of me."

Zelina nodded and continued walking, leaving Rune behind. She would rather have walked up to the house with Rune beside her, especially when she turned up the walk and saw Lexy and Sloane sitting on the front porch. "Well, well, well, if it isn't Little Miss Forgetful." Lexy cackled.

"Well, at least you think you're funny. Reality is, you're a git." Zelina walked up the front steps and through the door. She did not stop to hear what Lexy or Sloane had to say; she had had an enjoyable day with Rune and she was not going to let them ruin it.

As she was headed up to her room Mr. Jared called to her. "Zelina, can I see you for a moment, please?" He shut the office door and Zelina huffed as she headed back down the stairs. All Zelina wanted was to go to her room and lie down. Her day had been filled with madness, and she wanted to process it all. Instead, she had to go deal with Mr. Jared and whatever nonsense he was going to tell her.

She knocked on Mr. Jared's door and opened it slowly, peering in to see where he was. "Come in, come in." Mr. Jared was sitting behind his desk and pointed to a chair in front of him.

"Is something wrong?" Zelina questioned as she trudged into the office.

"No. I merely want to have a talk with you. Sit down." He kept his eyes on the papers that lay in front of him on his desk. "How did your first day go?"

Zelina sat down, putting her book bag on her lap. "It was fine," she shrugged. "Nothing much happened, just school." She was not sure what she should say; she should have asked Rune about that. She could feel herself starting to sweat, she began to pick at the strap of her book bag and bounce her leg. What if Mr. Jared knew? What if he got mad that she had skipped school and was lying about it? What would happen then?

Mr. Jared kept his eyes on the papers, occasionally writing something on the notepad beside him. "That's good, dear. No problems then?"

"No, sir. Everything went fine. I didn't talk to anyone, kept to myself mostly."

"That's good." He finally looked up from the papers and put his pen down and stared at her with concern. "I feel like you're holding something back." He got up, walked to the front of his desk, and sat on the edge of it, crossing his arms and furrowing his brow. "If you're having nightmares again, I need to know. I need to know what's going on with you so that I can help you."

Zelina chewed her bottom lip, trying to think of a way out of this. She wondered if Rune was outside the window and was tempted to look over but stopped herself. She did not want Mr. Jared thinking she was indeed hiding something. "Well, I did have a dream last night. It wasn't really a bad one so I didn't feel the need to mention it."

"Please, continue."

"Well, I was running through a forest with some dogs chasing me. I looked over my shoulder to see how close the dogs were and I saw the dogs had the faces of Lexy and Sloane. I stopped running and faced them. I told them to leave me alone or I would hit them with a big stick, which appeared in my hand. They tucked their tails, whimpered and ran off. That was it. That's all I remember." She gave a half smile. She was not sure where that had come from but was glad it came to her quickly.

"Interesting. Are you, Lexy and Sloane having problems?"

"I wouldn't say problems. I'd say they are having fun picking on me a bit about my memory loss. I don't care much what they say or think."

"I see. Well, if it gets worse—both the dreams and Lexy—please let me know." He went back to his desk chair, grabbed his pen and began writing once again. "You may go."

Zelina was happy to be excused; however, as she got to the door,

Mr. Jared stopped her. "Zelina, have you seen Rune today?"

She stopped with her hand reaching toward the door, looked over her shoulder and said, "No sir. Is he in trouble?" She turned the doorknob slowly even though she wanted out of there so desperately.

"No. If you do see him, please send him to see me." He went back to his writing and Zelina walked out before he could stop her once more.

From Rune's notebook, page 72

Chapter Four

ZELINA WENT TO HER ROOM and looked out her window wondering where Rune was. Her head started spinning once again as she thought of all that had happened. There was so much to process, so much to think over. She threw her book bag in the chair and decided to curl up for a quick nap.

"Zelina, wake up."

Zelina awoke with a fright. She was not sure how long she had been sleeping, but she was glad she had not had any dreams. Rune was standing over her, smiling down at her. "What's wrong?" she asked groggily as she rubbed her eyes and sat up.

"Nothing. It's dinner and I think you should come down and eat. Have a good sleep?" He backed up and sat on the edge of the chair while Zelina swung her feet off the bed and stretched.

"Yeah. Felt good to sleep uninterrupted. Oh hey, Mr. Jared wanted to see you." She got up and looked out the window before heading to the mirror that hung above her dresser.

"I already spoke to him. It's no big deal. He asked a few questions about us and how my job was going."

"I'll never get this red mess under control." She grabbed a hair tie and pulled her hair back out of her face. "So, what did you say about us?" She was watching Rune in the mirror.

"Nothing. That we're only friends and like hanging out. That's all. Why? Did you want me to say more? Something deeper?" He walked behind her and leaned in, putting his head on her shoulder and batting his eyelashes at her in the mirror.

She spun around and hit him playfully on the arm. "Don't be gross. Get out of my room before I hit you again." She loved the way Rune made her laugh; she felt so at ease around him and felt she was safe with him.

Rune walked out, laughing. "I'll see you downstairs, my love," he said and blew her a kiss.

Zelina rolled her eyes and laughed. She tried to straighten out her wrinkled clothes, then headed down for dinner, which she hoped was edible. She could not remember the last time she had eaten something that was truly delicious. The food they served in the house was always bland or dry. She was unsure what food she was missing exactly, just that she was missing it. She missed spices and flavor—mouthwatering food. Zelina stopped midway down the stairs; for an instant she could almost taste a meal her mother had made for her. She tried to concentrate, even for a moment, on that memory. She grasped at it, attempting to reach it before it faded away, like one would grasp for a branch as they fell from a tree. It faded out as quickly as it had come. It made her sad; she felt she had been right behind her mother, yet never got to see her.

She closed her eyes. A throbbing started behind her eyes and she took a deep breath, trying to keep the headache at bay. She wanted the rest of her evening to be carefree; she needed that.

Zelina opened her eyes slowly, stood up straight and put a smile on her face as she descended the stairs. She entered the dining hall to see just about everyone sitting and eating; she must have been the last person there. She was quite surprised to see Ms. Nyx and Mr. Jared eating at one of the tables. She wondered if that was normal for them; they had not eaten dinner the previous evening nor breakfast that morning in the dining hall. Zelina grabbed her tray and food, trying not to think too much about it. She found Rune and sat across from him, the two administrators behind her. He looked a bit tense, though. He did not have his light attitude;

instead, he was concentrating on Mr. Jared and Ms. Nyx. "What's wrong?" Zelina asked as she took a bite of food, room-temperature bean and sausage casserole, only to find it was rubbish, as always. She thought about pushing it away and being hungry, then remembered she had to eat to keep up the pretense that she was happy there and coping once again.

"They've never eaten in here," Rune whispered after a moment, bringing Zelina out of her thoughts. "I find it interesting that I was asked about us today and then find they're in here. We need to be on guard."

He was eating without looking at his food and talking to Zelina without looking at her. He did not take his eyes off of them, as if he was afraid if he stopped watching them something bad would happen. For the first time, Zelina saw fear in Rune's eyes and she did not like it.

Zelina turned to look at the two adults. They both looked at her. Zelina smiled and waved at them and they went back to talking as Zelina turned back to Rune. "Is it bad that they're in here? You think they know something?" She was beginning to get nervous, making it even harder to eat.

Rune looked at Zelina; his eyes seemed to be on fire. He was definitely on edge. He fidgeted with his fork, moving food around. "How was school?" He almost hissed the words through clenched teeth.

Zelina debated whether to answer; she knew it was not a real question, and she honestly did not want to be around him at that moment. "It was fine," she replied reluctantly.

Zelina was very confused by it all. She wanted to go back to her room and sleep. She wanted peace right now, and she knew it was not going to happen while Mr. Jared and Ms. Nyx were in the same room. Rune would not relax—he was not going to joke with her or even smile. She decided to play along. "How's your job going?"

"Good. I may be up for a promotion." His eyes were back on Ms. Nyx and Mr. Jared. Zelina wanted to turn around, see if they were looking her way. She wanted to march over to them, find out what they were saying and what they were doing in there. She wanted to slap Rune, to bring back the happy-go-lucky guy, the one that made her at ease. She did not like this; he had made her feel that all would be fine, and that was not happening now.

"Wow. That's great. I'm not sure when I will be allowed to start working. Hopefully soon." Zelina continued to pick at her food, unsure of what else to say or do. She desperately wanted to know what was going on, and yet she knew there was nothing she could do.

"I'll talk to you later, Zelina."

Rune got up with a huff, put his tray away and stomped out of the dining hall. Zelina tried to eat more of the food, then gave up and moved it around on her plate. She wanted to wait until Mr. Jared and Ms. Nyx left, but they did not seem to be leaving anytime soon. Every time she looked their way, they were looking at her and whispering. Zelina gave up; she could not sit there anymore. As she got up and put her tray away, she could feel eyes on her. She decided to head up to her room and stay away from everyone for the evening. She would meet with Rune the next morning and they would discuss everything then. She had to let it go for now, or she would never get any sleep.

Zelina was so exhausted from the day's events that she decided to shower early and head to bed. She wanted to get a good night's sleep; it seemed she had not slept restfully in days. No one spoke to her as she headed down for her shower or even as she returned the book to the common room. She tried not to think about the day. She wanted her mind to be clear for rest. Zelina went to bed before the sun was fully set and drifted off to the sounds of a couple of children playing outside. That night, she did not dream of the three ladies or of the fire and water. She did not see flashes of stone with a circle made of fire. She did not dream of the factory and all that Rune had told her. She drifted off to sleep.

She was wandering in an old two-story house. The walls were discolored from age; she could not guess what color they once had been. Looking out a window, she saw it had a small back garden and what looked like a vegetable patch off to the side. If it was where vegetables were indeed grown, no one had taken care of it in quite some time. Everything looked long dead. The ground beneath her window was brown, there was no green grass, no trees, and no flowers. Turning from the window, she caught a glimpse of herself in a small mirror. He hair was still unmanageably curly but was light aqua and her eyes were deep purple. For some unknown reason, this did not shock her.

The room she was in was small, with space enough for a bed and a small wardrobe. The old wood floors creaked beneath her bare feet as she walked around the house. The windows were open, and a cool breeze blew through the house and smelled so sweet, something she did not expect after seeing the dead garden. She could hear children playing not too far away and smiled. She wandered about the upstairs, peering in each of the three bedrooms and the one bathroom before heading downstairs. Each room was about the same size, with only a bed and wardrobe in each. There was nothing fantastic about the furniture in the rooms; it was made of simple wood with no intricate details, all fairly plain and ordinary. She could see where portraits once hung upon the walls; now they were bare. Several broken frames lay on the floor.

She headed down the creaky stairs, which lead directly into the kitchen. There was a very small dining table in the center of the room; the top was covered in dirt and had many scratches and spots on it. One of the two chairs was broken into several pieces and lying on the floor. The old stove sat beside the sink, above which was an open window. In the sink were some filthy dishes. She turned from the kitchen and headed left into the main room where an old, torn sofa sat under a window. Across from the sofa was a chair covered in dust with a hole in the seat. The fireplace in the center of the room looked well- used, with the stone around it charred; it still had some wood sitting in it.

As she stepped out into the back garden, she heard a woman call her name. The woman's voice sounded scared and it put a panic in Zelina. She tried to find the woman, following the voice, but she never could track her down. It was as if she was always just out of sight, no matter what Zelina did.

Zelina began to run down the road, passing the children playing and people relaxing in their gardens or tending their vegetables. She ran, trying to concentrate on which way the voice was coming from, until she slammed into someone. She hit them so hard that she fell backward to the ground.

"Watch where you're going, will you?" The boy she had run into bent over and stuck his hand out to help her up. "Why are you in such a hurry?"

He had a beautiful smile, with dark mint green hair cut short on the back and sides and styled nicely on top. His eyes were amazing; they were big and a color Zelina had never seen before, almost white with fiery colors near the pupil. She was mesmerized by his eyes; she did not want to look away. For that moment she was no longer concerned about the woman calling for her.

"Zelina? Are you okay?"

"Yeah. Sorry for running into you. I wasn't paying attention." The woman called for her again, causing Zelina to jump. "I have to go." She took off running, not stopping to ask how he knew her, what his name was or even where she was. She was only focused on finding the woman calling to her.

The dream slowly faded into blackness, and the rest of the night she slept peacefully.

Her alarm went off and for the first time she did not want to get up. She had finally slept, and it felt so good. She dragged herself out of bed. Thankful she had showered the evening before; now she only had to get dressed and go meet Rune. She wanted to share her dream with him and hear what he would have to say about it. She was full of energy and, for the first time, felt good about things. She felt that everything was coming together, even if it was for only a moment.

She grabbed toast again for breakfast and ran out the door to meet the bus on time. She was hoping Rune would be there, but only the same old lady from the day before was sitting on the bench.

"Hello, dear. You look much more chipper this morning." She smiled at Zelina.

"Yes, I slept well last night. How are you?" Zelina sat next to her.

"Very well, thank you. Off to school then?"

"Yes. Another day at school. Where are you off to?"

"Ah, the bus is here, my dear." With that, the lady stood and waited for the bus to stop.

Zelina stood behind her. "Well, wherever you're off to today, I hope you have a fantastic day."

She smiled as she got on the bus and found an empty seat. The old lady sat farther back on the bus and every time Zelina looked back, her head was down as if she was reading something.

Zelina got off the bus and walked down to her school; there was no sign of Rune. She sat on the front steps, watching all the kids talking and laughing, and she wished she could be that carefree. She wanted to have friends, laugh and have some fun. She began to wonder about her friends back at her real home and what they were doing at that moment.

The sun was out, and there was not a cloud in the sky. It was the complete opposite from the day before. The breeze was soft and cool and felt great against her face. She smiled, thinking the weather was matching her mood, and she hoped she would have more days like this. She felt lighter, as if she had no worries in the world. She leaned back on the stone steps, face up to the sky, and closed her eyes, fully enjoying the moment. That perfect moment ended too soon as the kids started running up the steps and into the school building. She opened her eyes and looked around for Rune, but he was nowhere in sight.

"Where are you, Rune?" she asked quietly.

After everyone was in school, she decided to head over to the tea shop and wait for him there. She had no idea what to do if he did not show up. Zelina did not want to start worrying or stressing over where Rune was or what she was to do if he never showed; she did not want her great day to end so soon. She walked calmly over to the tea shop, hoping, willing him to be there.

She realized upon entering the shop that she had no money to order anything and decided it would be better to wait for him outside instead. She felt foolish for not thinking about money and how she would pay for things. She crossed back over to the school and sat on the steps watching for Rune. She wondered how Rune had been able to pay for their tea the day before, or for his food every other day, for that matter. Her mind began to wander to her most recent dream. She thought about the boy—who was he and how they knew each other. She had no idea who he was, and yet, he seemed to know her. She was also curious about whose house she had been walking through, and who the voice yelling for her belonged to.

"Come on! We don't have time for your daydreaming!"

Zelina opened her eyes slowly and smiled as Rune walked past the steps and across the street, past the tea shop. She ran to catch up to him. "Hey, where have you been?! I've been waiting."

"Well, I'm so sorry to keep you waiting like that, my little princess; however, I had some things to take care of. Now, stop whining and talk."

Rune was walking rather quickly and Zelina was having a difficult time keeping up with him. "Talk? Talk about what? Why are you walking so fast? Slow down."

"We need to get to the factory, we can't dilly-dally. Tell me about what you were thinking when I arrived."

Zelina did not say a word; she watched him while he kept looking over his shoulder as if expecting to see someone. She grabbed his arm to slow him down, but he did not seem to notice as he continued at the fast pace. Zelina felt she was practically running to keep up with him.

"Rune, can we please slow down? What's going on?"

"Nope. We have to get to the factory. If you aren't going to talk, then move your behind faster. I haven't got all day." He looked at her and grinned. "I'll tell you when we get there." He mumbled something else, something Zelina could not make out.

They arrived at the factory and went upstairs to Rune's room. Once inside the room, Zelina sat in the chair, catching her breath, while Rune walked around the room speaking in a whisper. Zelina caught several words as he walked past her: "*Celo*" and "*Contego*." She was not sure what they meant; nevertheless, they sounded serious. When he was done, Rune stood at the window not saying a word.

"So why were you in such a hurry, Rune?" Zelina spun in the chair, making herself dizzy. She giggled.

"You first. Tell me about the dream you had last night." Rune kept looking out the window as if he was watching for something or someone. He was tense, his arms crossed over her chest, eyes squinting as he surveyed the area, and he chewed his bottom lip. Zelina wondered why he was so stressed.

"How do you know that I had a dream? Maybe I slept peacefully all night."

Rune looked away from the window, watched Zelina for a moment and said, "Would you stop spinning in that chair, little girl, and tell me about your dream?"

She stopped spinning and tried to steady herself. Giggling, she got up unsteadily and sat on Rune's bed. "I still don't know how you know I had a dream last night, but I'll tell you all about it once you tell me why you were so tense last night and why we practically ran here."

Rune looked at her, confused, as if he was trying to figure out what she was talking about.

"Remember? Last night in the dining hall, you wouldn't even look at me, wouldn't speak to me. You were absorbed in what Mr. Jared and Ms. Nyx were doing. What was going on?"

Rune turned back to the window. "Right. That whole thing. In all the years I've been at that house, not once have they eaten in there. They eat—well, I don't know where they eat, but it's not in there with us. I can feel that something is happening, like they know something. I'm just on guard. Zelina…" He turned from the window and looked at her sternly. "You have no idea what could happen. You don't know how dangerous this truly is." He turned back to the window, picking at his nails and tapping his foot. "When I began finding out the truth about everything, I was told it could get dangerous if anyone found out. I was told about the Medjay, who are basically assassins where we come from."

Zelina's eyes widened and tension rose through her back and into her shoulders.

"They hunt people that start to get their memories back or those that help people get their memories back. It's not allowed; none of what we're doing is allowed. I'm hoping that they were just in there watching you, since you are so new. Honestly, I don't know, Zelina; however, I feel that something *is* different."

"The magi? Who sends them?"

"No, they aren't magi; they aren't wise men at all. They are, like I said, assassins—soldiers doing as they are told. They are Meh-jay, not magi. No gifts from them, other than death." Rune took a deep breath and exhaled slowly. "It's really hard to explain everything right now and I know you are getting tired of hearing this from me, but it's something that'll come to you. If you're having dreams every night, then your memory could come back a lot faster than mine, faster than I expected or even hoped."

"Rune, are we safe?" Zelina got up and stood on the other side of the window and began watching with Rune, as fear twisted in her gut.

He smiled at her. "As safe as we can be, for now." He ran his fingers through his hair and took a deep breath. "On to something better—tell me about your dream. I know you had one last night."

"You're a know-it-all, aren't you? Okay." She sat back down on the chair, scooting it closer to the window, and told him about the dream.

"The boy in the dream, did he say or do anything else?" Rune stared intently at Zelina.

"No, I don't think so. It was right after I ran from him that my dream went all black. I don't remember anything else. Does it mean anything?"

Rune did not answer; instead, he started pacing the room, rubbing his chin.

"Rune? Does the dream mean something?" Zelina was beginning to worry; the look on Rune's face was not one of peace or amusement. Rather, his expression was one of worry and stress, and it made Zelina's stomach turn.

"I'm trying to think, Zelina, I'm sorry. I'm not sure what it means. I understand the whole dream of the three ladies; however, this one is new to me." He paced the room a few more minutes while Zelina watched him. She did not speak as she wanted to let him concentrate on the dream and what it could mean for her. Finally, Rune stopped pacing and turned to Zelina. "Possibly the house you saw was yours, the other houses around you are the town you once lived in, and the boy…" His voice trailed off and he began pacing once more.

"What about the voice calling to me?"

"I'm not sure on that one either, Zelina. I'm sorry I'm not much help with this one. Give me some time to think about it."

Zelina stood and looked out the window. The sun was still shining; with a few gray clouds moving in. It was a beautiful fall day, and the longer she stood looking out the window, the more she longed to be outdoors. It was beckoning to her and she yearned to be outside, not stuck inside talking of dreams and memories.

"Hey, Rune?"

"Yeah?" He stopped his pacing to stare at her.

"You said you met an older lady at the tea shop and she wound up showing you the truth."

"That's right. What about her?" Rune meandered over to the window to look Zelina in the eye.

"Well, yesterday and today, I met an older lady at the bus stop. She didn't ask me to meet her anywhere, though. She seemed nice enough."

Rune's face turned ghost white, all the blood draining from it. He grabbed her arms, shaking her slightly. "Why didn't you tell me about this sooner?"

Zelina shrugged and her eyes widened. "How was I to know it was important? I'm sorry. She is just a sweet old lady; I didn't think anything of it. Let go of me." She threw his hands off her arms, taking a few steps back. "Have you gone mad?"

Rune did not look at Zelina; instead, he turned to peer out the window, chewing his top lip, lost in thought for some time. The silence was finally broken by Rune clearing his throat. "I'm not sure what the old lady is all about, but she could be watching you. She could be working for them." He turned from the window, looking at Zelina. "Has she asked you any questions? Seemed abnormally curious?" His expression hardened.

"No. She's only asked where I was off to and I told her school. Today she didn't say anything really—she noticed I seemed happier than yesterday, that's all. What is it, Rune?" Zelina stayed several feet away from him, unsure if he would snap at her again.

"It could be nothing. If she's there tomorrow, let me know. I'm sorry, Zelina, we have to be careful." He forced a smile, but it did not put her at ease as it normally did. She could feel the tension and knew he was on edge. He would not share, and she did not understand why. She wanted to help him as much as he wanted to help her. He would not give her any way to help, never gave her any information on what was happening.

Zelina hated all the tension in the room. She wanted to clear the air and decided to change the subject. "Well, what else are we going to do today?" Zelina sat back down on the bed, relaxing on her elbows, hoping they could do something outside; it was too beautiful to be indoors.

"I do have a few things I could show you. I think you're ready for this. Your memory is coming back and I think this may help." Rune's genuine smile was back and it relaxed Zelina slightly.

"Okay. I'm ready. What are we doing?" She sat up straight on the edge of the bed, smiling. She was excited to be learning something new in hopes it would help with her memory.

"Just watch my hair. You'll like this." He sat down in the chair, closed his eyes and brought up his right hand. He curled his last three fingers in. The first finger stayed straight out, and his thumb was on this first finger. He raised his arm out to the side and wiggled his hand. His hair turned a light mint green color and Zelina gasped. "Like it?" He opened his eyes and smiled. "This is my real hair color."

Zelina sat stunned for several seconds, unsure of what she had witnessed; it had to be some sort of illusion. "Rune, that is crazy! How'd you do that?" She got up from the bed and walked over to him, touching his hair to make sure it was real. "This is amazing. You're like a magician or something, huh?" She kept touching his hair and laughing. "Truly amazing."

"No, I'm not a magician. This is simple. I can't wait to see how you react to the harder ones, the more intricate spells." He smiled and stood up, forcing Zelina to back up a couple of steps.

"Spells? So, you're like a witch?" She laughed and sat in the chair, finding what he said absolutely ridiculous. She was in awe of his hair changing color; however, she knew there were no such things as witches or wizards, and it made her laugh.

"No, you're the witch." Rune crossed his arms and stuck his tongue out at her. "No, it's not like that. We're from a different place and have different abilities than the people here. We don't have wands or ride brooms, although I've always thought that would be super cool. I've probably said too much." He walked over to the window, looked out and then turned back to Zelina. "Now to change it back. I can't walk around like this; people would find it odd. I don't believe Ms. Nyx would like me having my memory or my abilities." With that, he took his right hand and curled the last three fingers under, just as before. He tucked his thumb with his three fingers, kept his first finger out and brought his hand to his forehead. He touched the left side of his forehead and flicked his finger across, which turned his hair back to black. "I have to do this almost every day. My real hair doesn't like to be in hiding." He sat on the bed and crossed his ankles in front of him. "Now it's your turn." He pushed her up off the bed. "Let me see what you've got." He beamed

Zelina stood in front of him, unsure of what to do, still amazed at what he had shown her. "Rune, I don't know how to do this. I'm still shocked at your green hair. This is insane to me." She dropped back down on the bed next to him. "I think you're losing your mind." She rubbed her hands on her thighs as she tried to make sense of it all.

He stood, pulled her up and grabbed her shoulders. "Listen, you can do this. I'm not losing my mind. I'm no magician or wizard. You have the same abilities I do—they are locked up in there." Rune tapped her forehead with his finger. "You have to work at letting them out, setting your abilities free." He winked at her and sat back down on the bed. "Now, work."

She turned to face him. "Rune, I can't—"

Rune frowned and wiped an imaginary tear from his face. "What? You don't trust me? I'm hurt. Relax and don't think about it. Close your eyes and breathe."

"I can't relax with you in the room. I don't trust you." Zelina ran her fingers through her hair and rolled her shoulders back.

"Come on, the sooner you do this, the sooner we can head outside. I promise I won't do anything. I'll stay right here. I won't even make faces at you." He made an ugly face at her, which made her laugh. "Okay, starting now."

Zelina took in a deep breath and closed her eyes. She began concentrating on the air around her, the sunshine outside and the birds chirping. She giggled a few times; Rune scolded her and told her to keep trying. After about ten minutes, Zelina finally was able to fully relax. She slowed her breathing down and thought of being outside, in the fresh air. She saw herself in the house from her dream. There was light music playing from outside. The garden was green and lush; the day was warm and inviting. She stepped out the back door and looked down to find she was barefoot. The green grass felt so good on her feet. She lifted her face up to the sun and remembered. Her hair was blue in her dream. It was a light blue, the color of the sky on a clear sunny day. She concentrated on the color and brought her right hand up beside her face, bringing her thumb in to her palm, her four fingers together, and pointing up. She waved it slightly and heard Rune clap. She opened her eyes; Rune shot up from the bed and began touching her hair. "Did it work? What color is it?" Zelina could not stop smiling, and neither could Rune.

"Amazing, Zelina! You got it. Here, here's a mirror." He rummaged through some trash on a small table that sat in the corner of the room and found a little handheld mirror. "Look at what you did!"

Zelina snatched the mirror from his hand and gasped. Her hair was exactly the color she had seen. That was it. She did it. Her excitement quickly faded and in its place was panic and fear. The color drained from her face, and she felt she was going to faint. "Rune, how did I do that?" she asked. Breathless, she sat in the chair, placing the mirror on the floor and putting her head in her hands, elbows on her knees.

"Calm down. This is exciting. You did it; you harnessed your power slightly. That's great news and we should be celebrating. Just breathe." He patted her lightly on the back.

A part of her wanted to be excited, but the other part was in full panic. She had no idea what was happening, and she was unsure if she liked this or not. Her face glistened with sweat and she trembled. She thought it would be easier to just accept who and where she was, to be happy with what she had. She did not need to learn about these abilities that Rune kept speaking of or about a home she truly had no memory of. Her head started pounding and her eyes burned and watered. She lifted her head slowly, looked back at Rune and smiled wanly. "This is crazy." She had difficulty speaking; her mouth felt dry. "My head hurts." She closed her eyes and put her head back down. She was having a hard time breathing and she was scared. Scared of what she did and scared of what Rune was telling her. She had to be honest—she did not like any of this.

"Zelina, look at me." Rune knelt next to her and pulled her chin up toward him. "Open your eyes and look at me."

She lifted her head slightly to look at Rune, but she had a hard time opening her eyes. She rubbed them, saying "I'm sorry. This is all a bit too much for me, I guess. I don't mean to be a prat. I don't know if I can do this." She lowered her head. Her eyes were burning intensely, and the light made her headache worse. All she wanted to do was run from there.

"You're not a prat and I understand. Please open your eyes. Let me see something." Zelina wiped her eyes with her shirt sleeve and opened them slowly. "Zelina, this is amazing. Better than I thought. Oh my gosh, this is—" Rune jumped up and was clapping and jumping around the room. He was so excited and Zelina had no idea why. She only knew her head hurt, and her eyes would not stop burning and watering. "I can't even—I can't even describe how great this is." He sat on the bed. "This could also mean more trouble, but it's worth it."

Zelina wiped at her eyes again, using her shirt. "Rune, what is so amazing?" She hardly had any energy and was not in the mood for more mystery. Her head was pounding even worse and all she wanted to do now was to lie down and sleep.

"Look in the mirror again. Look at your eyes this time. They are amazing! Beautiful!" Rune grinned from ear to ear and his eyes beamed; this was the happiest she had seen him.

Zelina picked up the mirror from the floor, trembling she slowly raised her hand up and opened her eyes wide. She gasped. "What in the world is this all about? Did I do this?" She looked to Rune for the answers. Her hair was not the only thing to change color; her eyes had also changed. She was supposed to have yellow eyes with red specks; however, the color was entirely different when she looked in the mirror. They were purple—a light purple that covered her entire eye. It was amazing and terrifying. She had no idea what it meant.

"Well, what do you think?" Rune asked as he knelt beside her, taking the mirror from her shaking hand and putting it on the floor.

"Rune, I think we need to call it a day. My head is killing me." A tear trickled down her cheek.

"Well, we can't. I mean, you have to change your hair and eye color back before we can leave." He grabbed her hands and spoke softly. "Take deep breaths. I know this is all a bit much, but—"

That was it; Zelina had enough. "A bit much? A bit much?! Finding out I had memory problems was a bit much! Finding out I live in an orphanage is a bit much! This?! This is—well, this is pure madness!"

Zelina was out of the chair like a rocket. She was furious, her face turned red. Everything she had been told was a lie and she was not sure that Rune was telling the truth either. If he was, then what did that mean? Her head hurt and she wanted to go home and sleep. She stormed over to him, poked him in the chest, her lips drew back in a snarl. "You think this is all fun and games, but what you're telling me is *too* much, not a bit much! This is too much, Rune! Take me home, now! I'm done with this madness."

Zelina headed for the door. Rune reached out and grabbed her arm. "Zelina, you can't go out like that. You have purple eyes and blue hair." There was a tremble in his voice. "They'll know you're getting your memory and power back, and they'll send the Medjay to take care of you. I can't let that happen. Just lie on the bed, please."

Rune took her by the hand and pulled her gently. She did not have the energy to fight him. He walked her to the bed, where she lay down and closed her eyes.

Zelina woke a short time later, unsure of how long she'd been asleep, although her head was no longer pounding, and her eyes were not watering or burning. She sat up and saw Rune sitting at the small table; it looked as if he was writing. "How long was I asleep?"

"Hey." He turned and smiled at her. "A couple of hours. How do you feel?" he asked softly.

"Better, thanks. Sorry about the whole freak-out thing earlier." She smiled weakly back at him.

Rune closed the book he was writing in and got up from the chair. "No need to apologize. I know it's a lot and honestly, I probably moved too fast. I'm sorry about that. If you're feeling better, and up to it, you should probably put your hair back to red and hopefully your eyes will change back as well." He walked across the room to sit beside her on the bed.

"Okay." Zelina closed her eyes and concentrated on her breathing. Just as before, she saw her curly red hair and red-yellow eyes, brought her index finger up to her bottom lip, and her thumb held her other three fingers in her palm. She brought her finger down toward her chin, slightly curling her finger. Her eyes began to burn slightly, although not nearly as bad. Zelina wiped her eyes with her shirt and slowly opened them.

Rune was beaming at her and squeezing her hand once again. "Great job. You did it! You're back to normal, and by normal, I mean you have your red hair and yellow eyes back. You're a fast learner, little one." Rune patted her leg before getting up and going back to the table where he shuffled some papers. He turned back to her. "We should probably get some food and head back home. You've got to be famished. I know I am."

He took Zelina's arm in his and led her to the door, muttering "*Demitto*," and the doors creaked open.

"I'm hungry; however, I was hoping to talk a little bit more about what happened." She pulled slightly on Rune's arm, hoping he'd stop or turn around.

"I think we should move slower with this—don't you think that would be better? Besides, you accomplished a lot today, more than I thought possible. I don't need your brain exploding." The doors closed behind them as they began to make their way through the factory. "We can talk a bit while we eat. I can't think on an empty stomach." He smiled, tugging her faster.

"Okay. There's so much I don't understand." She sped up so Rune would stop pulling her. "Something easy to start with: What were you writing back there?"

"Oh, that's nothing. I was writing some notes about what's been going on and how quickly you caught on. Which you have, you know?"

"Yeah, you've told me. Are you worried I'll break down again? 'Cause I won't."

"You can't say you won't. What you did today was basic stuff, things we learn as babies. You don't know how you'll handle doing the more powerful spells, like taking someone out."

"What do you mean?" She stopped him. They'd just stepped out of the factory and standing outside in the warm sun felt so good to Zelina.

"Medjay, Mr. Jared, Ms. Nyx, Damon… Who knows who'll come after you when they find out?" He took hold of her arm once more and began walking with her. "Listen, this isn't something you need to worry about right now. All you need to do right now is relax, and let's enjoy some food."

Zelina sighed. "All right. Let me just ask you one more thing."

Smiling, face up toward the sun, Rune replied, "One more and that's all you get, little one."

"I've heard you say '*Demitto*' twice now. What does that mean?"

Rune stopped. He looked around as if someone was watching them. "Don't say that outside the room, understand?" Rune turned to her, looking her dead in the eyes. "I'm serious," he snapped.

"Yeah, okay. Relax." She began walking, leaving him behind. "You wouldn't let ask you any questions back there. *You* relax now. I promise it won't happen again."

She heard him huff as he hustled to catch up to her. "I'm sorry. It's just that saying those things outside a safe room can be danger- ous; it can alert the Medjay. We don't want that."

Zelina continued walking fast, and Rune stepped in front of her to stop her. "I said I was sorry. Now to answer your question, it's basically a spell that releases a locking or blockade spell. It allows the doors to open." He took her arm in his and they walked slowly side by side, not uttering another word.

They found a quaint fast food restaurant with outdoor seating. They both ordered the fish and chips with peas. To Zelina's surprise, the food was rather delicious. While they ate, they discussed many things, none of which Zelina wanted to talk about. She knew, of course, that they could not discuss their "abilities," as Rune called them, or why he was so amazed at the color of her eyes. She did want to tell him that she liked his green hair and that made her smile. She wished, beyond anything in the entire universe, that he would tell her everything. She believed she could now handle anything he told her. However, they only talked about things they liked, some of which Zelina wondered whether she really liked or if they were something that was planted.

"I'm no good with computers or anything like that," Zelina stated after Rune informed her how he had hacked into the school computers. "It seems like I've never used one." She laughed.

"Well, technically, you haven't. We don't have those, or really any electronics, where we come from. We don't need such things," he said with his mouth full of food.

"Rune, that's disgusting!" Zelina rolled her eyes and threw a napkin at him. "Clean yourself up. You're such a child sometimes."

Rune wiped his mouth with the napkin, sat up straighter and put his pinky in the air as he took a drink. "Is this better, madam? Shall I be serious then?"

Zelina threw another napkin at him. "No. You're ridiculous."

"I am a child, remember? I'm only sixteen. Relax and enjoy your food before we have the slop they give us at the house."

Rune made Zelina laugh several times, once so hard that she snorted, and several patrons looked her way. He had a way of making her relax and forget all about the trouble they could get into. She loved laughing with him; she felt so at home when they were together. She dreaded returning to the house and facing Mr. Jared and Ms. Nyx. She had not seen Damon since Monday and she hoped Lexy and her little lackey would leave her alone. She wanted to ask Rune for a spell to make someone shut up; she was so tired of Lexy's bashing. It was hard to believe she'd only been at that house since Sunday—four long, difficult days.

After eating, they strolled back to the bus stop. "Zelina, I won't be around tonight. I have to work," Rune informed her as they sat waiting for the bus.

Zelina frowned. She hated to be in the house without him and his support. "Who will I eat dinner with?" She elbowed him and smiled. "I understand, you have to keep up the illusion that we know nothing. Where do you work, anyway?"

"At a little grocery store not too far from here. Do I really go there, you may ask... the answer to that is no. I use the same charm on those at the store that I do on the school." He seemed genuinely proud of himself and his ability to trick people.

"Okay, how do you get money then? I mean, you paid for everything we've eaten lately. I have no money."

"That is another fun one, I'll teach you later. Also, they think I work there; therefore, I do get paid, so I have some real money on me." He leaned over, looking for the bus. "The bus is here. Be a good little girl."

The bus pulled up in front of them. Rune stood and helped her up.

"I'm always a good girl," Zelina replied. "You go off to work like a good little boy and stay out of trouble."

Rune walked away. Zelina watched him and shook her head, snickering. She got on the bus, which was almost full, found an empty seat and sat down with a big grin on her face.

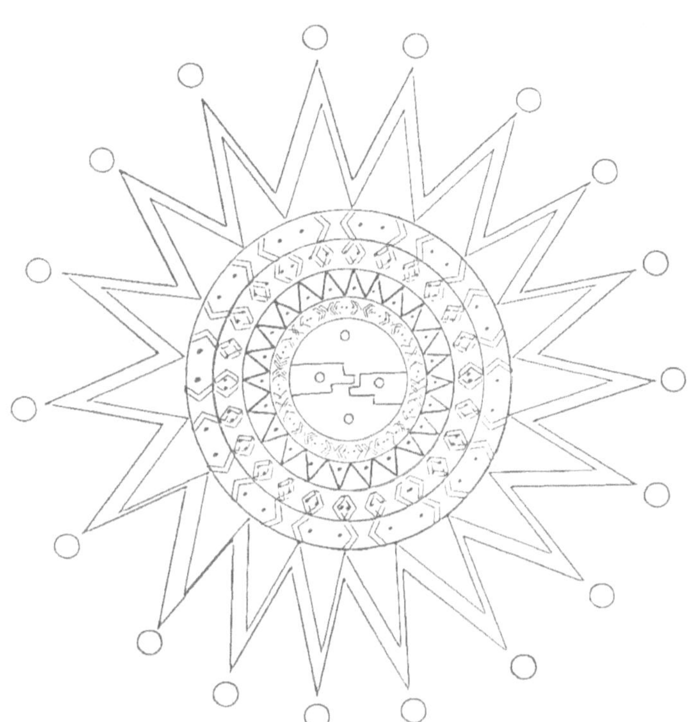

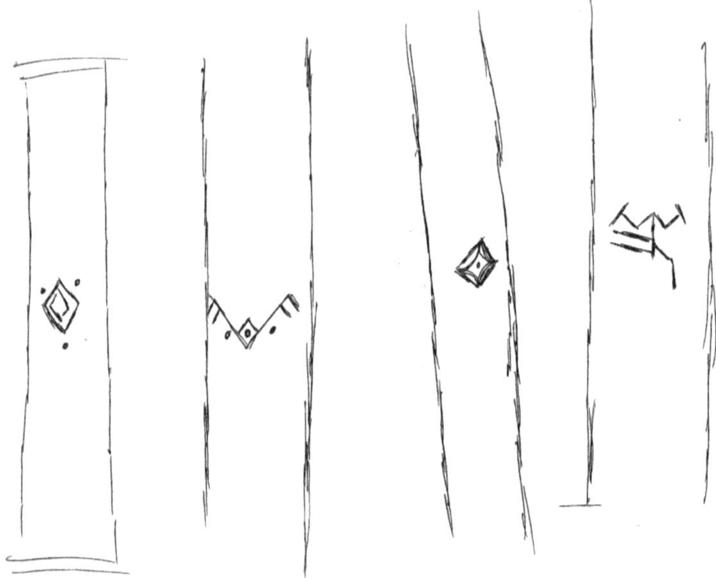

From Rune's notebook, page 3

Chapter Five

S HE ARRIVED at the house with the bus almost empty; she did not want to be there, especially since Rune would not be with her. She walked down the street and was almost to the house before she heard the shrill voice of Lexy behind her. "Well, if it isn't Little Miss Brain-dead. How was school? Did you learn anything new, like one plus one?" Lexy and Sloane both laughed.

"Oh, hello, Lexy. You look lovely today. You're such a wonderful, intelligent person." Zelina gave a half-smile. The other girls looked confused. "Oh, I'm sorry; I thought we were having a lying competition. If I throw a stick, will you leave?" Zelina turned and walked up to the house, wanting so much to hit Lexy and be done with it. She knew violence was not the answer, however, and knew she was better off walking away. She headed up to her room, reminding herself how truly ignorant Lexy was.

She threw her book bag on her chair, and pulled out schoolbooks and papers, throwing them on her bed to make it seem like she was doing schoolwork should anyone enter her room. She hoped that they would let her get a job soon so she could be away from the house, and Lexy, even longer. Out her window, she saw Lexy and Sloane talking with Ms. Nyx and wondered what they were telling her. She rolled her eyes and went to her mirror. She looked at herself with her curly red hair and yellow eyes. She wondered if there was a spell that would tame her wild hair. Even when it was blue, it was still completely out of control. She pulled her hair back, putting it in a bun on the back of her head; she wanted to get a better view of her eyes. She wondered if there was any purple in there at all. "Maybe that's what Rune was so excited about when I met him," she whispered to herself. As she leaned in closer there was a knock on her door. Huffing, she opened it. "Yes?"

Standing there was Ms. Nyx and Damon. "I just spoke with Lexy and Sloane; they said you tried to attack them. Is this true?"

Zelina stood in her doorway with the door only partially opened. "No, not all. They said some mean things to me, I replied, and that was it. Nothing else."

"So, they are lying to me then?" Ms. Nyx pushed the door open, making Zelina take a few steps back with it. Damon entered the room behind her, looking around.

"Yes, they are. Ms. Nyx, I have no reason to lie. I just got home and I have some schoolwork to do. Lexy started this entire mess. I know I shouldn't have said anything back to her; I apologize for that." Zelina stood at the door, hoping they would leave.

"Well, it seems to me you're causing trouble again." Ms. Nyx walked over to the window and looked out. "You'll need to help with dinner again tonight. If your attitude doesn't change, you'll help the rest of the week. Understood?" She turned to Zelina, arms crossed over her chest and eyebrows raised.

"Yes ma'am, but I don't think that's fair—"

"You don't need to think, my girl, and it doesn't have to be fair. I tell you what to do and you do it. Understand that?"

"Yes, ma'am."

Ms. Nyx walked to the door, snapped her fingers, and Damon followed her out of the room. The entire time Ms. Nyx was in there Damon had been snooping around her room, looking at everything from the objects on her dresser to the schoolbooks scattered on her bed. He seemed to be searching for something.

Zelina shut her door softly as Ms. Nyx and Damon headed downstairs. "Great, now I get to go be a chef and pretend I like these people." She sat on her bed, contemplating her life before coming to Ankerstone. She wondered if her mother was a good cook or if that is where Zelina got her inability to cook. She wondered if she had a job back home, and if her parents were worried about her or looking for her. She was curious if she had a boyfriend, which brought a smile to her face. The idea of a boy being interested in her made her giggle.

"Time to come back to this world." Zelina huffed as she pulled herself up from her bed. She went to the kitchen; the same two girls were in there cooking. "Hello, ladies. How are you today?" She smiled, grabbed an apron and set to work. "What are we making tonight?"

"Battered fish with chips. Fairly easy tonight—even you could make it," the younger one answered while the older one stared blankly at Zelina.

"You know, I never got your names. I'm Zelina." Zelina grabbed a bowl and started adding the ingredients for the batter.

The older girl was getting the oil ready for the frying. From the stove she snapped, "I'm Gwynn and she is Alix. Now enough chit-chat. Let's cook, shall we?" She concentrated on what she was doing, her mouth set in a hard line.

Alix smiled sweetly at Zelina and they worked together to make enough batter for all the fish. "We're going to be having dessert tonight as well, since we have time," Alix said with a squeal.

"Oh really, what is it?" Zelina was not hungry yet; however, the idea of having some dessert did sound fantastic.

"Chocolate truffles. Gwynn makes the best truffles ever."

Although Zelina hated being in the house, even more so in the kitchen, she was happy to be kept busy and away from Lexy. She thought maybe it was not such a bad punishment to be in the kitchen with these two. Alix seemed sweet, but Gwynn seemed a bit colder, more standoffish.

Zelina tried to carry on conversations with them, to no avail. At one-point Gwynn stopped cooking and told them, "No more talking," in a stern voice that even Ms. Nyx would have been proud of. After that, they were silent. It made no difference, Zelina kept her smile; she was happy.

Everyone entered the dining hall. Ms. Nyx, Mr. Jared, and even Damon were in line to get food. Zelina rolled her eyes and continued serving everyone as they came in.

"How did she do tonight, Gwynn?" Ms. Nyx asked as she was being served.

"Zelina did quite well. She did as she was told and we had no problems with her. We were glad for the help." Gwynn kept her eyes on the food, never looking at anyone as she served them.

Zelina smirked. "I actually had fun as well. I learned how to make battered fish, chips, and truffles. I can't wait to eat it."

"I'm so glad to see you adjusting well, Zelina. Excellent. Keep this up and you could be out working instead of in here working," Mr. Jared stated as he placed his dessert on his tray.

"Good evening, Damon. How was your day?" Zelina asked pleasantly.

Damon grunted, took his food and joined the other two at a table on the other side of the room.

After everyone was served, Zelina, Gwynn, and Alix got their food and sat down. Zelina decided to sit with them; she thought it would make it look like she had other friends apart from Rune. They did not speak, so Zelina ate her food in silence. Dinner was pretty good, and she really enjoyed the truffles.

After everyone finished eating and the room was empty, the three of them had to clean the kitchen, which did not take much time since they had cleaned most of it while the truffles were setting. This was Zelina's least favorite of the chores.

She decided to shower since she was sweaty from cooking and cleaning, then head to her room and pretend to do schoolwork while waiting for Rune to return.

She fell asleep early and missed seeing Rune that evening. Her dreams were random and made no sense to her.

It was as if the dreams were pictures, snapshots of things. The first series of shots was her house, her real house. First, she was in a bedroom, with her blue hair and purple eyes. Then she was downstairs in the kitchen. Standing at the sink was a lady, her back to Zelina. She was humming a pretty song while washing dishes. The lady had long, straight, bright coral hair that was tied back with a red ribbon. Before Zelina could say anything to the lady, she found herself in the garden. She was getting frustrated; she wanted to know who the lady was. She wanted to go back in the kitchen, but she could not move. She was not in control. The garden was in full bloom and smelled wonderful. Zelina lifted her head to the sun and found she was now down the street, her house up and to the right. There was the boy from her last dream, sitting in front of a house and smiling at her. He was beautiful; his smile made her blush. As he got up, Zelina found herself in the same circular room from the first dream, only she was alone. The three ladies had not yet entered. She was confused and calling out, only she made no noise. The three ladies slowly walked into the room and the procedure started.

Zelina woke with a start. Her heart was pounding, and she was sweating once again.

"So much for taking a shower." She pulled the covers off and sat in the chair. Wiping the sweat away, she closed her eyes. She wanted to remember everything. She wondered if the lady at the sink was her mother, and if that was the last time she had seen her. She started thinking about her mother, father, and any siblings she may have. Did they miss her? Were they fighting to get her back?

How, exactly, had she ended up in this place? So many questions and she felt she was no closer to getting the answers. Rune would not give her any straight answers and she could not ask anyone in the house because who knew what they would do to her. She wanted—no, she needed, her memory to come back quickly. She was completely and utterly lost and needed answers to get her back home. She felt as if she was starting to lose her mind, starting to lose her grip on reality. She curled up in the chair, trying to imagine her real home life as cheerful and filled with laughter, with a mother and father that doted on her and loved her entirely. A single tear fell from her eye as she drifted off to sleep once more.

The alarm went off and Zelina jumped up. How she hated that wretched thing! She had had no more dreams that night—at least none she could remember. She sat for a few moments, thinking of the snippets in her dream. She pictured the coral-haired lady humming at the sink and pictured her looking for her. Zelina realized sadly that she could not live in the daydream; she had to get up and head to school. She had to head downstairs and eat some breakfast and, most horrifically, she had to face Lexy at some point in the day. She gave in and dressed, headed down to breakfast, and decided she needed to eat more than toast. Breakfast was eggs, bacon, sausages, fried bread, and baked beans. Zelina got a small plate of eggs with some sausage and fried bread. She took her time eating since the day before Rune had kept her waiting in front of the school. She would make Rune wait for her. It was rather quiet in the dining hall; only three other people were in there with her. Everyone else was already off to school or sitting in the game room catching up on schoolwork before heading out. Zelina finished her breakfast, enjoying the silence, and then headed out the door. Before she made it off the porch, however, Lexy and Sloane stopped her. They stood in front of her, side by side. Lexy's arms crossed over her chest while Sloane played with a lock of her hair and fidgeted.

"You think going to school is really going to help you? You should be in the insane asylum. A frontal lobotomy wouldn't even help you." Lexy laughed, twirling a finger next to her temple. Sloane stood at her side smirking, but never making eye contact. Zelina wondered if Lexy really thought she was witty, for she did not find her witty one bit.

Zelina rolled her eyes. "You're right, Lexy, so right. A lobotomy wouldn't help me; it would only make me like you two, completely witless, and I honestly don't want to be like either of you." She rolled her eyes back into her head, let her tongue droop out of her mouth, slumped over and walked like a zombie as she pushed her way between them and walked off, never looking back at them. She knew she should have kept her mouth shut and ignored them; it was getting more difficult to deal with them. She had enough drama going on and she did not need Lexy's input each day, especially so early in the morning.

Zelina barely made it to the bus stop on time; the old lady was nowhere to be seen. The bus was packed and Zelina had to walk all the way to the back to find a seat, sitting next to someone who smelled as if they had not showered in months. She was thankful her stop was not too far away. When she exited the bus, she took a deep breath in and laughed; it had already been an eventful morning.

Rune was waiting for her outside the tea shop. He waved to her as she got closer. "Hey, running a little late this morning? Was the limo late fetching you, my sweet?"

"Oh, shut it, Rune. You were late yesterday. I'm not hungry this morning. Let's get out of here," she said, pulling his arm.

"I'm hungry, though, so you'll have to sit down and wait for me." He walked into the tea shop and ordered two teas and a scone.

Sitting down next to Zelina, Rune sipped his tea and asked, "So, how was your evening while I was out slaving away at work?"

"You? Work? Yeah, right. My evening was fine. I had to work in the kitchen." Zelina fiddled with her teacup. "Lexy and her sidekick told Ms. Nyx that I was causing problems, so that was my punishment. Honestly, it wasn't half bad—I was kept busy and away from everyone. I might be sent there again tonight." Zelina watched Rune stuff the scone in his mouth as if he had never tasted anything so delicious in all his life. "Slow down—it's not going to disappear before you can finish it. Good grief."

"I love scones. Why are you going to work in the kitchen again? Did my little sweetness cause problems this morning?"

Zelina glared at Rune. "I seem to cause problems no matter where I go or what I do." She stuck her tongue out at him. "It's not my fault. Lexy starts all of this… I just finish it."

"No, you don't finish it. If it was finished, she wouldn't continue picking on you. You've got to just walk away. Eventually, she'll give up. She likes getting people in trouble. She did that to me the first year I was here. She's like an annoying bee, the more you swat at it, the more it'll buzz around you. When you're still long enough, it'll go away and find someone else to buzz around."

"An annoying bee? Really? I will swat that bee. I can't stand there and pretend it's not bothering me. I don't understand why she is after me all the time. She needs to find another hobby. It's getting old, quick." Zelina pushed some stray hair out of her face and forced a smile. "So, what's on the agenda today?"

"Same as always, I suppose. I don't really plan these things; they just happen. Finish your tea and let's go. I can't keep waiting around for you."

"So sorry, your majesty." She bowed slightly to Rune, and he put his chin in the air. They both laughed.

After finishing their tea, they headed to the factory, walking much slower than the day before. There was a slight breeze blowing, making the air smell of fall. Leaves were changing to bright red and orange. Zelina loved looking at all the colors and feeling the breeze on her face. She stopped every now and then to pick up interesting-looking leaves; Rune would laugh at her and coax her to follow him, patting his leg and calling her his 'little princess'.

As they approached the factory, Rune came to a dead stop and went white. Zelina almost ran into him as she was looking at a tree rather than paying attention to him. He pushed Zelina behind him. He looked around, saw no one and decided to continue walking, past the factory. He looked nervously at the factory.

"Rune, what's going on?" Zelina whispered.

He grabbed her hand and intertwined his fingers with hers. "Someone's in the factory. We can't go in there right now. Don't look back."

It was difficult for Zelina not to look back; she wanted to see if anyone was in the windows or leaving the building. "How do you know someone's in there? I thought you had a protection spell over the place."

"Zelina, I can feel when the Medjay are around. I knew something was wrong the other day with Mr. Jared and Ms. Nyx in the dining hall. I just knew it." His grip on her hand tightened.

Zelina frowned. "Oh, I forgot to tell you. Last night they were in there again. Ms. Nyx, Mr. Jared, and Damon. They all sat together and ate. I never saw them look at me, but then again, I wasn't watching them. You think it could be one of them in the factory?" She wiggled her fingers, trying to get Rune to loosen his grip on her hand.

"No. I know it's the Medjay. They're hunting for someone who knows their real identity. Just keep walking—don't look back," he snapped. They walked a bit longer and found an empty park bench. As they sat down, Rune put his arm around her shoulder and pulled her closer to him. Zelina looked at him, laughed and pulled away.

"It's in case someone sees us. They won't question us sitting here. Just go with it." He was still tense, looking around them. "As for the protection spell, it's only around the one room. They won't be able to enter that room; they won't even know it's there. They will detect a spell nearby, but that's about it. We've got to really watch ourselves now."

"How do they know when someone has their memory back?" she asked, biting her nails.

"There are people that are sent here to watch for signs of memories coming back, such as abilities." He raised his eyebrows. "Once someone suspects a person of getting their memory back, they contact someone back home and the Medjay are sent."

They both sat on the bench, tense, and watching everything around them.

"Rune, I had another dream last night. Is it safe to talk about it?"

"Quickly and quietly, I suppose. Go for it."

Zelina put her head on his shoulder and told him of the snapshot dream she had had. "What do you think? More memories, huh?"

"Yeah, that's great. Again, I believe that it's your house you keep seeing, and you actually saw your mother. Did anyone say anything to you in the dream?"

"No. Just quick moving pictures, no talking. I'm starting to see more, though." She bounced her leg, ready for the tension to be gone.

Rune looked around and got up, pulling Zelina up with him. They began walking back toward the factory. As they approached, Rune shook his head and they walked down another street. "We'll need to find another abandoned place, at least for today. Hopefully they'll leave when they don't find anything."

They walked for a while before finding an empty house. There were many empty houses on the street, several with boards on the windows and one with the roof completely caved in. It seemed the whole neighborhood was now a ghost town. No one was around, no cars in front of houses, no toys in the yards; it was an empty, run down place.

Rune told Zelina to stay outside for a few minutes while he went in and checked it out. Zelina did not like being left alone, knowing the Medjay were so close. It felt like hours before Rune finally exited and waved for her to enter. Inside, it was an ordinary empty house. It seemed as if it had been empty for a while; dust was all over the bare bookshelves and counters. It had an odd smell to it, and there were stains on the green carpeting. One room, at the back of the house, had cardboard over the window.

The color had come back to Rune's face, but not his smile. "I've put a protection spell around the entire house; it's only temporary, maybe a few hours. It's such a small, insignificant spell that it should take quite a while to find it." He had a slight smile on his face and clapped his hands. "So, let's get to work."

Zelina sat on the floor, back against a wall, to watch Rune. "What are we going to do? You said we had to go slow because of the meltdown I had yesterday."

"Well, with Medjay showing up I figure I better teach you some defensive spells, just in case. You ready then?" Rune pulled Zelina up to stand beside him.

"I guess so. I think I'm ready for this." She took a deep breath in and exhaled slowly. "Okay. Let's do this."

Rune smiled at her. "You can do this. It's basic stuff. If you can change your hair and eye color as quickly as you did, then you can handle these spells, nothing to it. All right, the first one is easy. It means to send away or push away. How hard you say it or how angry you are will determine how far something or someone is pushed." He watched Zelina, who was shaking slightly. "You ready?"

"Yeah. Just ready to learn some spells." She rolled her shoulders back and rubbed her hands together. Her first attempt at a spell had nearly made her pass out from the pain in her head and she hoped that there would be no pain today. She wanted to learn who she was and the only way to do that was to push herself out of her comfort zone, no matter how scared she was.

"All right. Let's put some trash in front of you so you can push it away. Sorry, I will *not* be your test subject—who knows how far you'd send me. Through walls, maybe." Rune snickered and picked up a plastic bag from the kitchen that was directly behind them. He placed the bag only inches from her feet, then stood next to her.

"Just look at your enemy," he pointed at the bag and laughed, "and say '*Amitto*' and that will push it away. See it in your mind—see your enemy flying backward."

Zelina did as she was told. She stared at the trash bag, struggled not to laugh, and repeated his word, "*Amitto*." The trash bag flew down the hall. Rune clapped and retrieved the bag. Zelina repeated the process three more times before Rune stopped her and had her sit down.

"You look a little pale. Take a break and I'll teach you something else. I'll show you first."

Zelina sat with her back against the wall, facing Rune. She did have a dull ache in her head, but nothing compared to what she had felt previously. "To add to what you just did, I will push it faster. It won't necessarily go further—it will just move faster. Watch."

Rune put the bag a few inches from his feet, then winked at Zelina before beginning. "*Amitto Velox.*" The bag moved so quickly, Zelina barely saw it fly down the hall. It was at least twice as fast as Zelina's attempt. "Whenever you are ready you can try it."

Rune sat next to her and waited. "No hurry, take your time. I don't want you to be in any pain."

Zelina gave a half smile. She knew he did not want her in pain; however, she also knew he wanted her to learn the spells as quickly as possible. He was on alert and she understood. She slowly got to her feet and retrieved the bag, placed it on the floor, and repeated the words. The bag flew faster and farther than with Rune's turn. It hit the wall at the end of the hall and hung midway up the wall for several seconds before falling to the ground.

Rune jumped to his feet, clapping again. "Great job!" He ruffled her hair and ran down the hall to get the bag. "If that wall had not been there, who knows far it would've gone. Ready for more?"

Zelina rubbed her temples. "My head hurts a little. Why does it hurt when I do this stuff?" She sat back down, resting her elbows on her knees and her head in her hands.

"It takes a while to get used to, Zelina. I suffered fom headaches as well. I promise it does go away. It's your mind fighting against their spell to erase your memory. You have to fight through the block they have on you. One day you won't have any headaches when you use your magic." He sat next to her, watching her, concerned.

"Magic? So, this is witchcraft." She huffed and raised one eyebrow at Rune.

"No, but I'm not sure what else to call it. Your power, your abilities. This stuff comes naturally to us; some are stronger than others and some hardly have any power at all. Those are usually the people they send here, at least from what I know."

"They? Who are they?" she asked, thoroughly confused. "Obviously we have abilities, some anyway, so why us? If we had these abilities, why were we sent here?"

"I'm not sure about that. I was told by my old friend it was normal because parents either couldn't afford the child or just didn't want them. However, I know that's not the truth. I have my memory and my family did want me. Although they weren't wealthy by any means, they never would've sent me away. There's more going on than I know about, honestly." He got up and began pacing. "It's not just us, Zelina. It's all the kids at the house—and who knows how many houses like ours there are across the country. There are people who get their memories back, but the Medjay always seem to find them."

"How have they not found you?" Zelina put her head on her knees, slowing her breathing down, hoping the pain would dissipate.

"I was taught to cover my tracks and only talk about my real life and abilities in certain areas. I was taught to be aware of my surroundings and how to sense the Medjay. I've been lucky."

Zelina lifted her head and sighed. "I think I'm ready to learn more. We don't have much time left anyway." She stood slowly. "Rune, at some point you have to explain all this better. Frankly, you have my head spinning."

"I've already said way too much. It's all supposed to come back to you naturally, no prodding or pushing. I'm sorry if I'm pushing you too fast."

"It's okay. It helps when you're able to explain the dreams I'm having, so you're helping more than you realize." She pushed the hair from her face and blew out her cheeks.

"Hey, don't worry about how much time we have, just concentrate on the spells. Okay, this one is easy; it'll start a small fire. Ready?" Zelina nodded her head. "Again, concentrate on your enemy and say '*Fiametta.*' That's all."

Rune backed away, causing Zelina to chuckle. She closed her eyes and cleared her mind. She pictured the bag as a Medjay. Since she had never seen one, she imagined a big seven-foot-tall, fully armored man coming at her. She muttered the words; she was scared that if she said the word too loud the fire would be enormous. She watched as the plastic bag caught fire for a moment, then quickly died out. She looked back at Rune with a smile. "Was that good?"

"Yes, but when you say it you need to say it louder and see the fire in your mind. It was good, though." He patted her back. "You're doing great. How about one more?"

Zelina chuckled; Rune looked like a kid on Christmas morning, he was so excited. "Yeah, one more." Her head began pounding a bit harder and she started feeling weak. She tried to ignore the pain and pay attention to what Rune was telling her. She had to learn this.

Rune moved the bag a bit farther away from her. The house was starting to smell of burnt plastic and it was making Zelina's head hurt worse. Rune waved his hand in front of his nose and said, "*Aria,*" and the smell was gone. He turned back to Zelina with a big grin on his face. "That one clears the air. Now, this one's fun. I used to love doing this one. All you have to say is '*Attollo.*' Got it?"

"Yes, but what will happen? I don't want that thing turning into a spider or something."

He shook a finger at her. "No, that's not the right spell for that." Rune winked and walked behind her. "Trust me; nothing bad's going to happen."

Zelina turned to look at him. He nodded and gave her a thumbs-up. "Okay, I'm trusting you, although I don't know why." Zelina took a deep breath and said, "*Attollo.*"

The bag slowly rose up into the air and hung there. Zelina walked over to it, waving her hands under it. There was nothing pushing it or holding it in midair. She turned back to Rune, who was clapping once again. "That's amazing, Rune. How long until it falls?" Her eyes widened and she covered her mouth with her hand as she laughed; she was astonished by what she was able to do.

"Depends on how long you want it to stay there. Most of our spells depend on how strongly we feel about the spell. In other words, if you're truly angry and that person was, say, Lexy, then she could be hanging in midair for months." He laughed at the idea. "Think about that, Zelina. When she is picking on you, remember you are stronger than she is." He walked over to her and patted her shoulder. "Great job today. How's your head?"

"It still hurts some; not terrible, though. Not at all like yesterday."

"Good. Also, so you know if you're playing around with someone, like me, and you use this spell," Rune said, pointing to the bag, "you can say '*Cado.*' It means to drop. You hungry? I know I am. Let's go eat," Rune stated as he patted his belly.

Before Zelina could respond, Rune took hold of her arm and they walked out the door. They continued down the street, away from the abandoned house and farther from the bus stop and home. They found a quiet restaurant and sat down to eat. It was another great lunch full of laughter and teasing.

Afterward, they headed to the bus stop, never going back to the factory. They stayed quiet the entire walk, enjoying the wind blowing and the cloudless afternoon. There were so many thoughts going through Zelina's mind. She wanted to talk with Rune about all of them. She chewed her lip to keep herself from speaking, though; she knew it was not the right time or place.

"I have to work again tonight, so be a good girl and be on guard," Rune finally said as they were nearly to the bus stop.

Zelina raised her eyebrows at him and pouted. "Me? I'm always a good girl."

"Just leave Lexy and Sloane alone. Ignore everything they say. You could request to work in the kitchen if that'll help keep you from getting into trouble. The less trouble you cause, according to Ms. Nyx, the more likely you'll be to get a job with me. Got it?"

"Yes, sir." Zelina saluted him and continued walking toward the bus stop alone.

"I want to hear that every time, soldier." He smiled and saluted back to her as she looked back.

She did not want to go to the house, but Rune was right. She would request to work in the kitchen, showing she was trying to do better, and then they would let her get a real job in the evenings. She thought about working late with Rune on her abilities and learning more of the truth of who she truly was and all about her past. The more time she spent with him, the more things were coming back to her and that made her happy. Her headache was completely gone by the time she arrived at the bus stop. There were already several girls milling about, waiting for the bus to arrive, so Zelina stood to the side by herself. There were three girls sitting on the bench. One looked up at Zelina, then whispered something to her friend, who looked at Zelina. The third heard what they said and looked over her shoulder at Zelina. Zelina raised her eyebrows and waved at them.

"Great hair. I like it."

"Thanks." Zelina was confused. She had not messed with her hair color and thought they must like red hair.

The third girl got up, walked over to Zelina and touched the tips of Zelina's hair. "I love that color. Where did you get it?"

Zelina looked down at the tips of her hair and saw they were light blue. She looked around, hoping Rune would still be close by.

Sadly, he was nowhere to be seen. "Oh, my mum did this. I don't know where she got the dye." Zelina smiled at them as her heart began to slam against her chest. How had that happened? Her hair should be red, entirely red.

"So are your eyes contacts then?" one of the girls asked from the bench.

Fear flooded Zelina. "Yeah. I hate my real eye color, so my mum finally let me get colored contacts." Zelina forced a smile.

The bus finally arrived, and she climbed on, sitting in the back by herself. She had to change her hair and eye color but could not at that moment. She wondered how it had changed on its own and why Rune did not tell her earlier so she could fix it safely. She was so worried she would get caught before she could change the colors back. Before she knew it, she was at her stop; the driver had to yell at her for her to realize where she was. She smiled and thanked the driver as she exited the bus. She headed for the house; she had to figure out where to change the colors back. As she walked, she found a small cluster of trees and decided to hide behind them to change the colors. She knew she should not use her power without some kind of protection. However, she could not remember the protection spell, and she felt she had no other choice. She remembered two words that Rune used several times in the factory, and she hoped they were correct. She crossed her fingers and whispered them: "*Contego, Celo.*" She hoped she did not have to say them loudly as there were other kids walking by. She took a deep breath and made the sign for red, as she did before, bringing her index finger up to her bottom lip, her thumb holding her other three fingers against her palm. She then brought her index finger down toward her chin, slightly curling her finger. Her eyes began to burn, only slightly this time. She grinned, thinking that had to be a good sign. She wished she had a mirror so she could make sure her hair and her eyes had indeed turned back to their correct colors. She had to believe it worked; she had no other choice. She waited to make sure no one was coming as she stepped back out onto the pavement to continue to the house.

She was relieved to see that Lexy was nowhere around when she came into the house. She made it to her room and had just shut the door when someone knocked. Throwing her bag on the bed, she turned and opened the door.

"You will work in the kitchen for the next week," Ms. Nyx stated, turning her nose up at Zelina, turned and stormed off.

"Thank you, Ms. Nyx," Zelina said as she watched Ms. Nyx walk down the hall. It did not hurt her feelings to be "punished" like that. It was fun the evening before, and she was sure it would be just as much fun that evening.

She read some of her schoolbooks; she was curious as to what everyone her age was learning. After about an hour she decided it was time to head down and help the girls in the kitchen. Alix smiled at her as she entered, while Gwynn kept her eyes on the food she was mixing. "Well, ladies, I'll be your help for the next week." Zelina put her apron on and began working.

They did not speak the entire evening, even when they sat together to eat. After cleaning the kitchen, Zelina showered and read her schoolbooks until she fell asleep; she really needed a quiet evening and hoped she would have a good night's rest.

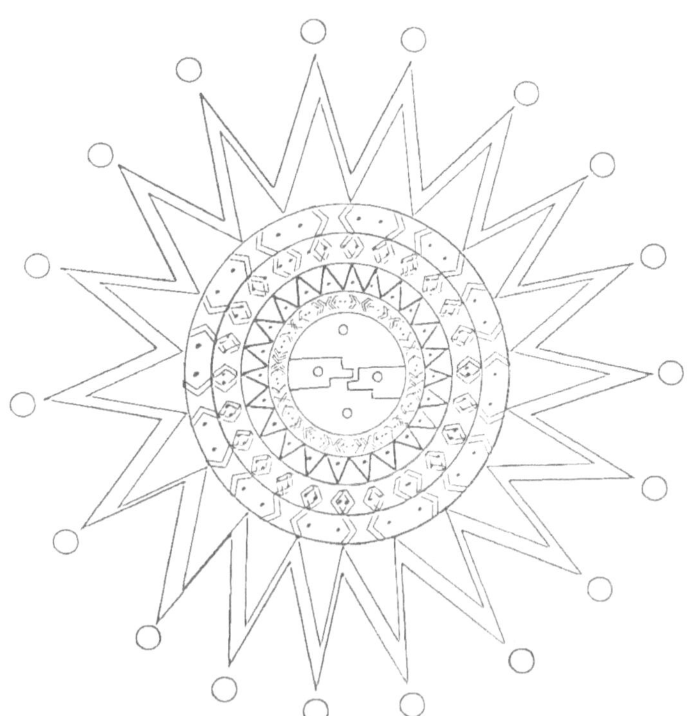

From Rune's notebook, page 8

Chapter Six

"ZELINA, WAKE UP," Rune whispered, shaking her slightly.

"What? I was actually sleeping." She rolled over, pulling the covers over her head. "It was wonderful, and you ruined it. Come back to me, my beautiful sleep."

"No, you need to wake up and listen to me." Rune sat on the edge of the chair, waiting for Zelina to fully awaken.

Zelina sat up slowly, rubbing her eyes. "What is so important that it couldn't wait until I woke up on my own? What time is it, anyway?"

Rune covered his mouth, trying to stifle a laugh. "Girl, you need to do something with that hair. It's out of control."

Zelina threw back the covers, ran to the mirror and started laughing. She must have been sleeping hard; one side of her hair was smashed to her head and the other was sticking out all over the place. "What? What's wrong with this hairstyle? I like it. It's natural beauty!" She pulled her hair back and sat on the bed. "So, what's the big deal, Rune? I'm so tired." She pouted.

"They're downstairs, the Medjay." Zelina's eyes bugged and she stiffened with fear. "They're talking to Mr. Jared and Ms. Nyx right now. Anything odd happen after you got home?" He sat beside her and put his arm around her shoulders. "We're fine, I need to know if anything happened."

Zelina thought it over for a few moments. "No, not that I can think of. Mr. Jared and Ms. Nyx didn't eat with us; I figured things were back to normal. Why would the Medjay be here?"

"Something must have triggered them to come to the house. Someone using power nearby, most likely." Rune let go of Zelina and looked at the floor. He seemed tense, one foot bouncing while he picked at his nails.

"Oh yeah." Zelina bit her bottom lip. She had forgotten about her hair and eye color, how she had had to change them back before entering the house.

Rune sat back, eyebrows raised. "What's 'oh yeah'?"

"When I arrived at the bus stop some girls were saying they liked my hair and eye color. The tips of my hair were light blue and my eyes were purple. I had to change it back before coming home."

"Zelina! Did you do that in front of them?" Rune was up and pacing, something Zelina noticed he did when he was thinking or on edge.

"No, of course not. I have some brains. I found a small bunch of trees near the house, hid back there and changed everything back. I thought I put a protection spell on before using the changing spell. I guess it didn't work. I didn't say it very loud." Zelina put her head in her hands. She felt like crying; she knew she had messed up and she had no idea how to fix it. "Tell me why my hair and eye color changed on their own."

Rune stopped his pacing and stood at the foot of her bed, looking rather pale. "That, I can answer. Once you start getting your memory back, everything in you wants to be normal again and that includes your real hair and eye color. I told you I have to change mine black every day; my green wants to be free. It could mean your memory is coming back or that your power is getting stronger. You just have to make sure you're checking your hair and eyes daily." He began pacing once again and rubbing his chin. "I don't know what's happening down there. Maybe they're simply asking around. Let's not panic here. We have to keep our wits about us.

Let me think."

Zelina was not sure he was even talking to her; it seemed more like a pep talk for himself. She decided to lie down again—even though she knew she would never get back to sleep, not now. Knowing the Medjay were right downstairs, how could she fully relax? She stared at her ceiling, listening to Rune pace back and forth.

She did fall back to sleep, however, and she woke up scared. She did not remember falling asleep and had no idea when Rune left or where the Medjay were. She got dressed in a flurry, grabbed her books and her bag and ran down the stairs.

"Slow down, Zelina. The food will still be there when you arrive," Mr. Jared said as he walked out of his office.

"Sorry, sir. I don't want to be late." She smiled and walked to the dining hall. Breakfast was the same as the day before. She grabbed some eggs and bacon this time and tried to eat slowly, but she had a difficult time of it. She wanted to get to the bus and meet with Rune as quickly as possible.

She finished her breakfast and left the house. Lexy was nowhere in sight, which made Zelina very happy. Once she was out of sight of the house, she sped up her walking, even running part of the way to the bus stop. Of course, she arrived early and had to wait impatiently. As she stood there, the old lady came up and sat on the bench.

"You look well rested this morning, my dear." The old lady put her purse in her lap and patted the empty space next to her for Zelina to sit down. "We have a few moments before the bus arrives—keep an old lady company?"

Zelina was not in the mood for idle chit-chat, yet she did not want to hurt the old lady's feelings. She sat down beside the woman, putting her book bag between her feet. "How was your evening? I don't even know your name." Zelina looked at her and smiled.

"Mrs. Leta, dear. My evening was grand, quite busy for an old lady." She grinned.

"That's nice, Mrs. Leta." Zelina looked at her and it was then that she noticed the odd eye color. Zelina realized she had never seen Mrs. Leta's eyes; she was always looking down or had big, dark glasses on. Today, however, Mrs. Leta raised her head up just enough for Zelina to get a glimpse of her eyes and it scared her. She had never seen eyes like that, eyes that color.

"What's wrong, dear? It looks as though you've seen a ghost." Mrs. Leta smiled and patted Zelina's leg, then grabbed her glasses from her bag.

"Oh, I just remembered I didn't finish some schoolwork. I hope I can get it done before class." She stammered and smiled through her shaking lips; in fact, her entire body was shaking. Zelina was petrified and completely unsure why. She wanted to run, run from the old lady, from Ms. Nyx and Mr. Jared. She wanted to run from there and never look back, but her feet would not move. She was frozen in place.

Thankfully the bus arrived right on time. Zelina let Mrs. Leta go first. Zelina picked a seat up front, sitting next to someone she had never met. Mrs. Leta went to the back by herself. During the ride to school, Zelina pretended to do homework so if Mrs. Leta was watching it would look like she had told the truth. She wanted to look back; she wanted to know if Mrs. Leta was watching her. It sure felt like someone was staring at her, boring into the back of her head. It took everything inside Zelina to keep her head down and pretend to do her schoolwork.

When Zelina was finally able to get off the bus, she ran for the school, not looking back. *Those eyes. What did they mean? Rune, please be there, please, please, please,* she begged to herself. She willed Rune to be on time today; she needed to ask him not only about the previous night, but about what Mrs. Leta's eye color could mean. What all of it meant.

She arrived in front of the school. A bunch of students were outside talking, but Rune was nowhere to be seen. "Of course," she said quietly as she sat on the stairs waiting for him, continuing to will him to show up. She looked over at the tea shop and saw someone standing outside. The man was wearing a pinstripe suit and a black fedora. Whoever it was gave her chills up her spine. She was not sure why; she just had an awful feeling in the pit of her stomach. Maybe it was the way he was standing outside the shop, straight up, stiff as a board, with his arms crossed over his chest. He was wearing sunglasses, so she was unable to tell if he was watching her, but it felt as if he was. She was tempted to wave at him, except she did not want him waving back. There was something off-putting about the man. Zelina, listening to her instincts, got up and walked up the front stairs to a small group of girls talking near the doors to the school. She stood there a few minutes before they stopped talking and looked at her oddly.

"Can we help you?" asked one of the girls in the group.

"Where is the closest restroom?" It was the first thing that came to her mind.

The girls laughed.

"New here?" one girl huffed and rolled her eyes. "Go in and it's on the left a few doors down—you'll see it." The girls went back to talking. "She acts as if she's never been here. I'm in two classes with her. I think she's lost her mind." They all turned to watch Zelina walk in.

Zelina had never stepped foot inside the school before that moment; however, she had a flash memory of walking around her school back home. She was laughing with several friends and the boy in her dreams was walking beside her. As quickly as the memory came, it was gone.

She found the restroom and an empty stall. She had no idea what to do next. A knot began to grow inside her stomach. For a moment, she felt as if the room was spinning—or maybe she was spinning. She could not figure out which way was up or down. It was like when she was a child and would spin in circles until she either fell down or got sick. Zelina put both her hands out on the walls to steady herself, closed her eyes and began to breathe slowly.

She knew she had to find Rune and not panic. After a moment, everything became clear to her, the knot disappeared, and she was no longer sick. She decided she would wait for school to start, then leave and head to the factory or the empty house. She had to get out of there and get to Rune.

She did not have to wait long; the bell rang, and she heard all the girls in the restroom run out. She waited a few more moments before exiting the stall. Zelina poked her head out the restroom door to make sure the hall was empty and then ran to the front door. She stopped right in front of the double doors, looking out the glass window to make sure the person at the tea shop was gone. Her heart stopped. There were two men walking up the steps, toward the front door, toward her. They were both wearing black pinstripe suits with red ties and black fedoras. One was the man she had seen at the tea shop. The knot in her stomach returned; she felt sweat on her forehead and the spinning started up. "Not now," she said as she backed away from the door. She knew that they were Medjay. She turned and ran as quickly as she could back to the restroom, just making it in the door when she heard them enter the school. They were trying to talk in hushed tones, however, their voices were rather deep and seemed to carry throughout the building. Her entire body was shaking; she could not remember ever being so petrified. Zelina put her head against the door and laughed quietly. "I have no memory, so how could I honestly remember if I've ever been this scared?" She laughed again. "Great, now I'm losing my mind. Rune, where are you?" she asked quietly, trying to calm herself.

She heard footsteps getting closer, then heard voices outside the door. "We have to make sure Zelina is indeed attending school daily like Jared says she is. Keep your hat low and your glasses on. Do not take them off for any reason."

"If she isn't here, where do we look next? The factory turned out to be a dead end."

"It will come to us, as it always does. Don't worry about it. We always find our person."

The two men walked past the restroom, their voices fading. Zelina had not realized she was holding her breath, and she exhaled slowly. *What now?* she thought. She was too frightened to leave. What if she got caught running to the doors? She did not take that chance. She put her book bag on the counter, looked at herself in the mirror and a great idea came to her. "Rune, you'd be proud," she said to her reflection, and at that moment the fear left, and she felt in control for the first time.

She splashed water on her face, dried it off a bit, and then headed out of the restroom to the main office. She was not sure where it was but decided to walk down the hall until she found it or someone to point her in the right direction. It was not hard to find; it was almost directly across from the restroom. She opened the door and asked to see a nurse. The two men were in there as well; they were standing to her left, asking where to find her. They were big men, quite a bit taller than Zelina. They had broad shoulders and it seemed as if their suit jackets were stretched to their limits; the fabric could rip if they flexed their arms. The one doing all talking was slightly bigger than the one standing quietly behind him. The smaller one turned toward Zelina and tapped the bigger man on the arm.

The nurse came around the corner and Zelina sighed with relief. "What's wrong?" she asked sweetly.

"My stomach is killing me." Zelina leaned in closer to the nurse and whispered, "Cramps." Zelina wrapped her arms around her waist and bent over slightly.

The nurse grimaced and said, "Come on back here with me; you can lie down for a bit and see if it passes."

"Thank you."

"What is your name?"

"Zelina, Zelina Smith. I'm fairly new here."

"Okay, lie down right there and I will contact your next class to let them know where you are."

Zelina lay down facing the nurse, whose back was to her. She was typing on her computer, looking up Zelina's next class, which was History. *Good to know,* she thought to herself.

There was a knock on the nurse's door and there stood the two men. "Sorry, ma'am, we need to check on Zelina." The bigger man tipped his hat at her and smiled slightly. He started to walk into the room when the nurse stood up, put both her hands up and stopped him. "It's okay" he assured her. "Her caregivers have sent us to make sure she is attending and adapting to the new school properly."

"If they are concerned, why don't they come down here themselves? Now, I can't let you in unless I get a phone call or note from the caregivers giving you permission to talk with her. She is sick, so if you will please leave." The nurse stood at the door, tapping her foot, arms crossed. Zelina had to fight back her smile. She liked this nurse; she was not scared or intimidated by the two men.

The man doing all the talking pursed his lips, crossed his arms and inhaled slowly before turning and leaving, the smaller man followed him. Zelina smiled weakly and rolled over to face the wall. The nurse shut the door and sat back down at her desk, looking at Zelina. "Sorry about all that, Zelina. Did you know those two gentlemen? Are things okay with you at home?"

Zelina turned over slowly. "No, I've never seen them before. Home life is interesting. It's fine. I mean, I'm being picked on by some girls, but it's nothing I can't handle. Everything's great."

Her forehead creased and her lips pursed. "Okay, just rest. I'll be right here if you need anything."

"Thank you." Zelina rolled back over. She had to figure out how to get in touch with Rune. For now, she was stuck in the nurse's office. At least she was safe, and she was grateful for that.

After about an hour, Zelina had had enough waiting. "Ma'am? Would it be all right if I head home? I really think I need sleep and a heating pad," Zelina asked, rolling over to face the nurse.

"I really can't let you leave without the permission of your parents."

"My parents are dead." She closed her eyes, hoping the nurse would fall for her fake sorrow.

She felt a hand on her shoulder. "I'm so sorry. I had no idea. Would you like me to call your caregiver then? See if they can come and get you?"

"No. They're working and shouldn't be disturbed. It's okay. I'll just tough it out and head back to class." She got up from the table, grabbed her book bag and headed out the door.

"Zelina, if it gets worse please come back. You can rest here for as long as you need." The nurse smiled at her and went back to her computer.

Zelina smiled at the other office workers as she left. She decided she would leave. *How would they know?* she thought as she headed to the doors. *There are no alarms on the doors.*

Before leaving, she checked to make sure the men were gone, at least from in front of the school. From what she could see, they were nowhere around. She took her time; she did not want to seem like she was in a hurry, which she was, or running from something, which she also was. Zelina decided to check The Enchanting Cafea first and make sure Rune was not in there before heading to the factory. She walked in and the lady behind the counter smiled at her. "Are you Zelina?"

Zelina was confused and cautiously replied, "Yes."

"I've seen you in here several times with Rune. He asked me to give this to you." She handed Zelina a small piece of paper.

"Thank you." Zelina took the paper and headed back out the door. She opened the paper from Rune. It read: *Zelina, Medjay are looking for us. I will find you. Do NOT go to the house or factory. Go to the park.* She was glad to know he was safe and knew the Medjay were around. Now she needed to find the park, the one they were at the day before, she assumed. They had wound through neighborhoods and stumbled upon the empty park. She hoped it would not be too difficult to find and that Rune would be there waiting for her.

As she walked, she kept looking over her shoulder, making sure no one was following her. She did not feel them around her; she felt normal. Zelina began recognizing the several neighborhoods they had passed to get to the park. This lightened her mood and made her feet move a bit faster. She knew she was heading in the right direction and would soon have some questions answered.

As she neared the park, she heard her name being called. She stopped dead in her tracks, looking around for whomever was calling for her. There was no one around. It unnerved her. It was not Rune or any voice she recognized. It sounded more like the female voice calling to her in her dreams, yet different somehow. Zelina could not quite tell which direction the voice was coming from, either; it was as if it was all around her. She continued walking to the park, which was in sight, and saw that Rune was sitting on a bench with his head down. She sighed with relief.

As quickly as the relief came to her, it deserted her. She felt a cold chill run up her spine, and the hairs on her neck stood on end. She wanted to turn and run, but again, her feet seemed to be stuck. She could not move at all. Zelina looked around. No one was there, yet she could feel eyes on her. She closed her eyes and inhaled slowly. As she exhaled, she opened her eyes. No one was on the bench. Was it just her imagination? No, she knew someone had been sitting there just seconds ago—someone trying to look like Rune, someone attempting to trick her.

Zelina's face paled and she began to tremble. She sat on the bench, trying to seem as if nothing was bothering her. She took a book out of her bag and began reading. She knew someone was watching her and she felt it was best to act like a kid who was skipping school. That made her giggle a little. *Would a student really leave school to come to a park and read a schoolbook?* she thought as she pretended to read. She thought of Rune, hoping he was truly safe, and hoping he would decide not to come to the park after all.

After a few minutes, Zelina slammed the book closed, shoved it back in her bag and headed over to the swings. She began humming to show she felt no worry or stress. She wanted to seem like a happy-go-lucky teen. She sat on the swing and began kicking her legs back and forth, swinging higher and higher. The swinging lightened her mood, slightly. She loved the feeling of the swing, it was as if she was flying and absolutely free. She closed her eyes and enjoyed it, even if it only lasted a few moments. She opened her eyes as she faced the sky and a memory came to her. Not a quick flash of one; on the contrary, it was filled with plenty of details that made her stomach drop.

She was running after the female voice calling out to her. She looked over her shoulder to see the beautiful boy with the short green hair following her.

"Zelina, what is going on?" he cried out to her.

She stopped, catching her breath. "Can't you hear her, Xan?"

"Hear who, Zelina?" he asked when he caught up to her.

"My mum. Something is wrong and I need to go find her."

"Wait for me and I'll help you." He ran back to his house and disappeared inside. Zelina waited several minutes and when he did not come back, she knew she had to go; she could not keep waiting.

"Sorry Xan, I can't wait any longer," she whispered. She stared a second longer at his house, then began running after her mother's voice. Something was very wrong with her; she could hear it.

She ran until she was in front of the Ecardia Sanctum. She stopped, breathless, and looked around. She could still hear her mother's voice calling out to her. Zelina hesitated before moving closer. She knew the rules; no one was to enter the Sanctum without first being told they are allowed by the Imperat. It was a very holy place and only those that had permission could enter. As a child, she had been told many stories of people that entered without proper permission and without the proper blessing—everything from them going blind to having their powers stripped or even them being turned to goo. Inside the Sanctum lived the three Ooras. They helped protect their realm from intruders, as well as from those within their realm seeking to harm anyone. The building was an entirely circular structure; it stood two stories tall and was the most foreboding place in the realm. The Sanctum had no windows and only one door. It looked as if the building had been there for centuries upon centuries, possibly before time itself. Its gray stone constantly appeared wet even when there was no rain and nothing else around the building was damp. Several stones had moss growing on them. There were no other buildings around the Sanctum as the land was considered holy, not only the building. The grass was always green, yet no flowers grew there. There were trees all around it, apart from the front of the building.

Her mother kept yelling for her, the urgency in her voice growing. Zelina had no choice but to proceed. She did not have time to seek permission from the Imperat and hoped she would be forgiven for her transgression. She ran through the lawn, which got the hem of her dress wet. *It hasn't rained in days. How is the grass wet?* she thought as she slowly pushed open the massive stone door. There was no handle on the outside, only on the inside. As she walked in, she could hear her mother's voice getting closer. Why would her mother be in here? What would she have done to be here with the Ooras? She could not think of any reason her mother would be sent to this place. Her mother was a good woman who never did anything wrong and worked hard to provide for Zelina. She had to find her mother and help her.

Zelina figured it would not take long to find her since there could not be many places for the Ooras to hide her. Upon entering, she saw there was only one door which was directly in front of her. To her right and left were enormous stairs. She only saw the back side of the floating stairs and thought the actual steps to head up would be straight ahead. Zelina walked through the open doorway into a vast circular room. There were stone columns engraved in the walls and they ran the full height of the room. She looked around wide-eyed, worried about her mother. The columns were lighter than the walls, the color of sand. On each of the dozen or so columns, midway down, was a symbol; each column had a different symbol. One column had a diamond shape with a smaller diamond in the middle and circles on it. One circle on the left of the diamond, one to the right and one at the bottom tip of the diamond. Another column had a stick figure missing a leg and with a "W" for a head, the arms pointing up and to the right. Zelina was fascinated by the symbols and wondered what each one meant. They were intriguing.

Zelina slowly walked farther in, looking around for her mother. There were three double doors: one set straight ahead, one to her right, and one to her left. She knew one of those doors had to lead to her mother. The doors were made of ancient wood, with intricate details carved in them. They were massive, almost the height of the room. None of the doors had handles or hinges on them. She hoped she would be able to push one open, just as she had done when she had entered the Sanctum. She walked to her left, noticing low fires burning in long, metal troughs. There were three fire troughs in the room and each one had the same symbols from the columns cut into them. She pushed on the door, but it would not budge. She called out, "Mum!

Where are you?" Zelina pushed once more before moving on to the next door. As she walked to the door directly in front of the entry, she noticed the gray-blue stone floor was shiny as if it had just been cleaned and left to air-dry. She walked cautiously to the door, afraid the floor was slick, and she would fall. She reached the door and pushed with all her might, but it would not budge.

"Mother! Help me find you! Where are you?!" Zelina screamed as loudly as she could. Tears started flowing. She put her head against the door, feeling lost and scared. She only had one more door to try, and after that, she was out of ideas. She stood up straight, wiped her tears and yelled out, "Mother, I am coming for you! Hold on!" She turned to walk back to the door that was to the right of the entry when she realized the entryway was gone. There was no door there—it was only a wall.

Panic began to rise. Now Zelina not only had to find her mother, but she also had to get them out of there. Was this her punishment for not having permission to enter? She held back her fear and the tears that were welling up inside of her. She had to focus; she still had one more door to test. She stood in front of it, staring at it, willing it to open. Zelina took a few deep breaths, then pushed the door. It did not move either. The tears flowed freely now; her shoulders slumped in defeat. "Mum, I'm sorry. I can't figure this out. Help me," she pleaded quietly as she slumped to the floor, her back resting against the last door.

After sobbing for several minutes, Zelina got control of herself and looked around the room once more. She noticed that at each door there was a circular decoration in the floor. These decorations were entirely different from the gray-blue floor, and she wondered how she could have missed that when she had entered the room. All three decorations were the same symbol: a triangle with a line running all the way through it and under the door. There was a fourth circle in the center of the room, and it was completely different from the other three. It was the same sandy color as the columns, plain, with no symbol or decoration of any kind. It was the only plain surface in the room.

Zelina walked back to each door, placing her feet in each of the triangles. She placed one foot on each side of the straight line and tried pushing once more. The doors still did not move. Having tried everything else, she decided to investigate the center decoration. She thought, perhaps, it was a release mechanism. If she stood upon it, then maybe the doors would open. It was her only hope to get out of there and to find her mother.

She walked to the centerpiece, looked around at each door and hoped that at least one would open for her. She stood in front of the sand-colored circle, took a deep breath, and exhaled slowly, saying, "I hope this works." She placed one foot on the circle, pushing down with her toe, hoping it would release a door. To her dismay, nothing happened. She knew she had to stand entirely on there if the doors were going to open. Reluctantly, Zelina stepped onto the center of the sandy stone piece and all three doors flew open. Excitement filled her; she just had to decide which door to go through to find her mother. Her excitement immediately turned to terror as she looked at the ground below her.

She was now raised up several inches and below was churning water. It was perfectly clear water but, Zelina could not see the ground below it. She looked up and saw the three Ooras walk through each of the doorways and stand on the triangles. The Ooras began to chant softly, their arms slowly rising out to their sides, one palm facing up while the other faced down. The fires began to burn hotter and rise higher. Zelina could feel the heat on her face and she began to sweat. She tried to speak, but nothing would come out.

As the women chanted, the water began rising higher and small waves moved out toward the Ooras. While the water hit their feet and splashed up, the fire from the troughs met with the water. The water got deeper as if there was no floor below, and the flames grew bigger. Amazingly, the water never reached Zelina or the Ooras. Even when the waves got near the ceiling, it simply splashed around them. The Ooras began to chant louder as the water and fire mixed together. Zelina stood, frozen, cold sweat running down her face and back. She could see a white foamy substance floating in the air directly below the Ooras' palms. The white substance moved slightly, bulging in and out and growing. As it grew, the Ooras lifted their heads to look at Zelina, their thick white veils completely covering their faces. Although she could not see the women's faces, she knew they were looking at her; she could feel their glares. The Ooras brought their hands in front of them, the white substance following wherever their hands moved. They brought their hands slowly in front of their chests, then at the same time all three Ooras pushed their hands forward and the white substance flew forcefully, hitting the platform Zelina was standing on.

Zelina slowly opened her eyes. She was still swinging, the sun still upon her face. She felt she had been gone for hours, reliving this memory, but it had only been a few seconds. She slowed the swing to a stop, looking around. No one was there and she felt she was alone, finally. She got off the swing, retrieved her book bag and began walking back toward the school. She was unsure of what she should do or where she should go next. She hoped Rune was someplace safe. She believed the Medjay would find no proof that she and Rune had their memories back.

She strolled, enjoying the warm sun on her face. She knew winter would soon arrive, along with the cold wind and rain. Zelina was not a fan of winter; she loved spring and fall. She enjoyed watching the trees come to life and watching the leaves change to beautiful colors each year. She did not like being bundled up in a coat and being cold; she loved being outdoors, and during winter she was not able to be out as often.

She thought about the carvings in the stones and one stood out to her. She had seen it before. Her head jerked up and she smiled broadly as she remembered where she had seen it. The moment she awoke at Stonehenge she had seen flash of a bright circle with an intricate design, set in stone, and made of fire. She stopped for a moment and closed her eyes. She tried to picture it again, what was it exactly? She searched her latest memory and could not place it. She opened her eyes and started walking. Her head hung down as she watched her feet move. She wanted to know what it was.

She arrived back at the tea shop and decided to sit out front on the bench to watch people and figure out what to do next. She thought about heading back to the house but ruled that out. She did not want anyone calling the Medjay to come get her, nor did she want a lecture about leaving school without permission. She had only been sitting there for a moment when she heard a light tapping on the window behind her. She turned and saw Rune waving at her to come in.

She jumped up and ran inside, throwing her arms around him, so thankful to see him. "Where have you been?"

He pulled her over to his table and sat down. "I was sitting in front of the school, waiting for you, when I felt the Medjay close by, so I ran over here, left the note for you and headed to the park. I sat there for nearly an hour before I felt their presence there. I ran into the trees behind the park and put a protection spell around me, hoping they wouldn't be able to detect it nor be able to find me. I wanted to be able to see the park in case you showed up and they were still there. Not too long after, I saw you sit on the bench, then swing. I wanted to come out and get you, but the Medjay were watching. You, by the way, did an excellent job covering. Where were you before showing up at the park?"

She rubbed her hands on her jeans and smirked. "This day has been crazy and it's not even over yet. I saw the old lady again this morning. She told me her name was Mrs. Leta, by the way. She looked up at me, only slightly, but it was enough. She doesn't seem able to stand up completely or look up fully since she has a hump on her back. Anyway, her eyes were red, like blood. I wanted to ask you about that." Zelina looked around the Enchanted Cafea and saw they were the only patrons in there; the only other person was the young girl behind the counter. "Should we be talking about this here?"

"It's safe. I put a spell on the place and her." He held up a hand so she would not interrupt. "It is detectable by the Medjay but it's a small spell and I did it correctly." He winked at Zelina. "You have to know what you're doing so the Medjay have a harder time detecting. Anyway, she," he said as he pointed his thumb to the young shop worker, "and others that walk by or come in, won't see us as we are; instead, they'll see us as a young man with his grandmother sharing tea and scones." He beamed. "She also can't understand what we're talking about. What she hears is an entirely different conversation. No worries. Continue."

"Why do you have to make me a grandmother?" Zelina asked, slapping his arm playfully.

"Well, I'm not going to be a woman. Not going to happen. Now, continue, the spell won't last forever." Rune took a drink of his tea and sat back in his chair.

"So, the Medjay can't track the spells you're using?"

"The longer they are used, the easier they can track it, so please get talking."

"I only saw her eyes a moment, but I know what I saw. They were definitely red. I wanted to ask you about that, but you never showed up at school. I was sitting there, waiting for you, when I looked over here and saw a man standing out front, staring at me. I could feel the stare, you know what I mean?" Rune nodded his head, fully understanding what she was talking about. "I had a bad feeling, so I hid in the restroom until everyone was in their classes, then tried to leave." Zelina told him about her morning at school and Rune listened with a slight grin on his face.

Zelina took a drink of the tea and a small bite of her scone that Rune orderd for her. "When I showed up at the park, I heard the female voice calling me, the voice from my dreams. Only, it seemed farther away than in the dream. What's more, there was a guy sitting on the bench. I thought it was you at first, but when you didn't look at me, I knew it wasn't you. I looked around, feeling like I was being watched, and when I looked back at the bench the guy was gone. The feeling of being watched didn't go away. Well, you saw the rest from your hiding spot, right?"

"Yes, I saw you sit on the bench and swing. I didn't see a guy sitting there, nor did I hear a voice calling to you. That's interesting." He gave a half smirk and scratched his head. "So, what made you decide to head back here?"

"I don't know really." She took another sip of her tea and began to tell Rune about her memory, the full memory of what had happened with the Ooras and the Sanctum. "What were those symbols on the columns?"

"They're runes. The runes have power, making the Sanctum a holy place. When you have enough runes, you can make a glyph, those are even more powerful."

"Interesting. I saw one when I woke up at Stonehenge." She rubbed her temples and tried to remember what symbol she saw. Her mind was blank. "Okay, so I don't understand why I heard my mother's voice calling me, and why did it come from inside the Sanctum? Don't you find it odd?"

"Your memory is coming back fast, and that's good with the Medjay coming around. You need to be extra careful with the spells and your hair changing on its own. I'm not sure why the Medjay are coming after us and that concerns me. I'm hoping they're checking all the students, making sure they're where they're supposed to be."

"Okay, so what's with the red eyes?"

"That's a Medjay." He sat up, pushing his tea aside and resting one elbow on the table. "A Medjay can shape-shift, basically changing into another person. They can't turn into animals, thank goodness."

Zelina looked thoroughly confused. "Why are you not freaking out about this? I've had a Medjay following me for days."

"Oh, I'm freaking out, but I'm thinking they are simply watching all the kids from our house. They don't know who's getting their memory back. And the good thing is Medjay don't have a lot of power, or abilities."

Zelina put her forehead in her hands. "So, how are they able to change their appearance like that?"

Rune took her hands in his and explained, "Okay, it's like this. I have an illusion put over this place, right?" Zelina nodded her head. "This spell is only for a short amount of time, a few hours if I'm lucky. The Medjay, however, can physically change their form instead of creating an illusion. They do have some abilities, but not usually too strong. However, they can't change their eye color. The red eyes are what distinguish them from regular people where we're from. So, the old lady has been watching you since you first arrived. When a person gets sent here, at least from what I've been told, someone picks them up and takes them to a relocation house. For kids it would be more like an orphanage, like where we are now. A place that helps people with memory issues. Are you with me so far?"

Zelina nodded her head and Rune continued. "These houses help finish planting the memories that the kids need to survive here. Once the memory is fully in place, if it's an adult, they get sent out in the real world to live out the rest of their lives. If it's a child, they get sent out once they turn eighteen. The children must stay in the houses until their eighteenth birthday. For some reason, when you were sent here, they had a Medjay following you, making sure the new memories were taking hold. All of it's odd, Zelina, and I don't have all the answer. Sorry."

"Okay, but you said earlier that they usually only send people without powers away, which is sad. I have powers, so do you, so why would they send us away?"

Rune shrugged his shoulders and slowly shook his head. "I don't know the answer to that, Zelina. I'm sorry. That's something we'll have to find out when we return home."

"Return? I know you said a couple of days ago that I could help you return home, but is that even possible?" She was excited now, thinking she would get to see her mother and friends again. She wanted to find out what happened, not only to her but to Rune as well.

"I've been told it's not possible. I feel differently, though. I believe the right person needed to come along to open the gate." He sat back, crossing his arms over his chest, watching Zelina.

"The right person? And you think the right person is me?"

"I don't know. It's possible, don't you think?"

"I don't know. That's a lot of pressure, you know, being the chosen one." She sat straight up, held her head high and looked down her nose at him, grinning. "However, I do like the title."

Rune stared at her, straight-faced. "I don't mean you are the chosen one. If anyone is the chosen one, it's me. You're just the first person I've met since my mentor that didn't have their memory completely wiped. I saw it in your eyes your first night at the house. I've seen people fight against the new memories only to have the Medjay show up and kill them or take them away. No one I know has ever come through with some memory, even a glimpse of it. This has got to be a good sign." He smiled at Zelina, which made some of her worry dissipate. "It's not only about finding another person with their memory—there's more to it than that. So, it's not like you are the chosen one or anything. Having someone with their memory helps."

"Hmm. That's what you saw in my eyes that night? I've wondered about that." She smiled back at him. "It wasn't the purple then?"

"Well, maybe I saw a hint of purple," he said with a smirk.

"So, what do we do now?"

"We go on like normal. We'll head back to the house and you'll work in the kitchen like the good little girl you are. Besides, you need to learn to cook if you are going to make your future husband happy."

Zelina playfully punched Rune in the arm and furrowed her brow at him. "Cook? Future husband? Yeah, right. I hate cooking and I'm not interested in any guy. I'm only in the kitchen to stay away from Lexy and to keep busy. Also, I'm only interested in finding out the truth. Why don't you learn to cook? That'd make a woman really happy."

"Oh, I know how to cook, girl. I'm not worried about making a woman happy. I'm the perfect catch."

"Oh gross." She threw a piece of her scone at him and laughed. "You would think that." She rolled her eyes and took one last sip of her tea. "So, we just act like nothing happened today? It's that easy?"

"Yeah. We go on like nothing unusual happened. We can't call attention to ourselves."

"Okay, got it. How long until I need to head out?"

"Soon. We have a little bit longer, though. Still hungry?"

"A bit; I can wait for dinner. I know you're hungry, so go get something to eat."

Rune got up and ordered a slice of blueberry pie and two more teas. "She's cute," he whispered in Zelina's ear as he sat down.

Zelina looked at the girl behind the counter. "I guess so. Stop staring at her; you're so obvious. Eat your pie." She turned Rune's face back to his pie, which he then took huge bites of.

"You eat like you'll never eat again. Slow down and chew with your mouth closed." Rune smiled at her and squished some blueberries between his teeth, which made Zelina laugh. "You are so gross." When she finished laughing at him she asked, "How do you pay for things? I mean, I know you said it's a spell. Can you teach me that?"

"Yeah, itsh eashy," he said with a full mouth.

"Please chew your food and then we can talk."

Rune finished his slice of pie, turned to Zelina and said, "It's all really an illusion spell. The same spell I use on the schools and even sometimes around the house. It makes people see what I want them to see. Simply think about what you want a person to see, whether it's money, you, a car, whatever. Then say softly, '*Exorior illusio*', and that person will see it. This spell doesn't have to be said loudly unless it's a big room with lots of people. Here you can say it in a whisper. It's easy. You want to try?"

"Okay, sure. You want another piece of pie?"

"Of course. Go for it."

Zelina got up, headed to the counter and asked for one scone and a slice of apple pie. The girl smiled at her, handed her the items and told her the total. Zelina thought about the money being in her hand and whispered, "*Exorior illusio*." Zelina opened her hand and there was the money. The girl took it, giving her some change back. "Thank you," Zelina said with a slight tremble in her voice.

Returning to the table, Zelina handed Rune the apple pie and placed her scone down as she sat next to him. "Isn't that like stealing? I feel bad; she gave me change back."

"It's real enough, Zelina. Sometimes we have no choice in the matter."

"Yes we do, we always have a choice to do what is right over what is wrong." She took a deep breath. "We can always get real jobs, like the one you have, and pay for this stuff."

"Oh, just eat your scone and shut it. It's not like I'm abusing it.

I'm not buying an expensive car or nice clothes. I'm simply buying some food."

"All I hear is an excuse and at this rate, this shop may go broke because of you."

"Okay, how about this? When I have real money, on days I get paid, I will use it here and not the spell. How does that sound?"

"Fine. I still think it's wrong using that spell, unless it's absolutely necessary." Zelina took a bite of her scone and a sip of tea while she watched Rune eat the slice of pie in two bites.

"Yeah, you feel real guilty; you've eaten two scones and had two cups of tea." He smiled at her as he pushed his plate away.

Zelina scrunched her face at him as she took the last bite of her scone, then sat back and patted her stomach. "All right, so do you work tonight?"

"No, I have tonight off, so I will get to taste your wonderful cooking." Rune stuck out his tongue and pretended to gag.

"Oh, stop. I am getting better at it. I'm glad you'll be around tonight. Having the Medjay following me has me worried, plus I have so many questions that need answers."

"No worries about the Medjay; they're making sure that we're doing as we're told. As long as we keep looking like we are," he smiled and winked, "then we have nothing to worry about. As for the questions, you know I can't answer a lot of them, but I'll answer what I can."

They sat in the tea shop talking until school let out. "I guess it's that time," Rune said. He frowned at Zelina and got up, pulling her chair out for her and walking with her to the door. "You first, my lovely." He looked back and winked at the girl behind the counter before leaving.

Zelina huffed and rolled her eyes. "Oh my gosh, Rune, you're such a flirt. It's disgusting."

"Don't be jealous, Zelina. You just aren't my type." He put his arm around her shoulders and winked at her.

Zelina threw his arm off. "Gross. Don't make me sick. I did

just eat. So quick question, the illusion spell will wear off when we reach the bus stop?"

"Yes, it slowly wears off when we leave a place. Once we reach the school or bus stop, everyone will see us for who we really are."

"No one will see us transform?"

He laughed. "No, remember they see what I want them to see and nothing more. Stop worrying so much."

"It's what I do."

Zelina and Rune walked behind a group of kids that we were walking to the bus. Zelina kept an eye out for any suspicious people, but she knew she would have no idea if any were Medjay unless they looked directly at her or until she learned to sense them. It would be their red eyes that gave them away and it seemed they were rather good at keeping them covered.

"Did you see those hot guys with the suits earlier today?" one blonde girl asked her friends.

"Yeah, they came into my homeroom first thing this morning looking for someone. Those suits were hot." The girl who replied fanned her face with her hand while the other girls laughed.

Rune looked at Zelina and winked.

They have no idea what those men were about. If they knew, they wouldn't think they were so hot, Zelina thought.

"I wish all boys dressed like that," said a younger-looking redhead.

"Yeah, that's just it, isn't it? Boys don't dress like that, but men do," the blonde stated. The girls all laughed and sat on the bench while waiting for the bus.

"Zelina, I'm going to sit in the back of the bus. We can't be seen entering the house together. My school is farther away than yours," Rune whispered in her ear. "Just keep watch and I will too."

Zelina nodded. Rune moved behind another group of kids that were standing behind the bench. That group was made up of a few boys, who were talking about the girls sitting in front of them. Zelina could only roll her eyes; she thought there were better things to do than giggle over boys or try to get a girl's attention.

When the bus arrived, Zelina took a front seat near the window so she could watch for anyone with red eyes. That idea made her laugh a little. Rune walked past her, all the way to the back, to sit on the opposite side of the bus. The little red-haired girl sat next to Zelina while her friends sat behind them. They carried on their conversation about the men in the suits and about the boys that were a few seats back. Zelina continued to stare out the window, looking for anything suspicious.

At the next stop, a few people got off the bus and only two people got on; both headed to the back. The red-haired girl asked Zelina the time, and Zelina apologized, stating she did not have a watch.

She looked back at Rune and saw Mrs. Leta. Her heart stopped and fear welled up inside her. What was she doing to do? How could she let Rune know that sitting next to him was a Medjay? She wondered if they were followed and if the Medjay saw the illusion spell and knew they had their memories—at least some of their memories. She also knew Rune was not supposed to be on this bus and that may alert the Medjay to him skipping school. Her stomach started flip-flopping and she stood up, covered her mouth and pushed past the red-haired girl, who screamed, "Ohhh, she's going to throw up." The bus driver threw the door open to let Zelina off.

She found the nearest trash can and leaned over it. She did not need to vomit; what she needed to do was buy some time for Rune to realize what was next to him. She had an idea. She wiped her mouth, pretending she had indeed thrown up into the trash can. She got back on the bus saying weakly, "Thanks for waiting." The red-haired girl had her leg across the seat, preventing Zelina from sitting with her again. Zelina shrugged and walked to the back, seeing the Medjay as the old lady sent shivers through her body. She knew what she had to do.

"Well, good afternoon, Mrs. Leta. I don't usually see you after school," she stated, trying to sound bubbly. Zelina sat behind Rune and the Medjay. "How are you this afternoon, ma'am?" Zelina asked, leaning forward, trying to see the old lady's eyes once again.

"Better than you, so it seems. Feeling okay, dear?" the old lady, or Medjay, asked Zelina.

"Much better now. Must have been a bad school lunch." Zelina scooted to the end of her seat, leaning forward to the point where she was almost in the aisle. She was trying to catch a glimpse of the old lady's eyes, but she had them covered with huge sunglasses. "So, are you on your way home now?"

"Yes, dear. Same as you. Heading home, making dinner, then will turn in early. The same as every day."

"Yeah, but I don't usually see you in the afternoon. Sure you're feeling well?"

"Yes, I'm all right. You don't need to worry about me; this old body is working just fine." She smiled and turned her head to Rune. "How was your day?"

Rune turned his head slightly, seeing Zelina. He looked up a bit at the old lady and smiled. "It was interesting, full of surprises. Days like this keep me on my toes." He went back to looking out the window.

"He likes action, I think," the old lady said to Zelina. "Good thing this world is full of action." She tried to smile sweetly at Zelina. It sent chills up Zelina's spine.

"Hey, Rune, you don't usually ride this bus home."

He turned toward Zelina. "Yeah, I decided to skip the bus today and walk a bit, now I regret it. I didn't realize how far the house was. I'm exhausted." He smiled and went back to looking out the window.

Zelina wanted to continue talking to Rune but could think of nothing else to say. She thought his story was a good cover for why he was on the bus, hopefully the Medjay bought it. Zelina began sweating. The bus ride could not end quickly enough. She wanted to get out of there and to be in her room, safe and sound.

"Well, my day was rather dull. Just plain old school." Zelina sat back, putting her back to the window and stretching out one leg to look relaxed. At least, she hoped she looked relaxed.

"You were at school all day? Most children nowadays skip school. They feel there is too much fun to be had when they should be in school, growing their minds."

"Interesting thought. I have skipped school several times, got in trouble for it and got switched to another school where I've had to start over with friends and so on. I try to be good now," Zelina replied with a smile on her face. She felt better not being able to see the Medjay's red eyes.

The rest of the ride was silent; Rune never took his eyes off the passing world outside the window. Zelina watched the bus riders come and go, always looking for another Medjay, but none came. The Medjay, or old lady, in front of her stayed quiet, head down the entire ride.

"This is my stop." Zelina stood up and began to walk down the aisle to exit the bus. "You have a great night, Mrs. Leta." She smiled and jumped off the bus, ambling down the pavement toward the house. She dawdled as much as possible to see if Rune got off the bus safely; however, she never saw him leave. She started worrying. She stopped and dug through her book bag to waste time. *Rune, where are you?* she thought. After about five minutes, Zelina closed her bag and headed for the house once again. She had to believe he could handle things and would be fine.

Zelina saw Lexy and Sloane sitting on the porch as she turned the corner to the house. She rolled her eyes and reminded herself to keep her mouth closed, no matter what Lexy said to her. She walked up the stairs, keeping her eyes on the door in front of her. It did not take long for Lexy to start things. "How was school, you daft monkey?"

"It was interesting. Two big guys were searching the entire school for someone. Thanks for asking." Zelina walked in the house without Lexy saying another word. She did it; she walked past Lexy without making eye contact or causing an issue, and she felt good about that.

"Well, move along, Zelina. You can't block the door and you need to get schoolwork finished before helping with dinner," Ms. Nyx scolded as she walked out of Mr. Jared's office. "Move along."

Zelina went to her room, spread out some books and paper on her bed and sat in the chair by the window, watching for Rune. A knock at her door made her jump. "Yes, come in."

Mr. Jared opened her door and walked in, eyeing her bed. "Lots of schoolwork?"

"Not too much." Zelina smiled, as she got up from her chair and grabbed a book from the assortment. "It's such a beautiful day out; I was having a hard time concentrating."

Mr. Jared looked over at her window and back at her. "Yes, I can understand that." He opened her door all the way, then sat down in her chair by the window. "I came by to talk to you about something I overheard. I heard you tell Lexy, just moments ago, that your school was searched by two men in suits. Is this true?"

"Yes, sir. They showed up right after school started. I don't know when they left, though."

"Where were you when they were searching the school?"

"I was in with the nurse."

"Are you sick?"

"No, I had—well, cramps. I thought if I could relax in the nurse's office for a bit then I would be all right." She gave him a lopsided grin.

"Okay. Did the two men talk with you at all?"

"No. I mean, they tried to, but the nurse wouldn't let them without my guardian's permission. I didn't see them after that. I stayed in the nurse's office for over an hour before heading back to class. I asked her, the nurse, if I could come back home." Calling the house "home" made Zelina's stomach turn. "She told me I couldn't without contacting my guardian and having them pick me up. I went back to class, thinking it would be better to finish out school than to bother you or Ms. Nyx." Zelina smiled at him.

"Thank you, dear. Yes, today was a very busy day for us; I

appreciate you toughing it out like that. Any other day, I would have sent Damon to get you." He sat there a moment longer, staring at the floor. "If you are still not feeling well, you may take tonight off from helping in the kitchen." Mr. Jared got up, walked to the door, and turned around to face Zelina. "Zelina, you are doing remarkably well. You handled yourself with Lexy wonderfully and I've seen a vast improvement in your behavior. Keep it up and we can talk about you getting a job." He walked out, closing the door behind him.

Zelina jumped up and began looking out the window once more.

"What are you looking at?"

Zelina spun around to see Rune standing in her room. "Where did you come from?"

"I've been here for several minutes." He sat in the chair next to her. "Were you worried about me?"

"Maybe, just a little. I didn't see you get off the bus." She sat down on her bed, crossing her legs.

"I got off at the next stop; it's not too far. I told the Medjay that I zoned out and missed my stop. So, what's on the menu for dinner tonight?"

"I don't know, Mr. Jared told me I could take the night off from the kitchen since my cramps were so bad." She patted her stomach.

"Wonderful, so the food will be edible tonight."

Zelina threw a pillow at him, which Rune caught and put behind him.

"So, what did the great and wonderful Mr. Jared want with you tonight?"

"You didn't hear any of what he said?" Rune shook his head. "He overheard me tell Lexy about my adventurous day at school, with the two men in suits searching for someone. Hey, how does that work? Your spell to have a fake me in the school and the real me shows up?"

"Yeah, like Mr. Jared didn't know anything about the Medjay

searching your school." Rune started at the ceiling and Zelina thought he must be talking to himself. "I wonder if they searched mine too. I'll have to look into that." He got up and headed for the door. "As for the spell, when the real you is in the school or building then the spell vanishes. So, there will never be two of you around and with a school that size, no one pays much attention to the new kid. No worries. I'll see you at dinner." Rune walked out of the room, leaving Zelina by herself.

She hoped the rest of the night would be calm, with no Medjay or Lexy messing with her. Zelina went back to her window and looked out at two younger girls playing dolls in the grass. All she really wanted to do was practice her spells; she wanted to get stronger and get her memory back. She was tired of not being able to remember anything other than what was planted there. She wanted to see the vision of her mother again; she wanted to see her face. No matter how hard she tried, she could not remember what her mother looked like, and that broke her heart.

From Rune's notebook, page 73

Chapter Seven

Dinner that evening was nice and quiet. Zelina missed working in the kitchen with Alix and Gwynn. She talked to them for a moment while they served her and Rune their food. Rune did not say much; he was too busy eating. Mr. Jared and Ms. Nyx were not seen in the dining hall. Lexy and Sloane sat at a table with several other girls at the other end of the room. After dinner, Zelina went to sit under a tree and watch the setting sun, knowing soon the weather would be too cold to enjoy being outside. Rune stayed in his room. Zelina was unsure what he was doing exactly. She figured that whatever it was, it had to do with them getting back to their real home. As she watched kids play and Lexy talk with two older girls, she wondered why they were there and if any of them had any idea of the power they may have running through them. She also began to wonder what life would be like if she had never known the truth, if her entire memory had been wiped. She wondered if she would be happy here, making friends and simply living her life. After all, that's all she wanted, besides the truth: to be happy.

Zelina went to bed later than normal and found she could not sleep. She tossed and turned, unable to get comfortable; she could not stop thinking about how different her life would be right now if she had not been sent here or if her memories had been entirely erased. Would she and Rune still be friends, or would she be friends with Lexy? Would she love going to school or hate it? Those thoughts kept churning inside her mind, never letting sleep take over. She gave up, threw back the covers, and looked at the time: it was three in the morning. She groaned and felt like crying. Zelina pulled her hair back, curled up in her chair and tried to relax. After about an hour she went to take a shower, thinking that would help relax her. As she walked down the stairs, she could hear voices coming from the common room. She tiptoed just outside the room, trying to find out who was up so late.

"So she was, indeed, at school? It was not an illusion spell then?" It was Ms. Nyx.

"No, she was there."

Zelina was unsure who Ms. Nyx was speaking to just by the voice; she guessed it was one of the Medjay who had come to her school.

"What about Rune? He's been acting odd ever since she arrived."

"We were not told to investigate Rune. We did see the two of them together for a short time, but we got nothing from them, they seem normal. If you would like, we can take a look at Rune. However, at this point neither one seems to be showing any signs of power or memory returning. We will continue to watch them, as well as several others here. During our initial investigation, there was one person who was always at the scene where power was spent the most. That person will be our primary focus now."

"Who are the others that need watching?"

"Ms. Nyx, we are in charge here—you are not. You need to let us do our job. Stay out of our way."

Zelina took a few steps back as she heard heavy footsteps heading toward the door. "So that's it? There's nothing else you can do about those two?"

Zelina could see a shadow under the common room door; she moved closer to the restroom. "I said we would continue watching them. There is nothing else I can do right now. If we can prove they have some of their memory back, then we can take care of things.

Right now, we will just watch. Have a great day, ma'am."

Zelina walked into the restroom, easing the door shut behind her. She knew she was not to be up this late; she could get in serious trouble for that and even more trouble now that she had overheard the conversation. She leaned against the door, listening for them to leave.

"Yes, you two have a great day as well," Ms. Nyx said with agitation as she shut the front door rather roughly. Zelina heard nothing else—no more footsteps, no breathing, nothing but pure silence. Where did Ms. Nyx go? Zelina began to open the bathroom door when she heard Mr. Jared.

"I told you she was doing fine. Everything has taken as it should have. If anyone is a troublemaker, it's that Rune character. He'll be out of here soon anyway; his eighteenth birthday isn't far off, only two years. You need to be watching Lexy. She is stirring up problems and the Medjay seem to be watching her as much as they are watching Zelina."

"Lexy? Lexy is perfect. She has no memory other than being here. *She* is the perfect one, not Zelina. Good night, Bevyn." Ms. Nyx stormed off and Zelina heard a door slam.

Mr. Jared went past the restroom and down the hall. Zelina stood, ear pressed to the door, for a few moments longer. She decided it would be best if she went back up to her room and tried to rest once more. She figured she would not be able to fall asleep with the Medjay being in the house, but she had to return to her room and try. Maybe she was starting to be able to sense the Medjay like Rune; it would explain her wakefulness.

Just as she predicted, Zelina did not fall back to sleep that night. She got up early, showered and ate a full breakfast. Rune showed up in the dining hall just as Zelina finished. Zelina went back to her room. She wanted to go to sleep; her sleepless nights were starting to affect her. There was no sun out, only clouds and mist. It matched her mood perfectly; she really wished she could curl up and fall asleep for the entire day.

"Good morning, sunshine." Rune walked into her room, quietly shutting the door behind him.

"If you say so." She continued to stare out the window.

"What's wrong with my sunshine this morning?" He sat on the edge of her bed and pouted at her.

"Just tired—didn't sleep much last night. I really need to talk to you about it."

"Not here. I'll have to figure out how to get you out of here. I'll tell you that I slept wonderfully, though. Even though the weather is gloomy, it's going to be a great day, my sweet sunshine face." He said with a high-pitched squeal and his face scrunched.

"If you say so." She was much too tired to play.

Rune left her room and several minutes later Zelina heard a commotion coming from downstairs. She could make out voices yelling, but she was unable to hear what was being said. She headed down to see what was happening.

Halfway down the stairs she heard Ms. Nyx yelling, "I don't know why Lexy would have taken off. She never does such things."

"Come into my office; you're causing a scene." Mr. Jared pulled Ms. Nyx into his office and closed the door.

"I won't let them harm her!" Ms. Nyx yelled. Mr. Jared must have said something because Ms. Nyx snapped, "I have had her since she was ten, Bevyn, ten. I can't just let them take her!"

That was all Zelina could hear from where she stood. She walked down the stairs and saw a small group of kids in the dining hall entrance, trying to listen. "What's happened?" she asked.

"Lexy is missing," one girl answered. "She hasn't been seen since lights out last night."

"Yeah, Damon's been sent to find her," a boy said.

"That's never good," an older girl stated.

"Why would Lexy take off like that?" Zelina questioned, looking around.

"She was following you and Rune."

Zelina turned around and saw Sloane sitting at the bottom of the stairs. "What are you talking about, Sloane?" Zelina's heart was beating rapidly. "Let's go outside and talk."

Zelina took Sloane's arm and they walked out to the yard. "What do you mean Lexy was following us?"

"Yeah, the past two days she followed you and Rune, hoping to catch you skipping school and stealing. She said that's why the police were here the other day."

"Police?"

"Yeah, those big guys that were here the other night and that showed up at your school."

"Oh yeah, those guys."

"She left this morning to get proof that you guys are the ones causing problems, not her."

"Who's accusing Lexy of causing problems?" Zelina questioned.

"She said she over-heard one of the policemen telling Mr. Jared they were investigating a few people here and that she was one of those people. She was angry. She said she knew you and Rune were the real cause of all the trouble around here and she was determined to catch you two."

They heard Ms. Nyx yelling as she left the house. She got in a car and sped off. "I hope they find her, and she isn't in any trouble," Zelina said softly. "Rune and I have done nothing wrong, Sloane."

"I don't know anything." Sloane never looked at Zelina, she kept her gaze down at her feet.

Mr. Jared yelled to her from the front porch, "Zelina, please come to my office."

"See you later, Sloane," Zelina said.

Zelina walked into Mr. Jared's office and sat in a chair in front of his desk. He paced behind her. "Zelina, what's going on with you and Lexy?"

"Nothing, sir. It's like I told you, she doesn't like me for some reason."

"Sloane says Lexy has been following you and Rune to an old factory on the other side of town. Were you with Rune yesterday or ever at an old factory?"

"No, sir. I've been going school and back here. I don't go any-where else. The policemen even saw me at school yesterday, sir."

"So they did."

He continued to pace, not saying a word, which made Zelina begin to sweat. She had no idea what he was thinking or what he might do. "Sir, is there something wrong?"

"No. Please send Rune in to see me."

"I haven't seen him since breakfast, but when I do I'll tell him."

Zelina headed back outside, sat on the porch and watched the sky. A few moments later Sloane joined her. "Are you in trouble?"

"I don't think so."

"Rune is in Mr. Jared's office." She sat next to Zelina and stared up at the sky.

"That's good."

"Are you two dating?"

"Oh gross, no! We're just friends, that's all. He's helping me with schoolwork." Zelina laughed at the idea of dating Rune. He was a friend and nothing more.

"Oh." Sloane sat staring up at the sky, expressionless.

They both sat in silence for a while.

"I actually have a bit of schoolwork to do. I'll see you later," Zelina said. She headed to her room; she was so exhausted that she decided to take a short nap.

Her nap was dream-free and she woke up feeling calmer and more at peace. She rolled over and yelled, "Good grief, Rune, please stop doing that!"

Rune was once again sitting in the chair, staring at her. It unnerved her how he could sneak in her room and watch her.

"Be quiet, girl. Ms. Nyx and Damon found Lexy before the Medjay did. They are talking to her now, downstairs."

"Where did they find her?" She sat up, smoothing back her hair.

"Near my school. She said she was trying to prove that we were up to trouble."

"Are they believing her?"

"Well, Ms. Nyx is, but it seems that Mr. Jared is on the fence about it. We've got to be super careful now."

"Then maybe you should get out of my room." Zelina got up and opened the door.

"Yeah, I'm going. I'll see you at dinner."

She shut the door and looked at the time, realizing she had slept through lunch. Zelina spent the rest of the afternoon alone in her room until she headed down to the kitchen to help with dinner. She ate with Alix and Gwynn; Rune ate with some other boys at another table.

The rest of the evening was spent cleaning the kitchen and dining hall. She had a good night's sleep and woke up the next morning much later than she had planned. As she headed to the dining hall, hoping they still had some breakfast, Alix stopped her. "No more food; you missed out." Zelina frowned and headed back upstairs.

She got so hungry within the hour that she got some fruit from the fridge and went to eat it out on the porch, which is where she found Rune. She sat next to him. "How's your morning going?"

"Good, and yours?"

"Missed breakfast, so I'm eating this lovely apple instead." She held up the apple and frowned.

"Apples are rubbish." He smiled at her. "We'll need to meet tomorrow morning, usual spot," he whispered.

"You got it." She returned his smile as he got up and headed in.

"So glad to see you and Rune together, a happy little couple."

Zelina turned and saw Lexy standing behind her. Sloane stood behind Lexy. "Good afternoon, Lexy."

Lexy sat next to Zelina. "I know you two are up to something and I'm going to find out what it is and have you both kicked out of here."

"Do whatever you need to do, Lexy, whatever makes you feel good." Zelina stared at the dark clouds moving overhead as she ate her apple.

Lexy grunted and headed to the other side of the porch with Sloane following her. Zelina shook her head and thought how sad it was to see someone that unhappy.

Zelina spent most of the day outside, enjoying the mild breeze and being alone. It was so peaceful outside; she thought she could be out there forever. As dinner rolled around, she headed in and helped in the kitchen. Once again, she ate with Alix and Gwynn, but this time there was another helper, Mandy.

That night, Zelina had another dream of her last day at home, her real home. She saw it all, just as before; she could smell the fire and feel the water. She woke up sweating and her heart was racing. Zelina took a few deep breaths and closed her eyes, trying to sleep once again. However, sleep never returned. She was miserable the next morning getting ready for school. She ate breakfast and headed to the bus.

Mrs. Leta was not at the bus stop and Zelina was thankful for that; she felt it was a good sign that the Medjay were not there. Zelina arrived at school just as everyone was going in. She saw Rune head into the tea shop, and she followed him.

Sitting next to him, she asked, "Why don't you ever eat at the house?"

"The food is better here. Why do you eat there?"

"It's free there."

"Be happy, little one. It's going to be a great day." He smiled.

Zelina wanted to slap the smile off his face. "Rune, we need to talk so hurry up." She watched all the kids run up the stone steps into the school, thinking she should be in there with them. She felt things were getting out of control and a part of her wanted to join in and be like everyone else. That part of her felt it would be better to be clueless about her real life.

"All right, calm yourself. I'll take this with us and eat it later," he said with a huff.

"Good. Where are we going, factory or empty house?"

"We'll walk by the factory and see what's going on there before heading to the house." He got up and grabbed a to-go cup for his tea, scowling at Zelina. "I wish you would lighten up. It's going to be a great day, have I mentioned that?"

"Yes, Rune, you did. Now, can we go?"

"Yes, master, we can go." Rune grabbed his tea and a few biscuits. He hunched over and dragged one foot while he walked to the door. "Master, first."

Zelina stifled a laugh. She could not help but smile and that irritated her more; she did not want to smile at him.

"So, what's wrong with my sunshine this morning? You should be happy the Medjay are gone."

"No. They aren't gone, and yet again, I didn't sleep well last night."

He stopped walking, pulling her arm to turn her around and look at him. "What do you mean they aren't gone?"

"Can we please talk about this where it's safe?" She began walking once more.

"Yes, your highness."

They stood outside the factory. Zelina waited for Rune to say it was okay to enter; Rune stared at an upstairs busted out window. "Someone's up there, only it's not Medjay."

"Okay? Who would be in there?"

"Not sure. Let's move around to the side and wait a few minutes—maybe they'll leave."

They went around the right side of the building. She had not seen this side of the building. It was still a mud pit but there were several bushes beyond the mud. They sat behind the bushes and waited. It did not take long for them to see who was in the factory. It was Lexy. Zelina gasped, holding her hand over her mouth. Rune looked just as shocked.

Lexy looked around. She seemed to be making sure no one saw her and then she ran down the road back the way they had just came.

Zelina stood. "What in the world? Sloane told me she was following us last week, but I'd hoped she would've quit."

"I have no idea what she was doing. Mr. Jared asked if we'd been going to a factory, but I didn't think she was really following us. What was she hoping to find up there?" Rune asked biting his lower lip, staying hidden behind the bushes.

"She's trying to prove we're causing problems. I guess she overheard the Medjay stating they believed she was the one getting her memory back and they would be watching her."

"Oh, that's good to know." Rune's eyes widened. "So, they are following her, which means they could be watching her now." Rune pulled Zelina back down and looked around.

"This is getting insane, Rune. We've got people following us; we should take a break from meeting." Zelina stood back up and began to walk off. Rune stopped her, pulling her back down behind the bushes, once again.

She started to say something, but Rune put his hand over her mouth. "Shh. Look over there." He pointed to the left side of the factory and there they were, the two Medjay that were at Zelina's school the day before. The Medjay stood there, watching Lexy run down the road until she could no longer be seen. They started talking, then leisurely followed Lexy.

Rune stood, looking around. "I didn't feel their presence." He lost all color in his face; he sat back down in the dirt, looking stunned. "I can't believe they didn't see us."

Zelina rubbed his arm. "It's no big deal, Rune. They must've hidden themselves. As for not seeing us, I can only think they were too busy watching Lexy to notice us approach." She got up and headed to the front of the building while Rune sat staring off in front of him. "Rune, come on. We need to go in and make sure your protection spell is still intact." Zelina walked in and headed to the room upstairs; she heard Rune behind her.

"*Demitto*," Zelina said. The doors creaked loudly as they opened and she went in. Nothing seemed out of place; the entire room was still dirty with food wrappers on the floor. "I should come in here and clean one day."

"No, it's perfect the way it is," Rune said as he came in, closing the doors behind him. He walked around the room, making sure it was fully protected.

Zelina looked out the window. "Rune, the Medjay are now watching Lexy."

"Obviously," he said as he sat at the small table, looking through papers.

"I was up late Friday night and decided to head down to shower. I overheard a conversation between Ms. Nyx and the Medjay."

Rune spun around in the chair. "Why didn't you tell me about this earlier?"

"When? In the tea shop? How about over the weekend with everyone around and on edge with Lexy taking off? Seriously?"

"No matter. Tell me now."

Zelina raised her eyebrows at him then turned back to the window.

"Please," Rune added in a huff.

"That's better." Zelina moved from the window to the bed. "I only heard the end of the conversation. They don't believe we have our memories back, but they think Lexy does. They think it's Lexy that's using power. They said something about them seeing only one person near where power was spent. They never said who, but after the Medjay left, Mr. Jared told Ms. Nyx it was Lexy the Medjay were watching. The Medjay said they would keep an eye on us, but we weren't their main focus."

"Well, that's good for us, not so good for Lexy."

"Rune, she could be in trouble. Don't you think we should help her?"

"Zelina, we can't help her. If we try, then they'll know for sure it's us. They'll investigate, follow her around for a while and see it's not her. They won't do anything to her without full proof."

"How do they know?"

"How do they know what?" Rune pulled a notebook from the table and flipped through it.

"How do they know that someone is getting their memory back or using power?"

Rune got up from the table and began pacing the room. "It's basically another sense. They can see and sense when power's been used within a certain amount of time. I'm not sure how long that time is. They must've sensed the power here and when you used it to change your hair and eye color back. Lexy must've been close by and they put the two together. You said she was following us, so it makes sense."

"So, are the Medjay more powerful than you?"

"They are stronger physically. Have you seen how big they are?"

"Yes, quite big, but I mean more powerful with their... power."

Rune smiled. "With some spells, yes, but other spells, no. It depends on the Medjay. Some Medjay are more physical than powerful, while others have more power than physical strength. From what I've been told, there are certain powers they have that none of us have, like the ability to change their appearance." He continued pacing. "They are not taught these abilities—the ability to see or sense power or to be able to kill without remorse. They are born that way and then trained to harness those abilities." Rune stopped and looked at Zelina. "Where we are from, to murder someone either gets you killed or sent here. The only ones allowed to eliminate someone—they like that term better—are the Medjay. They get their orders from the Imperat or the Palviers and can't act until the order is given to them. They are the police or soldiers where we're from." He sat down in the chair, moving it closer to Zelina so he could look her in the eye. "Very few people have been able to defeat a Medjay in battle—very few."

"But it has been done?"

"Yes, by people that were quite powerful. From what I know, those people are no longer around."

"What do you mean?"

"I mean, they were eliminated. The Imperat and Palviers couldn't have people being able to defeat the Medjay, their most powerful weapons."

"Okay, wait. What exactly are the Imperat and Palviers? I remember 'Imperat' from my vision when I was on the swing, but I'm not sure what it is."

He bit his bottom lip as if he was nervous about answering the question. "I'm not supposed to say, but I will. The Imperat is the one who makes all decisions concerning our land and people. The Palviers are his counsel; they help with smaller decisions and help the Imperat make major choices. Make sense?"

Zelina nodded. "So, if we ever encounter a Medjay and have to fight them, we won't win?"

"We can stun them and hide. Some of our abilities are much stronger than theirs, like illusions. You've seen them change their appearances; they can't hide those eyes, whereas we can hide better without getting caught. Our protection spells can't be broken by them, either. They can sense the power but can't see exactly who is using it or who is under the protection spell; they can only sense the general direction or see if power has been spent. So, we do have some advantages." Rune gave her a comforting smile and spun the chair around, moving it back to the table where he laid the notebook open, flipping through the pages once more.

"So, what do we do now?" Zelina asked as she lay back on the bed, staring at the discolored ceiling.

Rune shrugged. "If you are up for it, we can learn more spells."

"I'd rather hear more about where we come from." She sat up and smiled sweetly, batting her eyelashes.

"Nope, I can't do that. I keep telling you too much. I think the more we practice spells, the more it will help your memory come back."

Zelina rolled her eyes, flopping back down on the bed and staring at the ceiling. "I feel like I'm being left out of something all my friends know about. I'm on the outside looking in. Can't you tell me about the weather, the food, the clothes, anything?"

He spun the chair around, his left eyebrow shot up. "Friends? Like plural? What other friend do you have?"

"None. Shut it and tell me something."

"You're a pain in my—"

"Shut it, man."

"Well, if I shut my mouth, how I can tell you about where we're from?"

She sat up, pursing her lips and glaring at him. "Okay, you may only speak of home."

Rune sat looking at her for a few moments. "Fine. I will tell you about the weather there." He got up, stared out the window and then began pacing the room.

"Tell me."

"The weather there is… the same as here. It rains, it's cold, it's warm, it's sunny, and it's cloudy. Fantastic stuff, weather."

"Ugh, you're mean." Zelina stood up and crossed her arms, tapping her foot. "Fine. Let's learn some spells."

"Good." Rune stopped in front of her, patted her head and walked to the door. "I have a few; however, you can't practice them on me—or anyone, for that matter. One is to take away memory; it's only to be used in case of a true emergency. If it were back home, it could get you sent here. You simply face your opponent, look them in the eye and say, '*Abduco manin.*'" He faced the wall, said the spell and, then looked at Zelina once again.

"Okay." She dropped her arms. "Do I need to say this one loudly or can it be said under my breath?"

"No, it can be said either way, and not everyone can do this spell. This one is quite powerful and is only to be used when attacked. Usually the Medjay use it."

She nodded, looked at the wall and repeated the words. "*Abduco manin.*"

"Perfect. I pray we will never have to find out if you are powerful enough to actually use that spell."

"Have you ever used it?"

"No. I was taught it by my mentor as a just-in-case spell. I don't know if I can even pull that spell off. Okay, moving on." He picked up an empty candy box and set it on the table. "This one will freeze someone or something, then shatter them. Again, this one should only be used in a life-or-death situation." He smiled and backed away, standing behind Zelina. "Now, you simply say, '*Gelu fracta.*' The box will freeze for just a moment, then it'll shatter. Ready?"

Zelina nodded, stared at the box and repeated the words. The box froze—a white sheen appeared on it for a moment, then it shattered into tiny pieces.

Rune hooted and danced in place. "You catch on so quickly, my little grasshopper." He knocked the frozen pieces to the floor. "How are you feeling?" Rune walked in front of Zelina, looking into her eyes.

"Fine, actually. No headache." She thought it had to be a good sign that she was not having any side effects.

"Okay, a very important spell. If anyone is ever hurt and needs help immediately, this one'll do it. It'll stop bleeding, close wounds, and so on. It won't fully heal a person right away, but it does speed up the process quite a bit."

Zelina looked confused, brow furrowed and eyes squinting.

Rune clarified. "Okay, so if I were to get shot, you can pull the bullet out and close the wound; however, it will take time for me to get full mobility again. Using the spell would speed up the process, though. Instead of it taking weeks or months, it might only take a few days to be fully healed. Does that make more sense?"

"Yes. Now, how do I do this?" she asked, pushing him behind her once more.

"Okay, pushy. Once again, the person must be in front of you, and you must have eye contact with them. You simply say, '*Cito sano.*' Now go."

She repeated the words to the wall and felt a chill flow through her. "Something is wrong, Rune."

"What do you mean?"

"I just got a chill. I can feel something is wrong."

"Sit down and breathe."

He helped her to the bed, sitting her down, and then went to the window to look outside. "What are you doing?" she asked in a weak voice.

"I'm making sure there are no Medjay around. Maybe that's what you're feeling."

Zelina shrugged her shoulders, laid back, closed her eyes and saw it.

She was home; her mother was at the sink, humming. "Zelina, please go water the garden."

"Yes, ma'am." Zelina turned around to see herself much younger. She was now seeing her past, as a spectator.

The younger Zelina walked past her mother and out the back door to their little garden; spectator Zelina followed and was amazed at how the garden was thriving. The flowers were in full bloom to one side, and the other side had a few interesting plants growing. Zelina recognized some of them; however, there were a few that she had never seen before. She saw some tomatoes and strawberries. Next to the strawberries was an unusual plant that was growing on a vine; she did not know the name of it. The plant was almost clear. She could see inside the plant, its pink core and seeds. Out behind her yard, a shimmering tree caught her eye for a moment; it was a beautiful sight, not clear like the fruit but bright and shining like a crystal. The tree did not seem to have any fruit hanging from it. It stood taller than her house, and each time the wind blew, the tree shimmered, sending glistening light over her yard.

She could hear kids playing down the street. The sun was out in full force, no clouds in the sky and only a slight breeze blew. Younger Zelina turned the water hose on, but nothing came out. She shook it, and then looked into the hose to see where it was clogged. The water shot out, hitting younger Zelina in the face. Spectator Zelina laughed while her younger version wiped her face angrily with her hands and yelled, "Xan, I will throat punch you!" She dropped the hose on the ground and took off running after the boy.

"Run! She's coming!" Xan yelled to someone hiding behind a tree. "Run!" Both boys laughed as they ran down the dirt road.

Older Zelina followed as the younger Zelina ran after both boys. She stopped after a few moments and yelled, "I'll get you both back." Both Zelinas turned around and headed back for their home. Her mother was outside, watering the plants. "Sorry, Mum. Rune and Xan soaked me," the younger Zelina pouted. "I want to punch the both of them."

"You will do no such thing, Zelina. You will conduct yourself as a lady."

"I'm not a lady, Mum, I'm a girl. I'm only ten." She put her hands in the water and splashed her mother. In response her mother instantly turned the water completely on her daughter, soaking her from head to toe. Zelina laughed as she watched the two play in the water for a few moments.

"Go in and dry off. You can help me with dinner," her mother said as she turned off the water.

"Do I have to?" she whined. "I'd rather go catch Rune and Xan. I'd rather water the garden all night."

"Yes, you have to. You must learn to do these things for when you're married."

"Eww…marriage is gross." Younger Zelina stuck her tongue out and went into the house.

Zelina did not follow her younger self, instead she stayed outside. Her mother turned around and seemed to sense someone was there, watching her. She stood frozen, staring directly in front of her. Zelina took it all in, exactly what her mother looked like. She had the same straight, bright coral hair pulled back with a ribbon. Her eyes were a bright, vibrant green, set against skin darker than Zelina's. She figured her father must be fair-skinned. Her mother stood about the same height as Zelina and had thinner lips. Zelina smiled at her, wishing her mother could see her.

"Mum, I'm all cleaned up! Let's start dinner," younger Zelina hollered from inside the house.

"On my way," Zelina's mother called back. She wiped her hands on her apron and went inside, looking over her shoulder with concern in her eyes.

"Zelina, are you okay?" Rune was asking her. It seemed he was talking to her from a tunnel. "Zelina?"

"What?" she asked as her eyes fluttered open. "What's wrong?"

"You tell me. You were saying something about throat punching someone," he said as he covered his throat with both his hands.

She rubbed her eyes and sat up slowly. Rune sat beside her, looking very concerned. "I'm fine—just another vision is all."

"Tell me about it," he said grinning. "Every time this happens it means you are getting closer to getting your memory back."

"We knew each other when we were kids, a bit better than you let on." She put her feet on the floor, knees bent, elbows on her knees and head in her hands, staring at the floor as she recalled all the details.

Rune laughed when she told him about the water spraying her in the face and how the two boys ran off.

"Who is Xan?" she questioned, glancing up at Rune.

Rune looked down at the floor. "He's my older brother. He's a year older than me; we were very close when were young." He sighed heavily. "I think about him all the time." He lay back on the bed, head almost hitting the wall behind him, resting a bent arm across his eyes. "I totally forgot about that time." He chuckled.

"We used to pick on you and your friends. Throwing mud at you, taking the heads off your dolls, stuff like that. You always wanted to hurt us, but never did." He smiled at the memories of his childhood. "My parents died not too long after that and my grandparents moved in to take care of us."

"What happened, Rune? Why were you sent here?"

"I've told you, I don't know. I've been here since I was eleven, right after my parents died. I have no clue why."

He sat up, wiping his eyes. Zelina thought she saw tears but said nothing about it and stood up. "Do you want to teach me anything else?" She wanted to take his mind off missing his brother, she wanted him to focus on something positive.

"How is your head doing?" Rune stood up and tapped her on the top of the head. "Do you still feel that something is wrong?"

Zelina stood still, trying to feel something. "Nope, nothing there. Maybe the strange feeling was the memory coming back."

"Okay, one more today." He stood behind her, facing the wall. "This one will put your opponent to sleep and give you time to run or cast another spell at them, if you are mean enough to do so." He winked at her. "*Velox obdormio.*"

"Got it." She repeated the words to the wall and then turned to Rune. "How long would the person stay asleep?"

"Depends on how hard you say the spell or how angry you are. Most spells are that way."

"Okay." Zelina sat in the chair, moved it to the small table and picked up Rune's notebook. "What's in here?"

Rune snatched it from her hands. "Private stuff. For my eyes only." He put it behind his back and winked at her.

"Oh, am I in it?" She got up, trying to get it from him.

"No. Don't be gross." He put it above his head and ran around the room, with her chasing him and trying to grab the book from his hands.

"Just let me see what you're writing about."

"Nope. You're not privileged enough to see."

"I put up with you on a daily basis—that should earn me the right."

He stopped running, looked at Zelina and handed her the book. "Here, read it."

She took it from him and sat on the bed. Inside were drawings, some with crayon, and others with pencil. The drawings were no masterpieces, most seemed to be drawn by a little child, no straight lines, coloring outside the lines and so forth. Several drawings made Zelina giggle, but he was able to capture the details and that was what was important. The first drawing was of Stonehenge, and the second was the circular room, the Ecardia Sanctum. The next few pages were the pillars that were in the Sanctum. He drew the pillars with great detail; the symbols etched in each pillar were recounted perfectly. The next several pages were writings of his memories as they were coming back to him, about his brother and his parents and grandparents. Several times he mentioned a blue-haired girl that he liked to tease. She smiled at that; he didn't mention her by name in the book.

"I've been writing in that since my mentor showed me this place and began training me." He looked out the window. "Storm is coming in. We'll have to leave soon."

Zelina raised her eyebrows and gave him a slight grin. "Okay."

The things in the book were very personal to him. She did not read everything he wrote, thinking some of it may be too private. Zelina looked at all the drawings though, until she saw he had drawn purple eyes. "Why did you draw these?" she asked him, showing him the picture.

He turned from the window long enough to see the picture, then turned back. "It was something I saw in several dreams, years ago."

"Don't you find that interesting? I mean the first spell I ever did showed my eyes as being purple. That has to mean something, don't you think?" She closed the book.

"I'm sure you're right, but I don't know what it means."

Zelina placed the notebook back in its spot, under some old

papers on the table, then stood on the other side of the window. "What's wrong, Rune?"

He smiled weakly at her. "Just missing home, I guess."

She smiled at him and then began poking his chest and ribs, mimicking him from that morning. "Come on, Mister Sunshine. Don't be a prat—smile. It's going to be a great day."

"I do not sound like that and I never said that," he said, smiling his real smile. "You are an odd one, Zelina, very odd." He slapped her hands away, keeping her from tickling him and went to the door. "We should go before the rain lets loose."

"Okay, you crotchety old fart, let's go get you some food so you can be annoyingly happy once more."

Rune made sure to cast the protection and hiding spell once more before they left. They walked slowly from the factory and down the road. The wind was cooler than it had been that morning, and the clouds overhead were no longer gray, but instead, almost black. The day turned darker the closer they got to the tea shop. "Rune, can we please find a different place to eat? I just can't continue to eat scones or biscuits."

"Sure, if it'll make you happy."

They walked past the tea shop. Rune looked in for a moment, grabbed Zelina's arm and began to walk faster.

"What did you see, Rune?"

"Ms. Nyx, in the tea shop. Now, move."

They turned right down the next street and left at the street after, only when they were out of breath did they slow down. "Why would she be there?" Zelina asked.

Rune spotted a restaurant, grabbed Zelina's hand, intertwined their fingers and walked in. "Table for two, please."

The woman at the front looked them up and down, nodded and began walking, Rune and Zelina followed.

"Not near windows, please."

The lady nodded and sat them at a small booth in the corner.

"Is this all right?" the lady asked before setting down the menus.

"Yes, this is perfect. Thank you." Rune smiled, motioning for Zelina to sit down.

Once the hostess left, Zelina leaned in toward Rune. "What in the world is going on?"

"Maybe Lexy said something about seeing us at the tea shop. I really don't know. Let's rest here, eat a bit, then head to the bus stop." He looked at his watch. "We have about two hours, maybe a bit more." He picked up the menu and began reading it.

Zelina pulled the menu from him. "Shouldn't we talk about this?"

"I can't talk about what's on the menu if I haven't looked over it properly," he said. He snatched the menu back and began reading it again. "I don't know what to say, Zelina." Rune looked at her over the top of the menu. "You think I have all the answers, but I don't. All of this is new to me; I don't know what's going on any more than you do. Now, find something to eat." He picked up his menu once again; Zelina sighed and began looking over her own menu.

They ordered food, kept quiet and enjoyed the downtime. It seemed that since Zelina had arrived, everything was thrown into turmoil. Now, she tried to enjoy the bit of tranquil time with Rune.

They left the restaurant, hand-in-hand, walking in silence until they rounded the corner to the tea shop. Zelina hoped that Ms. Nyx was already gone, maybe back at the house since school would be out soon and kids would be heading home. Rune let go of Zelina's hand and crossed his arms. "I have work tonight, so I won't be around. Just relax, act normal. Nothing happened out of the ordinary today." He smiled stiffly at her and walked off past her school as she turned right toward the bus stop.

Ms. Nyx was nowhere to be seen and that lessened Zelina's worry slightly. School was not out, so she slowed her walk. Thunder rolled overhead, making her jump slightly. The sky looked ominous, completely black, and Zelina prayed it wasn't a sign of what was to come. She hoped the bus would arrive before the rain hit; it looked to be a dreadful storm.

She got to the bus stop just as school let out. Sitting on the bench, Zelina watched the other kids approach. She tried listening to their conversations about the day, any tidbit of news that she could pass on if anyone asked how her day was. The same trio of girls from the day before stood behind her talking about boys and clothes. She found it all pointless. The bus ride to the house was uneventful, something she was truly thankful for. She did not see Mrs. Leta at all; there were no Medjay following her, at least none she knew about, and she felt her shoulders relaxing and caught herself smiling in the window.

The drizzle began to fall from the dark sky as she walked down the road to the front of the house. She was grateful she had arrived when she did. Just as she opened the front door, a loud crash of thunder hit so close that the house shook and at that moment the clouds fully opened, the rain falling with such intensity that leaves were torn from their branches. The wind increased dramatically, causing the trees out front to bend abnormally and a howl to be heard. Zelina thought several of the trees might break in half. She thought of Rune walking to and from work in this weather and hoped he had a spell to keep himself dry. *I'll have to ask him about a weather spell tomorrow,* she thought as she closed the door and began walking up the stairs.

From Rune's notebook, page 4

Chapter Eight

THE HOUSE was eerily quiet. By this time, on a typical day, most of the kids were there running around, making all kinds of ruckus. Zelina stopped midway up the stairs, turned around and headed back down to the common room. There was only one person in there and that was Sloane, sitting by herself. Zelina debated about going in; she wondered why Sloane was without Lexy and her curiosity won the debate.

Zelina entered, looking around. "Sloane, where is everyone?" she asked.

"I don't know—in their rooms, maybe. The weather is bad, so that makes the most sense."

Zelina sat next to her on the sofa, putting her bag between her feet. "Where's Lexy?"

Sloane had her feet curled under her and was leaning on the arm of the sofa. She looked at Zelina; her eyes were red and puffy. She wiped a tear from her cheek. "She got sent to another home, one for kids that no longer need Mr. Jared's help. She left." Sloane began to cry, putting her head down on the arm of the sofa.

Zelina was unsure what to do. This girl had not been very nice to her since the day she arrived, yet here she was crying and Zelina felt horrible for that. "Well, that's a good thing, right? That means we all have a chance for a normal life, and I'm sure you'll see her again." Zelina smiled and looked around the room, uncertain of what else to say.

Sloane lifted her head, wiped her tears with her hand and smiled. "Yeah, I guess so." She sat up, put her feet on the floor and leaned closer to Zelina. "See, I don't think that's the truth. I don't think Lexy was sent somewhere else—I think those big guys took her. You know? Those big guys that have been around a lot lately? You've seen them, right?"

Zelina's eyes widened; she had not even thought about the Medjay taking Lexy. They had said they would have to investigate first. All she could think at that moment was that Lexy was gone and she had no idea if the Medjay were going to eliminate her or just question her, then place her in another home. "I saw some big guys, yes," she stammered. "They actually came to my school wanting to talk to me." Zelina sat back, crossing her legs and trying to look at ease. "Why would they take Lexy? I mean, she's a total pain to me, but she wouldn't do anything bad enough for them to take her away."

"I don't think they're police," Sloane said. "I think there is something more going on around here, more than they are letting on." Her expression hardened as she looked over her shoulders.

"Who told you they were police?" Zelina questioned, her brows knitted.

"Ms. Nyx and Mr. Jared told me, told all of us that. They said they were investigating some teens causing problems in town and that we were to cooperate with them in any way."

"I was never told that."

Sloane got up. "I think I'll go to my room and take a nap before dinner." She motioned for Zelina to follow her, at which Zelina nodded.

"Okay. Have a good nap and try not to stress too much over it. It'll all work out for the best."

Sloane went upstairs and Zelina followed a few minutes later. She was unsure which room was Sloane's; she had never gone into anyone else's room. There was only one door left open slightly, and she assumed that was Sloane's. She gently pushed the door and saw a room that looked exactly like her own, except the chair was newer and was light blue. She stepped inside.

Sloane shut the door behind Zelina, causing Zelina to spin around. "It's just me." Sloane walked over to the window, looked out, and then turned to Zelina. "Those men were not police; Lexy told me she saw them following her a couple of days ago when she followed you and Rune." Sloane was expressionless, her eyes boring into Zelina.

"Really? Did you tell anyone about that?" Zelina sat on the edge of the bed, watching Sloane.

"No, but Lexy did. She told Ms. Nyx that she skipped school for several days to see what you and Rune were up. Ms. Nyx was furious about all of it." Every few seconds, Sloane would look out the window as if she was watching for something or someone. "What were you two doing in an old factory?"

"I really don't know what you're talking about. I've been at school every day, Sloane, and so has Rune. I hardly see him at all."

"I know you're lying. Everyone here is lying. I can feel it; in my bones I can feel it." Sloane sat next to Zelina on the bed, which made Zelina rather uncomfortable. "I can see it in your eyes— you know more than you should." Her eyes lit up and she gave a lopsided grin. "See, I've always had an idea that they were doing something to our brains," she said as she tapped herself on the side of the head. "They are messing with us, planting ideas, memories that aren't real."

"Have you told anyone this? Lexy?" Zelina questioned as she got up from the bed and began pacing.

"No. I can't 'cause I know they'll get mad and have those big guys take me away like they've done to other people that have come here. Oh no, I wouldn't tell anyone. Maybe I shouldn't be telling you." She jumped up from the bed and stood in front of Zelina. She leaned in really close to Zelina's face; their noses almost touched. "You wouldn't tell anyone, though, would you?" There was craziness in her eyes, almost pure madness.

"Of course not. You can trust me." Zelina rocked back on one foot and have a nervous smile.

"No, I can't. Lexy and I were mean to you and you'd have every right to turn me in and get rid of me just like—Did you turn Lexy in?" Sloane's hand tightened into fists and she backed up to the door.

"No, Sloane. I don't even talk to anyone unless I absolutely have to. As much as I don't like Lexy, I'd never want harm to come her way and I'd never help anyone do her harm." Zelina sat on the bed and patted the space beside her. "Sit back down and talk to me while we have the time." She softened her expression and relaxed her shoulders. She wanted Sloane to trust her.

Sloane watched Zelina for a moment and then sat, relaxing slightly. "I can trust you, can't I?"

"Yes, Sloane, whatever you tell me won't leave this room, I promise." Zelina smiled at her, reassuringly.

"Good, 'cause I really need someone to talk to. I feel like my brain is going to explode." She giggled and rubbed the top of her head.

"Well, I'm here for you." Zelina was worried for Sloane, she was afraid she would snap and hurt herself or someone around her.

Sloane got up and paced the room, just as Rune always did when he was thinking. She spoke slowly. "I came here a few years ago, when I was thirteen. My first memory is of Stonehenge." She looked over at Zelina and smiled. "Just like you—just like all the others here, I guess. I had a meeting that day with Mr. Jared; he was telling me about how my parents died and my last name was Martin and blah, blah, blah. As he was telling me everything, I could feel my mind fighting it. I knew none of it was true; something in my gut knew none of what he was saying was true. I could never grasp why I was here and where my parents were. I've never been able to figure that out. Do you know why you're here?" She stopped, turned to Zelina, looking for answers.

"I honestly have no idea." She shook her head and shrugged her shoulders.

"Me either." Sloane began her pacing again. "I found if I kept quiet and acted like everything was fine, then I would be left alone. Lexy was here when I got here. She said she'd been here almost her entire life, although I doubt that's true. I think most of my memories are made up, but when I try to see the truth my head hurts and I wind up crying myself to sleep." She stopped pacing and slumped in the chair. "Like now, I'm tired and think I should sleep. Do you mind?" She pointed to her bed and Zelina got up.

Sloane curled up under the covers, facing away from Zelina. "Thanks for listening to my rant. Please don't think I'm crazy because I'm really not. I have so many thoughts running through my mind, sometimes it just all spills out into a big mess. I try to write a lot of it down." She yawned, pointing to her dresser. "Since the rooms get inspected every week, I have to hide it. It helps put things into perspective so I can see the big picture." Her breathing slowed and she started to snore lightly.

Zelina smiled at the sleeping girl, wondering how she fell asleep so quickly and wished she could do that. She walked over to Sloane's dresser and started rummaging through the drawers looking for papers or a notebook. She was about to give up when she saw a sock pinched in the back corner of the bottom drawer. Of course, it would be in the bottom drawer, under socks and underwear. Zelina lifted the sock and the bottom of the drawer pulled up. Inside was a small, pocket-sized notebook. Zelina sat in the chair and began reading the notes in it. The first page had Sloane's name written over and over, in different styles of writing. The next page blew Zelina's mind—it was the Sanctum. It was not drawn with as much detail as Rune's, but she was sure it was the same room. The next three pages were drawings of the Ooras. Several more pages were people's names, including Lexy's, and places that she had been. One note said: *My parents are not dead; I can feel it. This place is false.* She wrote so hard that it was pressed into the following three pages. Several pages had so many notes written that it was hard to tell where to start—notes written from top to bottom, in the margins, and really small in the corners. Some notes were crossed out and other notes written on top of them. Quite a few times she called Ms. Nyx and Mr. Jared the biggest liars she had ever met and wrote that she wished she could run away. She mentioned several times that she wanted to tell Lexy everything, but she could not fully trust her. She thought Lexy would turn her in to Ms. Nyx. Sloane also called Ms. Nyx the most vile woman to ever step foot on the earth, and Zelina giggled at that. Toward the back of the book were pencil drawings: a dirt road leading to a run-down house with holes in the roof. The last page that was written on said: *Lexy is following Rune and Zelina. They know something; I want to know what they know. Maybe they can help me get out of here. Maybe Lexy is catching on too. Surely she's never believed anything Ms. Nyx or Mr. Jared have told her. Surely not. Maybe Zelina will convince Lexy of the absolute truth that this is not our real home, we are not orphans and do not belong here. One can hope. Oh, how I hope.*

Zelina closed the notebook, stared at Sloane and wondered how she had handled not being able to talk to someone for so long. Zelina thought her mind would snap if she did not have Rune to confide in. She wondered if she and Rune could help Sloane in some way. She put the book back in its place, making sure the sock did not get stuck in it. She slipped quietly from Sloane's room.

"What were you doing in there?" Ms. Nyx was standing outside Sloane's room; she scared Zelina so hard that she let out a yelp.

Zelina held a hand to her chest and slowed her breathing down. "Sloane was crying over Lexy leaving and I was consoling her." Zelina forced a smile and began to walk down the hall to her own room.

"Lexy told me about you and your little boyfriend, Rune, sneaking off every day." Zelina stopped and spun around, glaring at Ms. Nyx. "Oh, yes, she told me about the old factory on the other side of town." Ms. Nyx stepped over to Zelina, grabbed her face and squeezed. "If any harm comes to Lexy, I will take it out on you, do you understand me?" Zelina tried to talk, but her face was being squeezed so hard it was making her eyes tear up. "I will find proof that you and your precious little boyfriend are up to no good and I will make sure those policemen take you away for good."

Finally, Ms. Nyx let go of Zelina and started walking away. "First off, Rune is not my boyfriend. He is my friend, the only true friend I have here," Zelina called out. Ms. Nyx stopped and spun around to face Zelina, who was rubbing her cheeks. "Secondly, you will not lay another hand on me, ever. Do *you* understand?"

Ms. Nyx looked shocked; astounded that someone was talking back to her. "You will not—"

"I will do as I choose to do. Those men followed me to school, saw me at school, and therefore I am in no trouble. I've done nothing wrong here, ever! I'm sorry that Lexy got in trouble and was sent off somewhere, but it's not my fault. She was going places she shouldn't have gone, skipping school and causing problems. You've been after me since day one and I'm tired of it! Get over yourself, Ms. Nyx! You are not all-powerful. You'll do no harm to me or Rune. If you even try," Zelina stormed over to Ms. Nyx, stood up as tall as she could, and got in her face, "I'll make your life even more miserable than it is now. Understand me?" Zelina thought, for a brief moment, she saw fear in Ms. Nyx's eyes.

Ms. Nyx's lips pursed together and her jaw tightened. "You may think you have this all figured out but let me set things straight. I run this place and with one phone call I can, and will, have you removed from here. I'll make sure your next home is not as nice as this one. Do not test me, little one." She put one finger in Zelina's face and glared. "Better yet, I'll have your precious Rune removed from here by those policemen. I'll make sure he's taken somewhere you'll never be able to find him." Fear shot across Zelina's eyes. "Yes, I knew you would understand that." Ms. Nyx glowered at Zelina for a moment, not making a movement or a sound.

Zelina shrank back. She thought she had Ms. Nyx, but Ms. Nyx turned it around on her. She wanted to stand up to her again and remembered what Rune said: "*Stop being scared! They can't do anything to you.*" She could feel confidence rising in her. Zelina giggled.

"Something you find funny?" Ms. Nyx questioned.

"No. I'm glad we've had this conversation, Ms. Nyx. Now if you don't mind, I have a lot of schoolwork to do. I sincerely hope you have a fantastic evening." With that, Zelina turned and walked to her room, slamming the door behind her.

Once in her room, Zelina could breathe. She did not realize she had been holding her breath that entire time. She could not believe what she had just done, what she said to Ms. Nyx. *Where did all that come from?* she thought as she paced the room, trying to calm down. She wondered what was going to happen now, not just to herself but to Sloane as well. She had no idea how long Ms. Nyx was standing outside Sloane's door or what all she had heard. She thought, again, about what Rune told her, that they could not hurt her. Was it because he believed she was too powerful? Was it because they had no abilities and she was gaining her abilities back? No matter what he meant, it gave her confidence. In that moment she was no longer afraid of Ms. Nyx.

There was a soft knock on the door. Before Zelina could say anything, Mr. Jared walked in and shut the door behind him. "We need to have a talk, Zelina." He walked past her and sat on the chair, resting his elbows on his knees and staring at the floor.

Zelina said nothing. She raised her eyebrows, unsure of what was about to happen.

It took Mr. Jared a moment to say anything. When he did, he sounded almost scared, his voice shaking. "What did Sloane tell you?"

She had to think quickly. She did not want the Medjay getting their hands on Sloane; she wanted to help her. "She's very upset about Lexy being sent to another home. I guess they were very close, I mean I never saw—"

Mr. Jared shot up from the chair and lurched across the room to grab Zelina by the arms. "I need to know what she said to you—the truth, young lady. Tell me, now!" He said through gritted teeth. His nostrils flared and his face was red and although his voice was still shaking, there was only anger in it.

He was within inches of Zelina's face, grabbing her upper arms tightly. "You're hurting me, Mr. Jared! Let go!" She tried to wiggle her arms free, but he did not let go. "Mr. Jared, please."

She tried pushing him away. His eyes burned with fury.

"She's very upset about her best friend leaving her! Why can't you understand that?" Zelina began raising her voice. She was getting scared and angry with how Mr. Jared was acting. "Now, let me go!"

Mr. Jared let go of Zelina, backed away slowly and sat, once again, in the chair. "I just have to know the truth of what happens around here if I am to fully help all you kids. I don't believe any of you know the pressures that are put on me or Ms. Nyx, for that matter." He got up, opened her door and walked out. Before shutting the door, he turned to Zelina. "If I find out you are hiding things from me, you'll regret it, I promise you." He took a deep breath, exhaled slowly, and relaxed his shoulders. "If I hear of you threatening Ms. Nyx again, you'll deal with Damon. Do you understand me?" His voice softened.

Zelina nodded and Mr. Jared slammed her door. She was alone and shaken. She sat on her bed, stunned by how quickly everything had escalated. She wrapped her arms around herself, her chest rose and fell with rapid breaths. It had only been a little over a week, nine days to be exact, since she had first arrived at the house, met Rune, and had her life turned upside down. So much had happened in such a short amount of time. She lay down on her bed, wishing her memory would come back entirely. She had to know why she was sent here and how to get back home. And she had to figure out a way to help Sloane and Rune get back home as well. *This is all too much for me. I'm only sixteen. I'm supposed to be crushing on boys and talking about the newest fashion trend and looking up silly videos, not trying to figure out my past and learn spells.* She giggled at that thought as a tear ran down her cheek. She wanted her mother there to tell her everything would be all right. She curled up on her side, watched the rain hit the window and fell asleep.

Zelina did not wake up until late the next morning. She could not believe she had slept that long, and with no dreams or nightmares. She smiled as she remembered there was no school for two days; she loved having no school in the middle of the week. She pulled her hair back and headed downstairs, wondering if she had missed breakfast. As she descended the stairs, she heard her name being called and she turned around. Rune waved for her to follow him back to her room. She sighed but followed him. Rune closed the door behind them and then walked quickly over to her window, looking outside. "They are taking Sloane away."

"What?" She ran to her window.

He thumped her forehead. "You can't see them from here; they're on the other side of the house. What happened last night?"

Zelina ran out of her room and down to Sloane's room. She knocked on the door. "Sloane?" She opened the door slowly and walked in, closing the door behind her. Sloane's hairbrush was still on her nightstand, the bed was unmade, and clothes still hung in the closet. Zelina opened the bottom drawer of the dresser, hoping that the notebook was still there. If they had found that, then they would have proof that Sloane had some of her memory back. She searched for it and began to panic; it was not there. She searched all the drawers with no luck. She looked around the room, trying to think of where else Sloane may have hidden the notebook. She searched the nightstand drawers, under the bed and the mattress with no luck. She gave up, going back to her room, finding Rune standing in the same spot.

"What was that all about?" he asked as he continued to look out the window.

"Can't talk about that here." She plopped onto her bed, laying her head on her pillow, hoping Sloane hid the notebook somewhere safe. She felt horrible that the Medjay had gotten to Sloane so quickly; she truly wanted to help her. "I'm hungry. Have you had breakfast?"

Rune spun around, looking shocked. "How can you think of food at a time like this?" His voice had a mocking tone, making fun of the many times Zelina had said the exact same thing to him.

"Oh my gosh, Rune, are you actually not thinking of food right now?" She got up and felt his forehead. "No fever. I thought maybe you were sick." She turned around and noticed, for the first time, that all her schoolbooks were on the floor. "I must have kicked these off last night." She picked them up and saw it: Sloane's notebook. "Here it is."

"Here what is?" Rune turned from the window again.

"Sloane's notebook." She handed it to Rune. "Read it."

Rune sat in the chair and flipped through the pages, looking up at Zelina every now and then. "Is this why you ran out of here?"

"Yeah, Sloane showed it to me last night." She looked to her door and thought of Ms. Nyx standing out there listening. "We can't talk about this here. We need to leave," she whispered.

"I don't have work for another three hours and there's no school. How are we going to leave?" Rune asked as he continued to look at the notebook.

"I don't know, think of something. Do whatever you need to so we can leave. Set the house on fire if you must." She walked over to her door, opened it slowly and peered out to make sure no one was listening in.

"I will not. They'll know one of us did that; besides, I want to eat." He put the notebook in Zelina's book bag and walked over to her. "We'll have to meet outside and use a protection or illusion spell. Let's eat—I think better on a full stomach."

She rolled her eyes. "You and your food."

"Hey, you said you were hungry. It's not just me."

"And, by the way, I was just joking about setting the house on fire. You head down and I'll be there in a few minutes," Zelina said.

When she was alone, she grabbed the notebook from her bag,

flipping through the pages again. Sloane must have somehow known they were on to her and hid her notebook with Zelina's schoolbooks. She flipped to the last page in the book. *Zelina believes me, and I wish she could help me, but it's too late. I can feel those big guys are back. I heard Ms. Nyx and Mr. Jared yelling at Zelina, so they called the big guys to take me. At least I'll go knowing that I wasn't the only one, that I'm not crazy like I always felt. I'm not sure what will happen to me, but it can't be good. Good luck, Zelina. I hope you and Rune find your way home, to your real home.* Zelina wiped the tears from her eyes; she felt helpless and frustrated. This was all falling apart too quickly. She wanted it to stop. She needed time to help Sloane.

She put the notebook back with her books and headed down to breakfast. As she neared the bottom steps, she heard yelling from Mr. Jared's office. There were several voices shouting on top of each other, so Zelina could not make out who all was in there or what was being said. She went to the dining hall, grabbed some food and sat next to Rune. "What's going on in there?" she whispered, leaning closer to Rune.

"Not sure. I saw the big guys," he said, clearing this throat, "walk through the front door with Sloane. They're all in there."

"Why would they bring Sloane back in?" She turned to watch the hallway leading to Mr. Jared's office, hoping someone would walk out, hoping she would catch a glimpse of something. She was not eating any of her breakfast, only moving it around on her plate.

"Don't know." He took a massive bite of eggs and sausage and tried to talk.

Zelina wrinkled her nose. "Chew, then speak."

"I bet it has something to do with that notebook hidden in your room."

"No way. How could they possibly know about that?"

"Zelina, stop playing with your food and eat it." Rune looked at her with disgust.

"Oh, this disgusts you? Me picking at my food? You are the

strangest." She took a small bite of her eggs and sausage but found it difficult to swallow. Her mouth was dry and she had butterflies in her stomach. What if what Rune said was true? What if they knew about the notebook? Maybe that's why they brought Sloane back in, to question her on the whereabouts of the book. Zelina could be in serious trouble.

She pushed her food aside and got up. "I'm no longer hungry. I'll be in my room if you need me." She got up and headed to her room. As she neared the top of the stairs, Mr. Jared's office door opened and the two Medjay walked out. It was quiet in the office and that worried Zelina.

The Medjay looked up at Zelina. She smiled and waved at them and they walked out the front door. Zelina stood at the top of the stairs as long as she could, hoping someone else would come out of the office. No one did. She went to her room and sat in the chair. She wanted so badly to help Sloane. It was all she could think about. After an hour of sitting in her room, she decided to go outside, hoping the cool breeze would relax her.

The day was overcast, the ground still wet from the previous night's storm. The front garden was covered in leaves and some fallen branches, as well. She closed her eyes, trying to relax her mind, which was running with so many ideas and scenarios of what could be happening to Sloane. She had to stop and rest, to clear her mind—then maybe an answer would come to her.

She was standing in front of a colossal stone edifice. Two massive wooden doors jutted out directly in front; the rest of the two-story building wrapped backward. The doors were intricately carved and stood nearly as tall as the building itself. There were runes and glyphs all over them. Some she recognized from the Sanctum while others she had never seen before. She looked around. There were houses on either side of the building; those houses looked nothing like her house. The houses were huge, with immaculate lawns. She thought they had to be four times bigger than her house and garden. Everything around her was pristine. A part of her expected everything to gleam and twinkle. There was no dirt where she walked, neither around the houses nor the massive structure she found herself in front of. Stone steps were leading up to the front doors. Looking up, she saw the windows were stained glass, with arches on some, points on others. Some of the stained glass had pictures of people while others were decorative patterns. She heard voices on the other side of the doors, laughter and chatter. The knobs on both doors were in the center of the doors. She pulled one door open; it was much lighter than it looked. Inside were dozens of children, all age ranges, moving about and talking. To her left, a slightly winding staircase led up to the second level, while to her right was a huge dining hall.

"Zelina, where have you been? I waited for you, but you never showed," said a young girl with curly, bright orange hair that stopped just above her shoulders. She walked over; her eyes were bright blue with specks of orange.

Zelina and turned and watched where the young girl was going. Behind her was a another Zelina. A shiver ran up her spine. This Zelina was by no means a ten-year-old; in fact, this memory had to be to very close to when Zelina was sent away. She was a spectator in her memory once again. "I had to help out in the kitchen, remember? This school isn't free for all of us." Zelina smiled as her friend threw her arm over her shoulders and they walked together.

"Right. I forgot it was your day in the kitchen. Glad I skipped breakfast, then."

"Oh, ha-ha! You are so funny, Talia."

Talia? That name did not sound familiar to Zelina.

None of this seemed familiar. She followed this Zelina and her friend as other kids started running around the school, getting into classrooms before they were late.

They made it into their class right as the doors shut. "Glad you made it. Now take a seat," their instructor barked.

The two girls laughed and found empty seats at the back of the room. There were at least twenty kids in the classroom. Four rows of long tables lined the middle of the room; the teacher's desk was in the corner, facing the room. Their teacher was a small, younger woman with bright red hair, yellow at the tips. It made Zelina think of fire.

Fire. Zelina eyes flew opened. She heard someone yell fire and she jumped up just as Rune ran out of the house. He grabbed her and ran off the porch. They ran down the walk, stopped by the gate, and turned back to the house, out of breath. Off to the left, where the kitchen was, flames could be seen through the windows. Other people were running out of the house toward them. After a few minutes, it seemed that everyone was outside, talking about how it started. "That girl, Lexy's friend, just walked in and said something odd. The whole kitchen went up in flames."

"I thought Alix said that someone set a cloth too close to the stove?"

"There is no way Sloane would set the place on fire."

On and on it went until finally Ms. Nyx came out. "The fire is out; it's safe to return to the house." She turned and walked back inside.

Slowly, everyone returned; the excitement was over. Rune and Zelina were the last ones outside. Suddenly they heard a scuffle off to the left of the house. Rune ducked behind a tree, pulling Zelina next to him, and they watched the Medjay put Sloane in a car and drive off. Zelina felt sick to her stomach as she sat on the wet grass. "Rune, they've taken her. What will happen?"

"Don't think the worst, Zelina. The Medjay don't just eliminate everyone. Maybe because she doesn't have her full memory back they'll simply do a memory wipe and send her to another home." He turned to her. "Don't think the worst."

Zelina sat in silence for a few moments before Rune grabbed her hand and helped her up. "There isn't anything we can do. We have to move on and figure out how to get home."

"I don't know, Rune. It feels somewhat selfish. I mean, all these people here need our help, don't you think?"

"We can't help everyone, Zelina. It's impossible."

"But we can help some. I wanted to help Sloane."

He stopped and turned to her. "I know you did. We can't help her now." He put his arm over her shoulder. "If they have no memory, we can't bring it back; that can't be done. If we run into people that have some memory, then sure, we can help them. I won't say no to that. However, if it's someone like Sloane, that the Medjay are already after, then no, we can't help them. I'm sorry, Zelina." He walked off, leaving her feeling empty and alone.

She dawdled back to the porch and sat down in a chair. Something had to change, and soon. She either needed to get her full memory back or maybe she needed a new memory wipe. The whole week had been entirely exhausting to her and she felt she was going to break soon.

Rune left for work without saying a word. Everyone continued to talk about the fire in the kitchen and the different ways it could have started. Zelina stayed outside in her chair the entire day, only going in for food, which was cold since the kitchen was ruined. She did not see Mr. Jared or Ms. Nyx the rest of the day; she figured they were trying to clean up the mess in the kitchen and were dealing with Lexy and Sloane being taken away. Her mind raced with the many details of the last week: the fiasco of Lexy and Sloane, her new memories coming back, and her abilities. She thought about the Medjay and what they were used for. It was all so much.

She stayed on the porch until one of the girls said it was time for lights out. She walked into the house somberly with her head down, and crawled into bed, hoping the next day would be a brighter, better day.

From Rune's notebook, page 3

Chapter Nine

ZELINA WOKE with the sun the next day. She was glad to see the sun; it put a smile on her face. She looked at herself in the mirror and laughed, as she did most mornings. "You have got to do something with that hair." She put on a pair of jeans and a shirt and headed down to see if she could help with breakfast. As she was about to walk into the kitchen, she remembered the fire and smirked.

"We will head to town today; workers are coming in to fix the kitchen so we can use it tomorrow." Ms. Nyx was standing behind her, arms crossed and looking as stern as ever.

"Oh, okay. Thank you."

"Be ready to leave at seven, please." Ms. Nyx turned and stormed out of the dining hall.

Zelina entered the kitchen. It was the first time she was able to see the damage from the fire. The entire side wall was scorched black, part of the flooring was burnt away, and the refrigerator doors were both opened—all the food inside was charred. The counters were scorched and the cabinets above the stove had fallen to the floor or were barely hanging on. The ceiling above the stove seemed to have caught most of the fire. The ceiling tiles were on the floor; only one was hanging by a corner. The entire kitchen smelled of burnt plastic. Zelina wondered how the workers were going to be able to fix the kitchen in only one day.

She sat outside, in the same spot as the day before, and watched the white clouds drift overhead. The bright blue sky seemed to lift her sadness, and the breeze felt good against her face. Fall had definitely arrived.

"Hey, sunshine." Rune sat next to her. "What are you doing up so early?"

Zelina shrugged her shoulders. "I could ask you the same."

"I have work in an hour." He winked at her. "What are your plans for the day?"

"Ah, Ms. Nyx informed me we're heading to town for the day. Workers are coming to fix the kitchen this morning, so we're leaving at seven."

"That sounds like a blast. A day with Mr. Jared and Ms. Nyx." He laughed. "Hey, the place where I work is hiring. I can talk to Mr. Jared about it if you want."

"Sure. That'd be great, so I don't have to spend another weekend sitting here staring at the trees." Although it was comforting to sit in the silence of the outdoors, Zelina thought she would enjoy working with Rune, more abilities practice, and more time away from the house. She did love the peace of sitting outside, doing nothing though. She loved watching the clouds roll by, listening to the birds sing and feeling the wind on her face. It relaxed her, helped her empty her mind, and relieved her anxiety.

"Okay. I better go get ready for work. I'll see you later tonight." Rune headed inside then turned around. "Hey, have fun with everyone." He stuck out his tongue and ran in.

Zelina rolled her eyes and thought, *Rune is such a child.*

As seven o'clock rolled around, everyone met by the garage to head to town. Ms. Nyx was the last one out, talking to Mr. Jared. "Bevyn, you cannot be serious! You cannot stick me with all these children for the entire day! Are you mad?!" She screeched.

"No, Ms. Nyx that is your job—to tend to the children. Damon will be with you; no one will wander off." Mr. Jared whirled around and went back into the house.

Ms. Nyx's face was red, a vein popped out on her neck; she was furious. She mumbled something, stamped her foot like a two-year-old throwing a fit, then walked closer to the group of kids. "Well, we have a slight change of plans." She smiled and handed Damon her purse as he started the car. "The younger children shall spend the day with me touring museums and having a leisurely day, while you older ones shall be on your own." She glared at Zelina. "This will be a test to see how well you can be trusted, so don't let us down."

Mrs. Nyx cleared her throat loudly as the younger kids began whining at the idea of spending the day with the older woman. "Now, you will stay in town. I have some money for you to spend, but you only get a little bit, so mind how you spend it." She began handing out money to each teen in the group. "There will be no wandering off to places you know you shouldn't go. Stay in Anker-stone; no going out of town." She kept her eyes on Zelina while she set the rules. "You will behave yourselves as if I am with you. You will be back here before lights out. Do we understand?"

Everyone nodded. The little kids climbed into the car while the older kids headed off toward the bus stop.

Zelina strolled to the bus stop, wondering what she should do with her day. As she rounded the corner, Rune jumped out and grabbed her, putting his hand over her mouth and pulling her back behind the trees.

"You absolute prat! What're you thinking?" She snapped at him once he removed his hand.

He was laughing so hard he had tears in his eyes and could barely speak. "You should have seen your face. It was priceless," he squealed. "Priceless."

Zelina stood, arms crossed over her chest, glaring at him. "What are you doing here? You're supposed to be at work, remember?"

He wiped a tear from his eye, catching his breath. "Yeah, but we both know how I work." He winked at her and began walking away.

Zelina stared at him as he walked away from her. She wished she had something to throw at him. "You're a pig." In her mind she saw water falling on him, drenching him and she said, quietly, without even thinking, "*Madesco*." In that instant Rune was soaked, water dripping from his hair and his shirt. Zelina doubled over laughing.

"Are you insane, girl?!" He ran back to her, hands on his hips trying to look stern. "You used a spell out in the open—no protection spell," he whispered as he took her hand and pulled her quickly down the road.

"Sorry, it just came to me." Zelina was still laughing; she could hear water squishing in his shoes as he walked. "I'm not really sorry, though. That was brilliant."

Rune continued walking, looking back every few minutes to make sure they were not being followed. He was not showing it, but Zelina knew he found it funny.

"Can we slow down or do we need to keep walking faster so you dry off?" Zelina asked as they turned right down the next street.

"You're so funny. Such a funny girl."

"Hey, seriously, I'm supposed to be heading into town. All the others will see I didn't go with them and they'll report me to Ms. Nyx, who is already out to get me."

"No worries, I did an illusion spell. They won't even realize you aren't with them. With a spell being used recently in the area I don't think it'll cause any suspicions."

"Oh, so you can do spells, but I can't. Well, aren't you just so special?"

"I am, yes, and it's about time you noticed."

They turned left down the next street and before Zelina knew it, they were standing in front of another bus stop. "We're heading into London today. It's a great day for touring, don't you think?" Rune said with a childish smirk on his face.

"I suppose."

At the bus stop Rune ran his fingers through his hair and whispered so low Zelina barely heard him, "*Siccare*," at which point he began to dry from head to toe. Zelina was amazed. They rode the bus to the nearest train station, at which time Rune paid for their tickets to get to London. Zelina was very excited to see the city, someplace new with no Ms. Nyx. They stayed on the train nearly two hours, which took them all way to London, where they got on the Tube taking them to the heart of London. They exited the Tube station, hand in hand, as it was very crowded. Then, they walked across a bridge to the London Eye. Zelina was amazed by the hustle and bustle of the city. All the people taking pictures, at all the sights and sounds of the city around her. "What do you think?"

"Rune, this place is amazing! Let's ride this, please." She grinned and batted her eyelashes. "Please."

"Fine." Rune sighed and took her by the hand. "Since you asked so nicely."

Rune and Zelina rode the London Eye, which to Zelina's surprise terrified her. She found that she hated heights, but Rune assured her it was safe. The view was phenomenal; she could see all of London from the top. After the London Eye, they went to Big Ben and then to Buckingham Palace. They stopped and ate lunch outside at a local cafe; the day was too beautiful to spend even a moment of it indoors.

Rune and Zelina spent the entire day sightseeing, never talking about their real home or their abilities. The Medjay were not mentioned once, nor was Ms. Nyx and Mr. Jared. Zelina felt this was the first day since she could remember that she was not worried about someone coming after her. She felt free and she loved it. She wished every day could be as wonderful.

As they finished a light dinner of homemade soup and bread, Rune took her by the hand and said, "I hate to be the bearer of bad news, but we have to head back now." Rune pouted at Zelina and put his head on her shoulder as they headed back to the Tube to take them back to Ankerstone.

"I hate to leave." Zelina patted Rune's head and laughed. "This has been an incredible day, Rune. Thank you."

"Hey, just don't say I never did anything nice for you." He smiled at her. "I had a great time, too."

They rode the Tube and then the bus back home without saying much. Zelina's thoughts were on all that she had seen that day and the freedom she had felt. Her favorite was the London Eye. Even though the height scared her, it was amazing to see all of London like that.

Once they were off the bus, Rune started talking. "I'm looking for a new meeting place. We can't meet at the factory anymore; it's too risky." Zelina nodded her head in agreement. "I'll have to meet you back at the house. I'm not supposed to be off work yet." He sat on the bus bench. "The life of the working man is so tough."

"Yeah, okay. You have fun." She walked away, feeling more like she was flying. It was the best day she had ever had, at least that she could remember.

She walked to the house and up to her room, where she lay on her bed, still smiling. There was a light knock on the door. "Come in."

"Hey, Zelina. How was your day?" Lexy walked in grinning.

Zelina sat up quickly. "What are you doing here?"

Lexy shut the door and leaned against it with her arms crossed over her chest. "Well, Mr. Jared decided that I should be here to continue working on my memory problems. He called the other house, talked with those in charge and had me moved back here. Isn't that sweet?"

"Yes, oh so sweet. What do you want, Lexy?"

"Oh, that's easy—to make you miserable." She smiled vilely at Zelina. "That's my goal."

"What did I ever do to you?" Zelina got up and stood in front of Lexy, her hands squeezed into fists.

"Nothing, really. I just don't like you." Lexy flicked a piece of hair off Zelina's shoulder.

"I'd really like you to leave my room, now." Zelina reached for the doorknob.

Lexy slapped her hand away. "I'll leave when I'm ready." She put her hand on the knob and held it there.

Zelina had had enough; she put her hand on Lexy's and a spell came to her. She whispered, "*Cham.*" The doorknob began to heat up as Zelina took a few steps back. "I think you really should leave my room and leave me alone as well." Zelina smirked and crossed her arms over her chest.

Slowly, the smile faded from Lexy's lips and her eyes widened. She yanked her hand away from the knob and looked at her palm. "What did you do?" she yelled as she held her palm to Zelina's face. It was bright red and starting to blister.

"I didn't do anything, Lexy. I was right here the whole time. What did you do to your hand?" Zelina grabbed her wrist, looking closely at the burn mark. "Maybe you should put some ointment on it. That would help, don't you think?" Under her breath, Zelina said, "*Cito sano,*" and dropped her hand. "I'm sure you'll be just fine."

"I'm telling Ms. Nyx."

"Go ahead, I'm not scared. You really should get another hobby, Lexy, and leave me alone." Zelina reached for the door once more; this time, Lexy did not slap at her. Zelina opened the door for Lexy. "You should put something on that burn—I'd hate to see it get infected." She gave a fake smile; Lexy walked out the door and headed for the stairs. "Thanks for visiting."

Zelina shut the door and lay back down on her bed. She had no idea why Ms. Nyx and Lexy were out to get her. She never did anything to them. *Maybe it's because I'm so beautiful, with gorgeous flowing locks,* she thought as she fluffed her hair. She got up from her bed and wandered to her dresser. *Maybe they don't need a reason to dislike someone, maybe they are just mean.* She looked at herself in the mirror and laughed. "Oh, that is just awful." She brushed her hair and pulled it back. She wondered how long her hair had been sticking out all over the place and why Rune had not told her.

If Lexy did tell Ms. Nyx about the burn on her hand, Ms. Nyx either did not care or did not believe her. Zelina knew her hand would be fully healed by the time she got down the stairs, and she hoped that Lexy would now leave her alone.

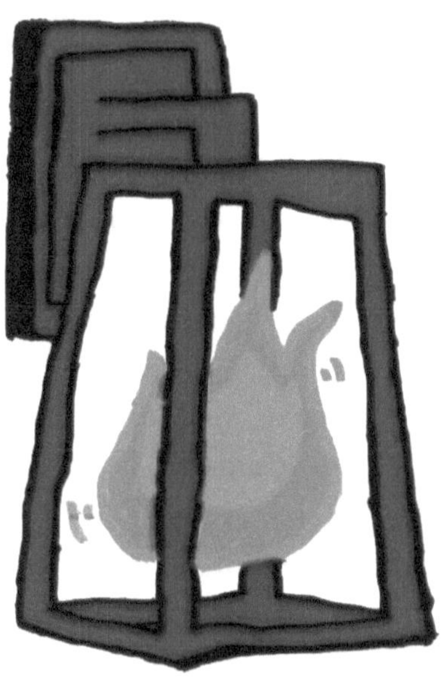

From Rune's notebook, page 11

Chapter Ten

THE NEXT MORNING, Zelina woke up slowly. She was sore from all the walking she had done the day before. She headed down for a shower and breakfast. The kitchen was, indeed, completely repaired, and Alix and Gwynn were once again serving everyone. "Did you guys have fun on your day off yesterday?" Zelina asked as the two served her food.

Alix smiled. "Yes, it was fun being served for once."

Zelina sat by herself at a table in the back of the room and took her time eating.

She made it to the bus stop just as the bus arrived. She sat at the back, looking at all the passengers as she passed by. Once again, she did not see Mrs. Leta, or any Medjay for that matter. She remembered Rune saying they could no longer meet at the factory or the empty house, so she had no idea where he would be meeting her. She got off the bus and headed for her school when she was suddenly drenched. She turned around and saw Rune laughing.

"I got you back," he said, laughing so hard he snorted.

Zelina ran over to him and punched his arm. "Do you have any idea how long it took me to tame this mess? I could beat you senseless right now." Water ran down her face, dripped from her hair and fingertips, and squished in her shoes.

He laughed and waved for her to follow him. "I'll show you how to dry off quickly if you'd like."

"No, I like being soaked from head to toe. It's a thrill."

"Okay. I don't want to take away your happiness," Rune said as he sped up. "I'll meet you here every day. We can't go to the tea shop anymore." He pouted and gave the Enchanting Cafea a sad look.

"Oh, that's a shame."

"Yes, it is. Especially since I was just getting to know that girl behind the counter."

"Oh, really? What's her name?"

Rune stopped and looked up at the sky as if the clouds would spell out the girl's name for him. "It doesn't matter now. Moving on." He walked off.

Zelina shook her head and rolled her eyes. "Can I please dry off now?"

"When we get there. Remember, we aren't supposed to use spells out in the open." He whispered sarcastically in her ear once she caught up with him. "We could get into trouble."

"You just used a spell. Use another one and dry me off."

He scratched his chin, thinking a moment. "Umm… not right now. I think you can wait."

They walked twenty minutes, weaving their way around town, before coming to an old park—not the same park as the day the Medjay were following her. "Here? This is where we're going to practice? What if it rains?" She threw her hands up. She was tired and still soaked from his stunt; she was not happy.

"What does it matter? You're already wet." He laughed.

Zelina no longer found it funny.

"Not here, back there." He pointed behind the park to a row of tall trees. There stood an old house; it looked as if it had caught fire years before and was never rebuilt or completely torn down. The house was still fully intact. The walls were charred, and a couple of windows were boarded up, but it was still the nicest place they had found so far. "It's the perfect place. No one ever comes out here; it's supposed to be haunted." Rune made a spooky sound and headed for the house.

Zelina looked around, remembering that Lexy had followed them several times before without getting caught, and now that Lexy was back at the house, there was a good chance she was watching them once again. She walked inside and Rune was already busy putting the shield around the charred house. "We should get some furniture in here—you know, really decorate it, make it a home." She smiled as she walked from room to room.

"Hopefully we won't be here long enough to call this home," Rune replied, smiling back at her as she returned to the main room. "Since we didn't talk much while we were in London, tell me what happened the other day with Sloane?"

"Isn't there any place to sit?"

"Oh, sorry, my precious one. Let me get on that." Rune hunched his back and dragged his leg again, bowing to Zelina. He went into a room off the hallway and brought out several discolored and stained throw pillows. "Will this do?"

"Oh, stop it." She snatched a pillow from his hand, tossed it on the floor and sat down. "Yes, this will do for now. However, next time I will require a soft sofa to sit upon." She stuck her nose in the air and turned her head away from Rune.

"Yes, your majesty. Sorry for letting you down."

"See that it never happens again, my dear boy."

"Okay, now will you tell me what happened?"

"Not until I am completely dry."

Rune repeated the spell he had used at the bus stop the day before.

"Much better. Thank you, my good boy." Feeling more comfortable, Zelina recounted the details of Friday evening. She told him how Lexy was taken away, that she was supposedly moving to a new house. She shared how Sloane was so upset by it that she was crying and how Sloane eventually told Zelina about some of her memory. She shared how Sloane never fully believed the lies that she was being told. "You saw her notebook, Rune. She had some memories."

"Yeah, it seemed that she had a few memories of her past. What I read in her notebook was a jumble of words, most of which didn't make sense to me."

"Me either, but I think it was to help her sort through her memories, through her thoughts."

"Yeah, maybe." Rune sat on the other pillow, with his back against the wall that led to the small kitchen. "You're right, we need a nice sofa." He smiled, looking around the room. "So, Lexy is back. What do you think of that?"

Zelina wrinkled her face and stuck her tongue out. "They should've left Lexy where she was."

"I heard her telling Ms. Nyx that you tried to burn her?"

"Me?" she asked, widening her eyes to look innocent. "She slapped my hand when I tried to get her out of my room. She kept her hand on the doorknob and I simply heated it up a tiny little bit. She's the one that kept her hand there too long. Besides, I healed it right away."

"You can't do stuff like that, Zelina. You're going to get caught."

"Yes, sir. I'm sorry; I had to get her out of my room." Zelina felt horrible, knowing that the use of her powers would get them both in serious trouble with the Medjay. She had such a difficult time dealing with Lexy. "It's difficult to control. You use it so often anyway." She looked down at her shoes and picked at the shoelaces.

"I know and really I shouldn't. I know how to control it and how to use spells without leaving a trace for the Medjay. You haven't learned that."

"Yeah, okay. I'm sorry."

"Don't be sorry. We both need to be better at using our abilities."

She raised her head and gave a half-smile. "Okay. So, on to a different subject, what happened in the kitchen, with the fire?"

"I honestly don't know. You heard the yelling from Mr. Jared's office. The Medjay came out by themselves and headed out to the garage through the kitchen. Right after that, Sloane came running through the dining hall and went into the kitchen. There was some yelling and then the kitchen caught fire, and everyone ran out. I don't think Sloane realized she had power."

"When I was sitting outside, before the fire, I had a memory come back to me. I was in school and had a friend named Talia, and I guess I worked in the kitchen to help pay for school there. I don't understand that one at all."

"No, it makes sense. We do go to school there; we'd have one more year left. Some of the schools—well, the best schools—are expensive and if parents can't afford to pay the tuition, the kids or the parents work there. So, that means you work in the kitchen to help pay for your education." He grinned. "It'll all make sense soon. Give it more time."

"What shall we do today?" Zelina asked, stretching out on the floor.

"I don't know, what're you up for?"

"I notice that some spells are coming to me, like when I soaked you and when I heated up the doorknob. I'm worried that if I get mad enough, my hair and eyes will change, and I'll do something like Sloane did."

"That's why I need you to keep calm around those that anger you, like Lexy and Ms. Nyx. Just be a good girl around them."

"I try, I really do, but they won't leave me alone. They're out to get me and I think Ms. Nyx suspects I'm getting my memory back."

"Well, until she can prove it, she can't do anything to you. So, don't give her the proof. Stay calm. Think of me and my handsome face—that'll help calm you." Rune smiled, lifting his chin up and framing his face with his hands "How could this face not calm you?"

"Really? 'Cause all I want to do right now is hit you." Zelina turned away, looking at the ceiling.

"Okay, close your eyes and relax. Tell me what you see."

She closed her eyes and tried to relax. "I see you turning me into a mouse." She opened her eyes and looked over at him. "I can't trust you—you'll do some spell on me and I'll end up with a tail or something."

"I would never do such a—Okay, you're right. I promise"—he put his hand over his heart—"I won't cast any spells on you or near you."

She studied him, looking him over for a moment. "Okay, I trust you." Zelina closed her eyes and fully relaxed.

She was back at school, again as a spectator, whom no one else could see or hear. She saw herself and Talia walking down the long hallway, talking about an upcoming match in some sport.

"So, are you guys ready for it? They are the best team in the area," Talia told her as they walked side by side down the hall and turned left.

"Yeah, we're ready for it. We're going to take them out. Hey, I have my Abilities lesson, so I have to head down. I'll see you for lunch."

"Have fun." Talia turned into her classroom while the blue-haired Zelina ran down a flight of stairs.

Zelina followed the other Zelina. Heading down the stairs, she noticed how much darker it got. This part of the school was not nearly as crowded as the upstairs. The main hallway was lit by old-fashioned, dark metal wall sconces, which should have had fires in them; instead, these sconces had glowing orbs floating in the centers, giving off just enough light to illuminate the hallway. The light was soft and warm. Zelina was mesmerized by the orbs; she had never seen anything like them before. There were only four classrooms, two on each side of the hall. At the end of the hall was a dead-end with one door. She could either turn left or right or go wherever the door went. Blue-haired

Zelina turned right. That hallway had fewer of the light orbs and more dark spaces. Only two classrooms were on the right side of the hall and she assumed it was the same setup down the left corridor. Blue-haired Zelina ran through the last door on the right. Zelina continued to follow her. The room had no desks, only one long table at the back of the room. The table had twenty or so people around it. She sat at one end.

"Just made it." Blue-haired Zelina sat next to a girl with multicolored hair that was cut right above her jaw line.

"She's not here yet, so catch your breath."

Zelina looked around the room. It was chilly in there and much darker than any room she had been in. There were only four light orbs in the entire room. She looked at each student, noticing their hair color. Each was so different and colorful. The girl blue-haired Zelina sat next to had bright yellow, orange, blue and pink hair while others had only one vibrant color of orange or red or green. She also noticed they did not have books in front of them.

"Quiet." A much older lady walked in, slammed the door behind her and stood at the front of the class. Zelina backed up against the wall and watched the entire class. This tall, thin lady had bright red hair and wore a long, flowing garnet dress. Her cheeks seemed almost sunken in and she had dark circles under her bright green eyes.

"I see everyone is here, and mostly on time." The teacher eyed blue-haired Zelina; Zelina smiled sheepishly at her. "Let's pick up where we left off. Nevan, you begin, please."

A boy near the middle of the table stood up. He was slightly shorter than Zelina, with dark blue, shoulder-length hair. He pointed at the ceiling and said, "*Illum.*" The entire room lit up.

"Good, now darken it slightly, please."

"*Nulla,*" he said softly. The lights dimmed moderately.

"Splendid, have a seat, Nevan." The teacher paced back and forth in front of the students. "Now, let's bring up Zelina and Paxton."

Blue-haired Zelina and a boy from the other end of the table got up and stood at the front of the room. Paxton glared in her direction and bounced from one foot to the other, rolling his shoulders. Blue-haired Zelina smirked at him. Zelina had a feeling those two did not like each other much. Paxton stood slightly taller, was wide-shouldered, and had short forest green hair. He had very light, almost colorless eyes with specks of blue in them.

"Okay, last week we talked about defense. We must always be ready if necessary. So, let's review before moving on."

"And what, Mrs. Zandra, would we be defending ourselves against?" Blue-haired Zelina questioned, not taking her eyes off Paxton.

Mrs. Zandra walked slowly before blue-haired Zelina. "I am here to hone your abilities. You will simply do as I say and not question me, do you understand?" Her brows furrowed and lips set in a thin line.

Blue-haired Zelina saluted her teacher. "Yes, ma'am."

Mrs. Zandra leaned into Zelina's ear, whispering, "If you didn't show such promise with your abilities, I would boot you, not only from this class, but from this school." She backed away from Zelina, turning to face the class. "Now, let's begin."

Blue-haired Zelina took a deep breath, stood up straighter and looked her opponent in the eye. She could see what he was planning to do; she sneered and said, "*Contego*," then raised both her arms in front of her and said, "*Amitto Velox*." Paxton's stun spell bounced off Zelina's shield and he was pushed backward, hitting the far wall. Blue-haired Zelina dusted off her hands with a big grin on her face.

Paxton launched toward blue-haired Zelina, his face red and twisted with anger. "*Attollo!*" he yelled.

Just as he spoke the words, Zelina put up another shield and said, "*Madesco.*" Paxton's spell once again bounced off, and he was soaked from head to toe. Blue-haired Zelina covered her mouth with her hand as she laughed.

"Okay, enough." Mrs. Zandra stood between the two students, forbidding them to cast any more spells. She looked at Paxton. "Dry yourself off and go sit down." She looked at Zelina and shook her head. "I don't know how you do it. If we could get control of your attitude, you would be a great addition to the Palviers one day. You may sit down, Zelina."

Mrs. Zandra walked back and forth in front of the students. "You both did remarkably well with your spells. Paxton, you need to work on your shields. Zelina, work on your attitude. Now, everyone up front, pair off and work on your shields."

Blue-haired Zelina and her friend paired off, laughing and talking as they practiced their shields. "I wish we could do more than levitate each other. I want to learn the fire spells," she said as she lifted her friend in the air several inches and then lowered her. "Cast your shield stronger, Flora. See it as a thick wall, not a bubble."

The class went on like that for some time. Zelina sat on the floor watching it all, watching herself do amazing spells, laughing and being carefree with her friend. It amazed her how strong she was with her abilities. To her surprise, she was helping others with their spells. The light dimmed in the room and the door opened; everyone grabbed their bags and walked out.

"Zelina, I would like to talk with you for a moment," said Mrs. Zandra. "Flora, you can leave."

"I'll catch up with you later." Zelina waved to her friend,

tossed her bag on the table and slumped down in her chair. "Have I done something wrong, Mrs. Zandra?"

"I heard you talking to Flora about the fire spells. Those are for last-years only. Are you currently practicing those?"

"No, ma'am. I know that we're not allowed to cast those, or the relocation spells either."

"Zelina, you're quite good with your abilities and that's why you are in this advanced class. However, I believe you need to move up further, to Mr. Nolan's class. It's for last-years, but I believe he'll be a greater help with your abilities than I. I believe there is more inside you, and I have reached the end of what I can teach you."

Zelina was thrilled. "Wow. Thank you, Mrs. Zandra." Picking up her bag, she began to walk out of the room, shaking with excitement.

Mrs. Zandra stopped her. "Zelina, understand you do have an attitude problem with certain people at this school—"

"Only those that think they're above me when they're not."

"There are people here, Zelina, that are quite wealthy and have a hard time accepting those of us that are not. That is true in just about every society. You have to learn to turn the other way, not set them on fire." She smiled at Zelina. "I think it will do wonders for you to be in Mr. Nolan's class. Good luck." With that, Mrs. Zandra waved her hand in the air and disappeared.

Zelina opened her eyes and looked over at Rune, whose eyes were wide. "That came to me quickly," she marveled.

"Yeah, it did. We should do that more often."

"I know you can't tell me a lot about where we come from—

you've stated that clearly several times—but let me ask you about our school."

"Okay, go ahead."

"I've seen it twice now, in two different classrooms. It's very different from the ones they have here. Not just in looks, but in how things are run, what they learn. We were practicing spells; I don't believe they teach that kind of stuff here."

"Right. So, what's your question?"

"Do we not learn history, math, languages, or anything like that?"

"Yes, we do. We learn our history, as well as the history of this place. We, of course, have math and languages taught to us. Our math is different from this math and we have languages that this place has probably never heard of. We learn most of that in our earlier years, while our later years are more focused on abilities, with the history, math and languages being optional in the last two years and not the main focus any longer. We also have sports, as well. It sounds like you were on a team there, getting ready for a match, and no, I will not tell you about it. If you keep going the way you are, all of it'll come back to you quite soon. Just lay back and close your eyes."

As much as Zelina tried, she could not fully relax again. She kept trying to focus on the school, her friends there or the lessons she had learned. After a while she gave up. "I can't see anything right now." She sat up with a huff. "What now?"

Rune smiled. "Just relax and enjoy not being in the house, surrounded by Lexy and Ms. Nyx."

All color drained from Zelina's face and she jumped up, ran to the front door and looked out the small side window. She could not see anything, but she felt them there.

"Zelina, what's going on?" Rune got up and stood beside her, trying to peer out the window.

"The Medjay, they're here. I can feel them."

"I don't feel anything. Are you sure they're out there?"

"Yes, Rune, they're here. How did they find us so quickly?"

Rune ran from the front window to one of the rooms, and Zelina followed him. They ran from room to room, taking quick glances out the windows, but saw nothing.

"Zelina, I don't think—"

An explosion ripped through the house, sending Rune and Zelina flying backward. Zelina hit the wall behind her and fell to the floor on all fours. She closed her eyes, which were burning and watering, and shook her head, trying to stop the ringing in her ears. She yelled for Rune but could hear nothing.

"Rune, are you okay?" she yelled again as she opened her eyes, looking through a dust cloud surrounding her. "Rune!" The ringing subsided and she could barely hear someone grunting. "*Contego*," she stammered as she slowly, shakily got to her feet. Wiping tears from her eyes, she choked, "*Aria*." The air cleared enough for her to see Rune in a heap in the corner of the room.

Zelina stumbled over to him, bent down and pulled his head toward her so she could see him. The back of his head had a small cut that was bleeding slightly; his forehead had a bigger gash running from his temple to his left eye. "Rune, can you hear me? You have to get up; we have to get out of here. *Cito sano*." She moved her hands lightly over his forehead and the back of his head. She could hear voices coming from the front of the house; she had to get them both out of there quickly. She thought of the dust cloud that had filled the room seconds before, then closed her eyes and said, "*Exorior illusio*." She curled over Rune, praying that the illusion would work, hoping the Medjay would believe they had escaped. She kept her head close to Rune, watching his wounds gradually heal.

"They were here."

"Maybe the explosion was too much?"

"Of course not. One, if not both, of them has their memory back and we must take them in immediately. You saw them come in here, did you not?"

"Yes. They came into this hovel not too long ago. We both sensed power being spent not far from here."

"The explosion was merely to knock them out."

The Medjay walked into the room. Zelina held her breath. "Looks like no one is here. They must have fled. We need to go after them now." The bigger of the two Medjay turned to leave while the other one stood, looking around the room. "Now, I said!" the bigger one yelled.

The smaller Medjay hesitantly turned and left the room. Zelina was unbelievably happy. "It worked, Rune," she said softly. "You need to get up so we can get out of here. I need your help, Rune," she pleaded.

Zelina sat by Rune's side while the Medjay finished searching the house. As the Medjay left, she heard them say something and she could smell smoke. They had set the house on fire.

"Rune, seriously, we've got to get out of here." She got up and walked down the hall. From there, she saw the fire in the living room; it was spreading their way. Zelina watched the fire grow. She inhaled deeply and said, "*Madesco*." She prayed it would be enough water to put out the fire, but it wasn't. The water did slow the fire and gave Zelina enough time to figure out how to get them both out. She ran back to the room and said, "*Attollo*." Rune floated off the floor, just a few feet, and hovered there. Zelina put her arms under him to move him to the far room down the hall and out the window. "Thank you for teaching me the spell to levitate someone; it's come in quite handy." She smiled down at Rune. His wounds were almost completely healed, and she hoped he would wake soon. She was able to get them both out the window and into the woods behind the old house before the spell wore off. She knew they could not go back to the house; they were running for their lives now. Ms. Nyx would hand them over to the Medjay if she saw them. "Rune, I swear if you don't wake up soon, I'm gonna kill you myself," she whined. Zelina put a shield around them and started a small fire to keep them warm.

After several hours of sitting in the woods, Rune finally opened his eyes. "What happened?" He tried to get up, but Zelina pushed him back down. "Where are we?" he asked raspily.

"We're in hiding. The Medjay burned the house down after they blew it up—well, part of it, anyway. Relax, and when you feel up to it, we can go get something to eat and find a better place to hide out."

"You got us out of there?"

"Yeah, I'm stronger than I look."

"My head is killing me."

"I'm sure it is. You were knocked out by the explosion."

Rune rubbed his head. "Thanks for getting us out of there. How'd you do it?"

"You're a great teacher; I used what you taught me. I handled it." She grinned at him and he smiled weakly back.

"How long have we been here?"

"A couple of hours, at least."

Rune sat up slowly. "How did they track us that quickly?"

"Maybe when we were playing water games." Zelina raised her eyebrows at him. "That's why you don't ruin a girl's hair," she said, trying to lighten the mood.

"I'll keep that in mind for next time." Rune moved closer to the small fire, looking at Zelina. "I don't suppose you've looked at yourself in the mirror lately?"

"Yes, because that's what I do when I go on the run—check to see how gorgeous I look."

"Your hair is blue, and your eyes are purple," he beamed.

How had she not noticed this? "What does this mean, Rune?"

"I'd say that you are pretty close to getting your memory back. Instead of changing it back, let's put an illusion over ourselves— disguises so we can find a place to eat and sleep. We need to get some rest so we can figure out what to do next."

Rune gave them the illusion of a young married couple. "This illusion will only last a few hours, if we're lucky. Our illusions are not as strong as the Medjay's, so we need to be quick about it."

"Where are we going to go?"

"Let's head back to London. No one knows us there and I'm sure the Medjay wouldn't think to look for us there either."

They walked out of the woods to the first bus stop they could find and headed to London. Once in the city, they made their way to the closest hotel, just making it to their room before the illusion wore off.

"Quick thinking with the credit card, Rune." Zelina threw herself on the bed and held back tears.

"I figured it was the same as the illusion for money, glad it worked." He stood tall, pulled his shoulders back and grinned from ear to ear. "I'm pretty good, aren't I?"

Zelina rolled her eyes. "Yeah, I guess so." She got up and went to the bathroom to splash water on her face. "I can't go out looking like this, Rune." She looked at herself in the mirror. "I need to find a spell to control these curls." She laughed.

"No, we'll order in food. That's why I picked this place—room service."

They were both starving, having missed lunch, and they enjoyed the room service thoroughly. The food was the best Zelina had eaten since she had come to at Stonehenge. They had grilled rib-eye steak with chips, grilled cherry tomatoes, sautéed mushrooms, and garlic butter. After eating, they sat back on one of the beds and planned for the next day as best they could.

"I think we should stay in London. The place is big enough to hide in and there are plenty of hotels with room service," Rune pointed out proudly.

"Yeah, because room service is the most important thing," Zelina said with sarcasm.

"It is. I'd love to have room service for the rest of my life. Want to order dessert?"

"Sure." Zelina got up and looked out the window. The city was busy down below: people coming and going, and the London Eye full of passengers. She wished she could be down there, carefree and having fun once again.

"Hey, don't get all miserable on me. We have dessert coming and that'll help you calm down and feel better." Rune got up, pulled Zelina away from the window and sat her on the bed. "Listen, we'll get through this. You're stronger than you realize. Just keep your chin up and we'll take each moment as it comes." He looked her in the eye and smiled; his smile always seemed to calm her.

The dessert was delicious and was like nothing Zelina had ever tasted before. It was a chocolate-glazed chocolate tart with ice cream, and she could not help but smile as she ate it. Just as Rune said, the dessert began to lift Zelina's spirits, and Rune cheered her up the rest of the way. He was such a kid, jumping on the beds, throwing water at her, and pushing all the buttons on the elevator. For a moment, it all made her laugh and forget about what was happening in her life.

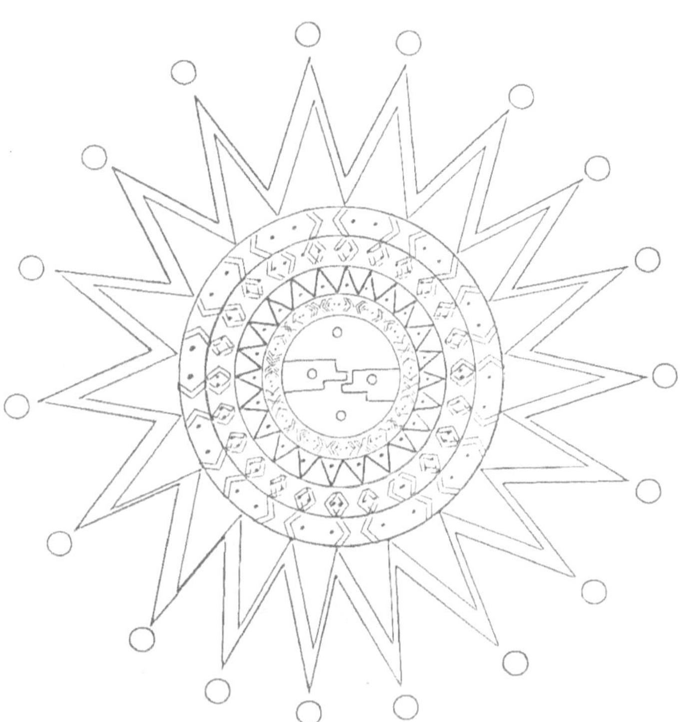

Can she get us back?

I believe so.

She just needs to realize
how powerful she really is.

From Rune's notebook, page 81

Chapter Eleven

THE NEXT MORNING, Rune ordered breakfast and they ate leisurely before heading out to find a new place to hide. They decided not to use an illusion this time, as the illusion spell would not hold long enough for them to walk around the city all day. Instead, Zelina and Rune decided to change their hair and eye color. Their bright locks and vibrant eyes were changed to more common place shades of blonde and brown. As another layer of camouflage, the pair bought new clothing. Rune wore a black baseball cap, a t-shirt, a black leather jacket, and baggy jeans. Zelina chose a long floral dress, sandals, and a cream-colored leather jacket.

"At least changing our hair and eye colors will last longer than the illusion spell, and these spells are harder to detect," Rune stated as they rode the elevator down to the lobby.

The day was overcast and gusts of wind blew Zelina's hair about; she finally had to tie it back to keep it out of her face. Despite the wind, Zelina and Rune enjoyed walking around town, looking in shops, and eating lunch at a very busy upscale restaurant. The hotel they decided to stay at was nicer than the one they had stayed in the previous night, and Zelina felt uncomfortable there.

"Shouldn't we be staying in a cheaper place, Rune?" Zelina asked as Rune threw himself onto one of the beds.

"Nope. How would staying in a dingy, dirty place be better for us?"

Zelina shrugged her shoulders. It *was* a very nice place. Before heading into the hotel, they decided to use an illusion spell rather than their disguises. Rune said that the illusion spell would not give off much of a trace since they would only need it for a short amount of time. He would not put much power into the spell, therefore, it should not be easily detected. The illusion made others see them as older business partners who were in town for two days. He gave them suits, graying hair, and even gave himself a gut. Rune got them a suite near the top of the hotel. The suite had two bedrooms in it, each with a king bed, and they got their own private restrooms. The living room was furnished with two desks and a huge sofa facing an enormous television. The view from their window was beautiful; all of downtown was lit up and it made Zelina's heart feel light.

"I'm exhausted," Zelina said as she sat on the sofa and put her feet up on the coffee table.

"Me too. However, I'm more hungry than tired. Shall we go down and eat tonight?" Rune asked as he sat next to her.

"I don't want to go anywhere tonight, Rune. I think I'll take a hot bath and relax. Why don't you go down and eat? You can bring me back some dessert." She patted his leg and headed to draw a bath.

"Okay, but you're missing out, little lady." Rune sprang to his feet and skipped out of the room.

Zelina took a long, hot bubble bath, after which she ordered a bacon cheeseburger from room service. She thought about heading down to find Rune but decided against it; she really wanted to stay in and put her feet up. Rune had them walking around all day, and the only time they sat down was for lunch. They had bought new clothes and shoes, which she thoroughly enjoyed, but now she was exhausted and her feet hurt. She ate on her bed as she watched television, enjoying the downtime. However, Zelina grew bored quickly and wandered into Rune's room. He had thrown his bag on the floor; Zelina picked it up and rummaged through it.

There was nothing exciting in there, except his notebook from the factory. "When did you go back and get this, you little bugger?" she asked as she pulled it out, sat on his bed, and began looking through it. Most of it she had seen before, but there were some new scribbles and sketches. There were drawings of her purple eyes and blue hair. He wrote about the kitchen fire and Sloane being taken away. There were several pictures, poorly drawn, of the two Medjay. On the very last page he had written: *Can she get us back? I believe so; she just needs to realize how powerful she really is.*

Zelina put the notebook back in Rune's bag, tossed the bag to the floor and flopped onto his bed. "I wish I knew how to get us home, Rune. I really do," she mumbled to herself. Then, she closed her eyes and fell asleep.

Zelina rolled over and rubbed her eyes, unsure of where she was. It took her a few seconds to remember they were in a hotel in London. She stretched and sat up, looking around the room. "Rune, are you in my bed?" she asked groggily as she crossed the living room to her room. He was not there. She began to worry. He should have been back. She looked at the clock by her bed; it was one in the morning. "Where are you, Rune?" Zelina mumbled. She walked over to the window, pulled back the curtain and looked out at the illuminated city. She rang down to the front desk to see if Rune was still in the restaurant.

"Good evening, I was looking for my friend and wondered if he was still in the restaurant. He has gray hair and a big gut. Not sure what he wore down though."

"I know who you are talking about. He left several hours ago with two men in pinstripe suits and fedoras. They seemed to know each other. Is everything all right ma'am?"

"Yes. He just didn't tell me he was leaving. Thank you," she answered in a tremulous voice. She was barely able to breathe, her heart drummed, and worry snaked through her.

She hung up and began pacing the room, tears flowing down her face. "Oh, Rune, what do I do now?" She knew the Medjay had him and she had to find him, quickly. Normally, Rune would be in charge, telling her what to do and how to handle the situation, and this petrified her. She had no idea how to handle a crisis like this. The tears continued to fall from her eyes, and as she wiped them away, she got angry. Not only angry that the Medjay had taken Rune, but that she was crying over it instead of figuring things out. "Rune would never cry over it. He would figure out how to find me." She wiped her face and inhaled deeply.

She remembered what she had read in his notebook. *She just needs to realize how powerful she really is.* That was it; that was all she needed. Rune was not there, yet he had somehow yelled at her and got her moving. She grabbed his bag, ran back to her room, and grabbed her own bag. She put up the illusion of the business-woman and ran out of the hotel. She stood in front of the hotel for a few seconds, trying to decide which way she should go, and then she saw it. Off to her right there was a slight glow, like tiny orbs floating in the air, and she knew at once that it was Rune's illusion leaving a trace. She followed the lights, and the farther she went, the more she could see it. She walked quite a while—the illusion spell ran out and her feet started hurting again—until there was no glow, no trace of Rune's illusion.

The path she had taken led her to a nice neighborhood, full of new houses with big yards. The streetlights were on; all the houses were dark and everyone was asleep, as she should be. Zelina had no idea which way to go; she closed her eyes and concentrated on Rune, picturing his face and his smile. She walked down a dead-end road where she saw a building directly in front of her. She stared at it, not sure if it was the right place. "I have nowhere else to look," she said to herself as anxiety swirled around her.

She walked up to the front of the building. It stood three sto-ries tall and was covered in windows. It looked to still be under construction with the dirt all around and building materials sitting on the ground. She peered through several windows. There was nothing inside—no furniture, lamps, or even any carpeting. She tried opening the door only to find it was locked. "*Diruo*," she said, and one of the two front doors crumpled at her feet. She stepped cautiously inside. She whispered, "*Deprehensio*," to detect if anyone was around. She wished that spell had come to her sooner; it could detect whomever she was thinking of. Zelina loved that spells were coming back to her, but she wished to be out of this situation, with Rune safe and by her side.

Zelina looked up and saw a blue glow, letting her know Rune was on the top floor. She knew the Medjay had to be with him. She found the stairwell and tip-toed up. Standing outside the door to the room Rune occupied, Zelina said, "*Pluo*," making it rain inside the room and causing a diversion. She heard running, so she tentatively opened the door, keeping low to the ground, and hid in a dark corner directly to the left. Suddenly, her chest tightened with fear.

"She's here, Brutus," one of the Medjay said as he looked out a window and whispered a spell that caused the rain to stop.

"Good. We can take her and be done with this place," Brutus said, as he crouched on the floor with a wicked smile on his face.

"I'm telling you, Brutus, we should have taken Rune in and come back for her. This isn't safe."

"Milo, you need to realize that we are the powerful ones here. We have full reign to do as we want."

"No, we have to take her alive."

"Ah, yes, but we can do whatever we want with this one." Brutus got up and kicked something on the floor. Zelina put her hand over her mouth when she realized that it was Rune he was kicking. Rune was a heap upon the floor.

"Brutus! Don't forget the Palviers want *her* alive," Milo snapped as he pushed the other Medjay away from Rune.

Zelina watched her friend, waiting to see if he would move. She wished she could get closer to him to make sure he was all right. Brutus walked past Rune, kicking him once more. Rune grunted and Zelina was blinded with fury.

She jumped up from the corner, yelling, "*Illum!*" as she ran to another corner of the room. The entire space lit up for a few seconds, so brightly that the Medjay had to cover their eyes.

"*Exorior illusio!*" Zelina yelled, throwing an illusion of herself next to the bigger Medjay, Brutus.

He swung at her saying, "*Abduco manin.*" The illusion vanished and moved to the smaller Medjay, Milo. Milo repeated Brutus' command and swung at Zelina.

"She has her memory back, Brutus!" Milo yelled as he took a few steps back. "Can you see her?"

Brutus pulled his shoulders back and lifted his chin up. "Zelina, you will surrender to us. We are to take you in alive, but if you continue to fight us, we will fight back, and you will lose."

"Is that what you believe?" she shouted. "You have been misinformed! You two may leave in one piece now. If you continue fighting me, neither one of you will walk out of this room. Be smart and walk away, the both of you." She threw a darkness spell over both Medjay and ran to another corner of the room as one of the Medjay threw a fireball directly at her. She felt the heat as it passed by, narrowly dodging the flames. "Okay, you've made your decision. Honestly, is that all you've got? You better come up with better spells than that. *Amitto Velox!*" Zelina yelled with all her might at Brutus, throwing him into an iron beam in the center of the room.

Zelina hoped the hit would knock Brutus out for at least a few minutes while she took care of Milo; however, Brutus hit the iron beam, fell to the floor, and jumped back up. He yelled a spell to take her memory away, while Milo yelled a spell for her to sleep. To their dismay, neither of their spells worked because Zelina yelled, "*Contego,*" protecting herself with a shield. She yelled it once more to protect Rune from the many spells flying around.

"Come on, Zelina, just walk out into the light and I promise we won't hurt you," Milo stated as he walked over to Rune. "*Illum,*" he said, putting a spotlight on himself and Rune. "I promise we won't hurt you."

Zelina saw movement behind Milo. Brutus was moving behind the light to move in on her. She yelled, "*Attollo! Velox obdormio!*"

Brutus started snoring as he was raised to the ceiling and was held there. Zelina crept to the edge of the light. "You will let him go!"

"Zelina, we can't," reasoned Milo. "When someone gets their memory back, we have to take care of them. It's our orders, and we always follow orders."

"Then this will not end well for you, Milo," she replied. She took a step back, put her shield in place again, and looked up at Brutus. Her eyes began to burn, and she saw a small curl by her eye turn blue. She screamed, "*Gelu!*" Brutus froze up against the ceiling.

"Zelina, you don't want to do anything you'll regret later. Come on out and let's talk."

"You *will* let Rune go! Do you understand?" Her annoyance flared and every muscle tensed as rage ran through her body.

Milo looked down at Rune and back to Zelina, who was standing at the edge of the light once more. "Fine. I will wipe his memory and let him go."

"You will do no such thing. Step away from him or you will regret it." She took one step closer to Rune. Zelina looked up at Brutus and snarled, "Just leave, Milo, and I won't hurt either of you. Leave us alone."

She looked up at Brutus, frozen in the air and hissed, "*Abduco manin.*" She looked back at Milo. "Unless you want your memory wiped as well, walk away now."

"Zelina, please listen to me." Milo put both his hands up. "I promise you that no harm will come to you or Rune. Just come with me and let me take you to the Palviers. We can get this all sorted out."

"You think I trust you?" She looked up at Brutus again and said, "*Amitto Velox.*" Brutus went flying out a side window without a sound, except that of shattering glass. "You're next, Milo."

Milo wiped his brow with the back of his hand. "Zelina, I won't do anything to him or to you. I promise, let's just talk."

"We aren't going with you, and you won't wipe his memory, or mine for that matter. If I let you walk out of here, you and another Medjay will return to hunt us down. How about I wipe *your* memory? How does that sound to you?"

"Please don't! I can help you! Do you have any idea—?"

Zelina had heard enough. Milo would not step away from Rune and she was tired of talking to him, so she snapped "*Madesco, mira!*" Milo was drenched in one second and struck by a bolt of lightning in the next. He crashed to the floor while Zelina held her position, trembling with anger. She was unsure of how she had beaten two Medjay. She wanted to make sure Milo would not be getting back up, so she brought down one more bolt of lightning. When she was satisfied they were safe, she ran over to Rune, sat beside him, and brought his head onto her lap. "Oh, Rune, I should never have let you out of my sight."

His face was swollen, one eye was black and blue, his bottom lip was bleeding, and he had a new gash above his left eye. She was unsure if he had any internal injuries; she had no idea what the Medjay had done to him. She placed one hand above his face and the other above his ribs and said, "*Cito sano,*" as tears rolled down her face. She repeated the spell twice more to make sure all wounds, even internal ones, would be healed quickly. Rune's breathing began to sound better, not so labored. The swelling and bleeding on his face stopped, and the gash above his left eye closed gradually. Rune never moved nor made a sound. "Okay, now to get us out of here and figure out how to get us home. You'll need to wake up real soon, Rune—I can't get us both home by myself."

Zelina got up from Rune's side and walked over to the shattered window where Brutus had flown out. She looked down, expecting to see Brutus on the ground below. She leaned over and saw nothing but the parking lot in the night. She looked around, beyond confident she would see some sign of Brutus, but all she saw was darkness. She hoped, at the very least, the memory wipe had worked and if he came to, he would have no idea who he was and would not have any of his abilities.

Zelina turned to look at Milo. She felt bad for electrocuting him; he seemed to be a nice guy, at least nicer than Brutus. She approached him cautiously, half expecting him to jump up and attack her. Nothing happened as she stood next to him, no movement nor any breathing from what she could see.

"Zelina?" Rune murmured. It was barely audible, but it made Zelina jump.

"I'm here, Rune." She ran over to him and knelt beside him once again, joy welling up in her heart. His eyes were still closed, but the color was coming back to his pale skin, and the black eye was no longer swollen. "Rune?"

She knew they needed to move; they could not stay in the building any longer. She was not sure if more Medjay were coming for them. She put her hands under him and said, "*Attollo*." Rune rose from the floor, and Zelina began guiding him down the stairs and out the door. She was thankful it was still dark as she exited the building and hurried past the houses. Zelina needed to find an empty place for them to rest for a day or two, so Rune could heal and help her get them home.

They were safe, for now.